BIGGEST
PLAYER

OTHER TITLES BY SARA NEY

Campus Legends

How to Lose at Love
How to Win the Girl
How to Score off Field

Accidentally in Love

The Player Hater
The Mrs. Degree
The Make Out Artist
The Secret Roommate

Jock Hard

Switch Hitter
Jock Row
Jock Rule
Switch Bidder
Jock Road
Jock Royal
Jock Reign
Jock Romeo

Trophy Boyfriends

Hard Pass
Hard Fall
Hard Love
Hard Luck

The Bachelors Club

Bachelor Society
Bachelor Boss

How to Date a Douchebag

The Studying Hours
The Failing Hours
The Learning Hours
The Coaching Hours
The Lying Hours
The Teaching Hours

#Three Little Lies

Things Liars Say
Things Liars Hide
Things Liars Fake

All the Right Moves

All the Sweet Moves
All the Bold Moves
All the Right Moves

Stand-Alones

The Bachelor Society Duet: The Bachelors Club
Jock Hard Box Set: Books 1–3
The Pucker Next Door
Not Your Biggest Fan

BIGGEST PLAYER

SARA NEY

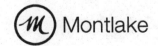

This is a work of fiction. Names, characters, organizations, places, events, and incidents are either products of the author's imagination or are used fictitiously. Otherwise, any resemblance to actual persons, living or dead, is purely coincidental.

Text copyright © 2025 by Sara Ney
All rights reserved.

No part of this book may be reproduced, or stored in a retrieval system, or transmitted in any form or by any means, electronic, mechanical, photocopying, recording, or otherwise, without express written permission of the publisher.

Published by Montlake, Seattle

www.apub.com

Amazon, the Amazon logo, and Montlake are trademarks of Amazon.com, Inc., or its affiliates.

EU product safety contact:
Amazon Media EU S. à r.l.
38, avenue John F. Kennedy, L-1855 Luxembourg
amazonpublishing-gpsr@amazon.com

ISBN-13: 9781662525513 (paperback)
ISBN-13: 9781662525506 (digital)

Cover design by Hang Le
Cover images: © Wander Aguiar Photography; © Volha Kratkouskaya, © Tartila, © Eshma / Shutterstock

Printed in the United States of America

Roses are red,
Violets are blue.
Don't swipe on me,
And I won't swipe on you.

Chapter 1

Dex

Swipe left.
Swipe left.
Always to the left . . .
I sigh, mindlessly trolling the dating app as if it were my job, my ass planted firmly in this reclining chair for the past hour.
Swipe left.
"*Everything in a box to the left . . .* ," I singsong humorously, continuing on my dating journey, proud of myself for having the strength to go on.
I'm not one of those dudes who goes on a binge when scrolling; I do not swipe right on every living, breathing person with a pulse. I look at all the photos and try to get a vibe.
I read the biographies.
I'm picky—some would say a little too picky—but I have my reasons.
Pfft. What does *picky* mean anyway? I consider it having standards and not settling, but if you want to be an asshole and judge me for it, *be my guest.*
I take a slice of pizza resting on a plate on the side table and dangle it in front of my face, aiming for my mouth. Take a bite. Chew. Swallow.
Swipe.

Chew.
Swallow.
Swipe.

This is my new favorite Sunday-evening activity, since I don't have to play in a game tonight.

See, that's something you don't know about me. Not to brag, but I play professional football and I'm kind of a big fucking deal.

It's the offseason right now, which means I have time to fuck around and try dating—which I've been going hard at for months. And months. And months of me looking for love in all the wrong places, and those places include these damn dating apps.

I have four of them on my phone, including the new Kissmet app, which my buddy Landon's girlfriend developed—sorry if that was a mouthful.

I think it's great he's dating someone who has her own thing going on—Harlow is a badass in her own right. The fact that she happens to be dating an old teammate of mine is a bonus.

I'm the least romantic guy you've ever met, but I have to admit, my best friend is one lucky bastard.

I figured it was time to join the club and be part of "couple goals," but damn. It's harder than it looks!

I stare at the profile of a woman named Madisson—yes, with a double *s*. From the looks of it, Madisson *loves* fishing, hiking, and new adventures. Has a golden retriever. Loves trying new food and traveling. And has several photos that are heavily filtered.

Already aggravated by the dumb way she spells her name, I swipe left to delete her.

Poof!

Just like that she disappears into oblivion, only to reappear once I run out of local matches. Ha fucking ha.

But the joke seems to be on me because finding someone I click with has been impossible. I'm fun, dude! It should not be this difficult to connect with a woman in person. Unfortunately, that has been my reality.

Biggest Player

Landon, my best friend, called me a fucking idiot to my face because on the dating app I am there as myself. He thinks I should create a different profile with a nickname, using photographs that don't reveal my true identity.

Which makes no sense to me.

Why shouldn't I be me? Isn't that what the ladies want?

And so, I use my real name, my real photos, my real age.

I even had my house manager, Ms. Dorothy, help with my bio, though Harlow and Landon offered to write it for me.

Ha. As if.

Dex, 25
Professional Football Player
Nice young man in search of a serious relationship.
Tall, dark, and handsome.
Funny. Sarcasm is my second language.
Loves eating but not cooking, unless you include frozen pizza.
Still discovering what it is I want.
No cat people. Dogs only (big dogs preferable).

The "serious relationship" part at the beginning of the bio? Still on the fence about including it, but I didn't have the heart to tell Dorothy otherwise. She's old enough to be my grandmother, which means she's old fashioned. The only real option *with her reading over my shoulder* was to write that I'm looking for something long term, even though I wouldn't mind a friend-with-benefits situation.

Or just the benefits.

See? Mostly honest.

Why should I pretend to be someone I'm not? Why should I use pictures that aren't mine to avoid gold diggers? Shouldn't a woman know who she's going out with before she goes out with him?

They should be so lucky! It's not my fault I am who I am!

I jam the remaining hunk of pizza down my gullet and thumb to the messages within the Kissmet app, the little heart icon bursting with tiny pink envelopes to indicate I have mail. Or a message. Or whatever.

It's like a party every goddamn time I log in, confetti and hearts and all that cutesy bullshit.

But it also gives me a confident feeling I don't get with the other dating apps. I mean, come on—who *doesn't* love confetti raining down on them? It's as if the app is congratulating me for making the correct choice to log in.

A photo of myself greets me, and I smile. "You handsome son of a bitch," I tell it, going to my stats.

One thousand three hundred eighty-two women have swiped right on my profile. Say whaaaaat?!

"Those are good chances!" I say out loud to no one, mentally patting myself on the back.

Oh, also.

Have I mentioned I have a date later tonight?

I'm playing the odds, still swiping and going on dates. None of them have worked out for me, and there have been zero second dates.

This date with a young woman named Claire I'm slightly optimistic about. We seem to have a lot in common. She loves football, sports in general, and parties, and has a dog named Snoopy. Plus, she's tall and blond and wants kids—*but not right now.*

Cool.

Works for me.

I don't want kids right now either.

Maybe not ever, if I'm being honest.

My *friends* are my family. I have one brother, and my parents are out of the picture, reappearing every so often to ask for money. I'm not close to any cousins and haven't seen any aunts or uncles in years. Not in person, anyway, although every so often they, too, reappear—again, *asking for money.*

So, yeah, I have an estranged relationship with them.

The last person who should be bringing up children is me, considering I can't get along with the people who raised me.

Actually, I had to go to therapy for two years to cope with the fact that my family is full of leeches and the guilt about telling them no, but hey, I learned how, and that's all that matters.

Which brings me to dating.

Wanting someone who loves me for me—the way Harlow loves Landon for himself and not because he is a world-class football player, and she didn't know his true identity when they met.

"Maybe I should go to a big city and sit in a park and wait for a woman to fall into my lap the way he did, instead of having to put myself on this stupid dating app," I grumble, thumb moving in the same direction, one swipe after the next in the wrong direction.

Left.

Always left.

"Don't they tell people in their advertising that we're supposed to find a match so we can delete this thing?" I complain.

"Are you talking to yourself?" My chef appears in the doorway, blue pin-striped apron tied around her waist. "Hold up. Why are you eating pizza?" She moves into my office, fingers clearly itching to snatch the paper plate off my side table and toss it in the nearby trash. *I can see it in her eyes.* "I thought you said you wanted to eat healthy."

"I do want to eat healthy. Once I'm done with this pizza."

"The giant pizza on the counter is why I'm barging in." Her lips curl in disappointment. "Yesterday I put lean chicken in the fridge to thaw out. Did you want me to make extra and meal prep the rest?"

"Yes, please." I bat my lashes in her direction. Lean chicken is my favorite. "You're an angel."

"Fine." She turns to go. "Don't let that ruin your appetite."

"This isn't going to ruin my appetite!" I protest and take another bite to prove my point, chewing vigorously.

Carrie squints. "When would you like to eat?"

My shoulders move up and down in a shrug. "Whenever. Doesn't matter. I'm in the middle of finding a girlfriend—then I'm having drinks in a few hours."

My chef laughs the kind of laugh that makes her a terribly unprofessional employee, but we grew up together and went to high school together, and when she moved to Arizona, I hired her to freelance as a personal chef.

Several of my teammates use her too.

Is she a pain in my ass?

Yes.

Does she make great food? Yes.

Do I occasionally wish she wasn't all up in my business?

Also yes.

But Carrie is really the only family I have in Arizona, and I wouldn't trade her for the world, though I do wish she was less of an asshole.

I'm sensitive, dammit!

"So you won't be here for dinner or you will?"

"I'll grab something before I leave but probably won't sit at the counter and eat, no."

If Carrie is annoyed, she doesn't show it. "Is this person you're meeting for drinks a *love interest*?"

My eyes narrow. "Don't you have something better to do other than harass me? Like bake my chicken?"

"Better you than me, that's all I have to say. I hate dating apps."

I roll my eyes. "You're en*gaged*."

"Thank God."

"Correct me if I'm wrong, but didn't you meet Tyler on a dating app?"

"Yes." Her chin notches up. "And I detested every loathsome minute of it before I met him and swept him off his feet."

I grin. "If I need any tips, I'll let you know."

Carrie nods. "Please do. I can't imagine what a train wreck it is being so well known."

My mouth pulls down at the corners. "I am feeling very sorry for myself, actually."

"I'm sure you are." She sighs. "Okay. I don't have all night to stand here; I have to get you fed so I can get Tyler fed."

I snort. "Oh sure. Rush home to feed your fiancé."

With a laugh, she walks out of my office to finish the task of making my dinner so she can clean up—the back end of a woman leaving me is a familiar sight. I don't have the best track record.

But I'm doing my best, which honestly is not all that remarkable, considering I haven't had a single successful date. At the moment, I have the time to put into this, so what the hell am I doing wrong?

Landon says if I show my face and add my career—which happens to be as the best quarterback in the league—it will attract the wrong sort of person.

The thing is, I don't know who the person is that I'm trying to attract yet! My plan: trial by error.

When you know, *you know*!

Bowing my head, I get back to swiping, a gob of pizza sauce smeared on my knuckles.

I lick it off, sadly noting I've eaten all the slices on my plate, before grinning down at a woman's pleasant photo. She's smiling at the camera, arms around a golden retriever; the caption above reads *my only nephew*.

Huh.

Cute.

Margot is active and 5 miles away! Swipe on her now! the app tells me.

For once, I take direction, swiping right without reading one word in her profile.

Hearts bubble up and flutter across my screen. Kissmet makes me feel as if I've made a wise choice with Margot, and my stomach drops when the words *You're a match!* are announced on my tiny phone screen.

More praise!

This is fun.

Chapter 2

Margot

Having to date online gives me hives.

Literal hives.

I scratch at my chest, itches occurring every so often, typically when I'm nervous or stressed out or have anxiety. The task of judging men solely based on photographs and brief biographies is daunting. And time consuming.

And more often than not? Fruitless.

Like finding a needle in a haystack.

I lean my hip against the kitchen counter, lifting the phone closer to my face to make it easier to see the photos clearly before swiping left on several more men.

Swipe left.

Swipe left.

"At the rate I'm going, I'm going to get carpal tunnel and need surgery on my thumb," I complain, squinting at a grainy picture of a man named Jacob, scrolling through his pics and frowning. "Apparently fishing is the only hobby you enjoy."

Not that I don't, but . . .

I cringe and swipe left.

Jacob meets the same fate as all the others, disappearing into the abyss.

All this unknown has my heart racing with excitement.

Apprehension.

Fear?

I glance at the time; it's past six, and I have accomplished no tasks around the house.

"What the hell are you doing, Margot? Put the phone down and go be productive!"

My daughter, Wyatt, is with her grandparents but will be home soon enough.

It's a school night, and when she arrives it will be bedtime for both of us. Wyatt is an early riser; her four alarm clocks, set each morning, are sure to have me moaning and groaning because I hear them go off from my bedroom, blaring loudly one by one.

Still, I don't put my phone down.

I do not move from the counter.

With hesitant fingers, I go through the gallery on my cell, searching for a better image to upload as the main profile picture. It feels like I've done this one hundred times, but can you blame me for wanting to strike the right balance between approachable and confident?!

I want to look cute but not cutesy.

Sexy but not *too* sexy.

I give up and go back to Kissmet, resume scrolling through the endless stream of profiles, each one blending into the next with their generic taglines, staged photos, and cookie-cutter bios.

"Come out, come out, wherever you are . . . ," I whisper, not being creepy at all. "Where are all the decent guys hiding?"

You know, *the ones who aren't going to murder me in my sleep?*

Dear Lord, please show me the guys who are looking for stability and long term and not just a casual fling. I've never had a one-night stand and do not plan on having one now, not with a young daughter as part of the equation.

Specifically, a ten-year-old daughter who encouraged me to download the app to put myself out there. She reminds me daily to enjoy the process of online dating and to *chill out, bro.*

Yeah. My child calls me bro, tells me to chill and take it easy.

Easy?

"Easy for *you* to say," I grumble. "Some of these people look as if they're going to eat me alive."

I scroll on, wishing like hell I had a bag of, like, cheddar puffs to munch on as I stand here, shifting on the heels of my feet.

Give my chest a scratch.

Then, I stand up straighter.

"Whoa." I stop swiping. "Who are *you?*"

Amid the sea of selfies and cheesy pickup lines, a profile catches my eye. His name is Dex, and he is ridiculously good looking.

Like.

Super hot.

So hot I gaze at his bio with my mouth gaping.

"Stuff a chip in your mouth and get a grip, Margot," I mutter, still staring at his photo.

Dex, 25
Professional Football Player
Nice young man in search of a serious relationship.
Tall, dark, and handsome.
Funny. Sarcasm is my second language.
Loves eating but not cooking, unless you include frozen pizza.
Still discovering what it is I want.

No cat people. Dogs only (big dogs preferable).

Several alarm bells go off when I read what he has written: *still discovering what it is I want?*

"Dude, you're twenty-five, shouldn't you have it figured out by now?"

My daughter will be a teenager in three years, for heaven's sake.

Got pregnant at nineteen, had her when I was in college—and, well, here we are.

Single mother of one at twenty-nine.

Good times.

My eyes home in on the career shout-out: Professional football player? He can't be serious—this must be a joke, yeah? Perhaps he plays football in the park on weekends. Pickup games, I believe they're called?

No way is he for real.

These photographs of a big dude in a uniform couldn't possibly be his.

I should report the account as being fake.

I should . . .

But I don't.

"What I should do is give him a piece of my mind for wasting everyone's time!" I announce to a room full of no one. "Then I'll report the fake account!"

Yes!

That's what I'll do.

Swipe in the guise of science—see if we match, then chew his ass out for giving women false hope that they're going to meet a player in the NFL.

With a knot forming in my tummy and a bag of mixed nerves from the impending excitement of catching a catfish, I swipe right, reminding myself not to be anxious.

"This is fun!" I chant. "*So* fun!"

Plus, if this is a fake profile, I'll never hear from him anyway, and even if I do hear back, that most likely means he's a bot. Right?

Seconds pass.

They feel like minutes.

Hours.

I set the phone down and go to the sink, then stack the dirty plates neatly so Wyatt can load them into the dishwasher tomorrow after school, then add the forks, spoons, and knives. I busy myself so I will not be tempted to fixate on my cell, putting it out of my mind so I can—

A notification pops up on my screen. *You're a match!*

Hearts flutter, floating over my screen as if they were balloons being released into the air.

"Okay, pal, let's see if you're who you say you are."

I'm not a detective, but I play one when I'm bored.

When no message instantaneously appears from Dex, I bite my lower lip.

"Sir, you are off the hook for having a life."

It will have to be up to me to make the first move.

I hesitate before typing out a message, fingers hovering over the tiny keyboard.

What do I even say? Should I play it cool—or let my nerves show?

In the end, I settle for something simple yet playful. What do you think would get you laid more often: pretending to be a professional football player on a dating app, or being one in real life?

I hit send, immediately regretting the harsh tone of my first note. He's never going to message me back when I sound like a bitter shrew! Ugh!

Why would he?

"So what!" I reason out loud. "He's a liar!"

And I'm going to prove it.

He deserves the lashing I'm about to dish out, and now *he* knows that *I* know he's a liar, so perhaps he'll delete his profile and create a new one.

None of this stops me from going back to studying his pictures. Why would a man who looked like him swipe on a woman like me? Why would a man who looked like him swipe on a single mother?

"Because he's fake, Margot."

He's big—massive, some would say. I can tell because he is surrounded by a few other dudes and stands a head above all of them.

Bearded.

So handsome.

Younger than I am by several years.

Something about him looks too perfect, too polished, as if his photos have been plucked straight from a stock photo website.

Men like him don't exist in the real world.

"Not in yours, anyway."

I'm tempted to do more investigative reporting, though that takes some of the mystery out of dating, does it not? Digging for details? I mean, shouldn't he be the one to tell me about his personal and professional life? Not the internet?

Yes.

Waiting is the right thing to do, and I have other shit to worry about.

Like my daughter, who's going to be home soon.

Setting my phone down again, I pick up tidying at the sink where I left off, a long sigh escaping my frustrated lips.

Chapter 3

Dex

To say my date this evening went horribly wrong is an understatement.

I lean back against my pillows, showered and shaved and exhausted, my fingers drumming anxiously on the mattress next to me as my brain recounts the train wreck that was my date with Claire.

It started off promising enough. Meeting someone new always comes with a nervous excitement and anticipation that this could finally be the one who frees me from having to masturbate in the shower, night after night.

But as soon as Claire walked through the door of the sleek bar I'd chosen to meet her at, I knew the night was headed straight for the gutter.

I'm sure you're asking yourself why.

Dex, what could have possibly been so bad?

Well. Let's just say the pictures she used in her profile must have been taken during the Paleolithic era because the woman who showed up? Looked nothing like the photos she'd posted.

Not even in the same decade.

Now, I'm all for embracing natural beauty—*but there's a limit to how much Photoshop and editing a person should be allowed to get away with*, and let's just say: she had crossed that limit by a mile.

I tried to hide my shock and disappointment behind a polite smile, but it was impossible to ignore the glaring disparity between expectation and reality. I also couldn't ignore the fifteen years that had been added to her face—Claire is nowhere near my age, not even close.

I hate being lied to.

Strike one.

"This was a waste of my time," I said, stifling any chance of salvaging the evening. "No."

"No? You're just gonna . . . leave?" She raised her thin eyebrows, frosted lipstick from another era sticking to her upper front teeth. "But I want to get to know you! You're Dex Lansing!"

She clearly only wanted to date me because of who I am, which was strike two. Plus, she was screeching: strike three.

My head was shaking.

No, no, God *no*! "Not happening."

I'm out.

Standing, I reached into my back pocket. Pulled out my wallet to retrieve a ten-dollar bill, then smacked it onto the center of the bar.

"Get yourself a drink."

"Wait." She shimmied herself onto a barstool. "You're leaving?"

I rolled my eyes—I couldn't stop it if I'd tried. "Uh. Yeah, I'm leaving. You didn't think I was actually going to stay."

Her flared nostrils told a different story. "What am I supposed to tell my friends, you asshole—I already told them all I was going on a date with a football player!"

Ergo, reaffirming my belief that she only wanted to go out with me because of my name and is worried about what her friends might think.

Strike four—which is more than baseball allows.

Ha!

"Great. Leave. It doesn't matter anyhow. The Kissmet app has all my data," Claire ranted, squinting her eyes. "They're watching us, you know."

But then, before I could formulate a response to *that*, Claire did the one thing no woman has ever done to my face: she launched into a passionate monologue about reptilian overlords and government conspiracies, hands gesturing wildly, voice booming.

It was so . . . weird.

And so random.

Strike five was my cue to get out of there before I lost my damn mind. In the comfort of my own home, my tense body relaxes, finally at ease. I can breathe.

I can open my app and see if any of my matches have left messages first, since I haven't had the chance. Now that I'm home, I can mark myself safe from my date with Claire and respond to people on Kissmet.

My mouth widens into a grin when I see a message from Margot, the woman I matched with before leaving for my disaster date.

Margot:
> What do you think would get you laid more often: pretending to be a professional football player on a dating app, or being one in real life?

Whoa.

Feisty little thing.

My hackles are immediately raised.

Me:
> No hello? Damn, girl, you get straight to the point.

I peel my socks off to get more comfortable as I wait for her response, wiggling my toes.

Ahh.

Margot:
> I hate wasting time. Love cutting to the chase, don't you?

Me:
> Sure.

Margot:
> So what's your answer?

Me:
> Depends on the day you ask—this app is turning into a disaster. So I guess the answer is playing football in real life is the best way to get myself laid LOLOL.

Margot:
> Guess I shouldn't have asked if I didn't want to hear the answer #CarefulWhatYouWishFor

Me:
> Why are you asking me about getting laid, anyway? Is adding to your body count your goal? You want to fuck a football star, honey?

A red stop sign appears on my screen, asking if I meant to send a message containing profanity and giving me the option to cancel the message—or send it.

I hit send.

Fuck it.

I said what I said.

Margot:
Whoa. Are you asking me if I want to SLEEP with you??

Me:
I wasn't asking you to sleep with me. I was asking if YOUR goal on this app was to sleep with a football player! Or to sleep around, because that's not what I'm here for.

I don't point out to Margot that on a whim I could close my eyes and run a finger down the list in my phone, text any number of the contacts, and have a girl down on her knees within ten minutes. Twenty if there's too much traffic.

Me:
I'm not the cleat chaser here, sweetie.

Margot:
Don't call me sweetie. You don't know me.

Well.

This isn't going well.

In fact, I'm beginning to miss Claire.

I take several seconds to exit the chat to give Margot's profile a glance, something I probably should have done before messaging her back in the first place.

Margot, 29
Single mom.
Fun professional who loves adventure. Date nights.
Spontaneous weekends, board games.
Loves: trying new food and restaurants.
I am on the short side, but sweet.
YOU: someone with their shit together—please know what you want!

Single mom?

Like—an *actual* mom? This means she has children, yeah?

Yikes.

Kids = do not pass go.

Do not advance to the next round.

Seriously. How many kids does this mom have? Her bio doesn't say, and in my opinion, that's need-to-know information.

Me:
Listen, babe. You're a great-looking woman. I'm sure you're a nice person and a lot of fun, but I'm not looking to be a stepdad any time soon.

I hit send, satisfied she'll be grateful I'm letting her down gently—not to mention, I'm being straight up and honest with her. No bullshit here, thankyouverymuch.

She's going to eat that shit up.

Margot:
> WOW. I didn't ASK if you wanted to be a stepdad.

Okay. So she doesn't exactly sound thrilled with my candor.

Margot:
> And don't call me babe.

Me:
> I'm simply responding to the information you have in your bio. Chill out. You don't have to get salty with me.

I learned the phrase *don't get salty* from one of the rookies on our team. The cocky little prick had the gall to say those words to my face after he'd taken the last flavor of Powerade I wanted from the locker-room fridge.

Been using it since whenever it suits my fancy.

Ha!

Margot:
> Chill out? That's a good one. A man with a FAKE account, using FAKE photos of some famous football player, telling me to CHILL OUT. Don't make me laugh.

I doubt very much that Margot is at home laughing.

Me:
> You can stop coming at me with those harsh, all-caps words, K?

Margot:
> You are a catfish! Why should I give a crap whether or not you're sensitive to my "harsh words?"

I sink farther into my pillows, luxuriating in their softness and staring at my cell phone screen because it is the most interesting thing in my bedroom at the moment.

This broad is on a bender, and I have no idea what has gotten her all worked up. Was it me?

Me:
> Was it something I said?

Margot:
> OMG. I can't believe I'm still wasting time talking to you.

Me:
> Your bio says you're short but SWEET! You're the one who's full of shit! You are anything BUT sweet.

I use all caps sporadically, mirroring her vibe.

Margot:
> How about we just stop talking altogether—I do not need to defend myself to you!!!!

Me:
> Nor I to you.

"Nor I to you," I repeat, laughing when I type out that sentence. "How proper do I sound?"

I give my nut sac a scratch, spreading my legs a bit to give my balls more air, wishing I had crackers or something crunchy to snack on.

Margot:
> Great. Have a nice night.

Me:
> Good luck with your search.

Margot:
> Yeah, you too. You're going to need it after I report your profile for being fake.

Me:
> To clarify, based on your personality, you're going to need all the luck you can get.

I smirk, firing off that last message.

My agent is always saying things like *to clarify*, and I dig how those words look in a written sentence. It makes me feel smart and stuff.

Then, as I prepare another message to Margot, grin spreading my mouth, her profile disappears completely.

Poof.

Gone as quickly as it had taken me to swipe on her.

For several seconds, I feel an odd disappointment settle in the pit of my stomach—a disappointment that should not be there. Margot is a nobody to me. A stranger. A single mom.

But damn I enjoyed sparring with her.

Is that wrong to say?

Our banter was fun, in a weird way, though it appears Margot didn't feel the same and wasn't willing to stick out the conversation. Good riddance.

I yawn, bored now that Margot has given me the axe.

Rude of her to delete me without saying goodbye, don't you think?

"Dating apps suck," I gripe, making a mental note to complain to Harlow, too, since this is her doing.

I exit the app and plug in my cell to charge, abandoning my efforts for the remainder of the night, and within minutes, I'm asleep, Landon's advice to use a fake profile ringing in my ears.

Chapter 4
Margot

I may be an adult, but that doesn't mean I don't love letting my parents take me to dinner and treat me to a free meal.

A nice meal at that.

I lean back in my chair so the server can set the plate in front of me, smiling and thanking her once she's through placing it, adjusting the white linen napkin on my lap.

A crystal chandelier hovers above us, casting a soft golden glow over the table, where a small vase of roses decorates the center, low enough that I can see my Mom, Dad, and Wyatt without leaning this way or that.

The sound of clinking silverware against porcelain fills the air.

I take a sip of wine, trying to savor the moment before what's coming next.

"So," Mom begins, eyes twinkling. "Been on any dates recently?"

She's never been subtle in her attempt at prying into my love life, not that I blame her. Now that I'm a mother, I'm sure I will be the same way once Wyatt is old enough to be in a relationship.

"Ah, the perennial question." I swirl the wine in my glass with a theatrical flourish, focusing on the red liquid inside simply to avoid answering the question. "You know, Mom, I've decided to focus on my career as a professional Wyatt wrangler. It's *very* demanding."

Wyatt titters, pleased that I've included her in my response.

Dad smiles patiently. He's not as invested in my personal life as my mother but occasionally gets curious enough to raise his brows.

"Mom is on a dating app," my daughter announces to the table, happy as you please.

She twirls her pasta on a fork and takes a bite, ignoring my gaze.

"Was that necessary?" I mutter. "Announcing it to the entire table?"

"Dating app?" Dad asks. "My buddy Roger is on a dating app." He makes quick work of cutting the broccoli on his plate with his steak knife. "Probably not the same one, though, he's in his seventies."

Wyatt does her best to stifle a childlike giggle.

I chuckle nervously, exchanging a knowing glance with my mom—she's the one who got us into this conversation. I had hoped to avoid it, not wanting to discuss men in front of my daughter.

"I don't have my search set to anyone that old." I lift a forkful of chicken to my lips. "But if I see Roger, I'll let him know you say hello."

"Margot!" Mom gasps. "You better not be swiping on old men!"

I can't help but laugh at the expression on her face. She's horrified at the possibility of me swiping on my father's golf buddy? As if I would do that, even to say hello.

"Yup, it's just me and a sea of men, swiping left, swiping right, hoping to find the one." I wink at my dad. "Swipe, swipe, swipe."

My father has had his eyebrows raised this entire time. "No luck?"

I hesitate for a moment, trying to choose my words carefully. "Well, let's just say there have been a few interesting men."

Wyatt smirks. "Interesting? Is that what we're calling them now?"

I shoot her a playful glare, trying to deflect and change the subject. "How is it you're only ten?"

She acts nineteen.

My mother leans forward, curiosity piqued. "But seriously, what's it like? Do you ever worry about meeting someone *dangerous*?"

"Dangerous?" I shrug. "Sure, but not really. Everything carries a risk, Mom. But I like to think I have a pretty good radar for detecting red flags."

As I've done with that *Dex* character.

What a douchebag that guy is!

I take a few mental jabs. Pow pow—take that, catfish!

Wyatt sits contentedly in her seat, nodding along. "Mom is like a dating app de*tec*tive. She can spot a catfish from a *mile* away."

Confession of a single parent: *I may have shared that Dex story with my child at bedtime the other night—don't judge me.* I'm a single mom, and hey, sometimes entertaining stories are hard to come by!

Plus, Wyatt knows I'm trying to date, and it's only fair that I keep her sort of informed.

Baby bits, anyway. She doesn't need to know everything.

"I wouldn't call myself a red flag detective, but I do smell bull poop from a mile away. That much is true." I smile at my daughter. She's too adorable. "I'm having fun at least. I've only pissed one man off so far!" I add. "But he deserved it."

Mom puts her fork down on the plate; it clinks. "What do you mean? What happened?"

My shoulders move up and down in a shrug. "He was lying in his profile and using fake pictures, and I called him out on it. It's not fair to women for men like that to prey on them."

"You're so brave." My mother holds a hand to her heart dramatically.

"It must be strange meeting someone for the first time after chatting online." My father wields the butter knife, waving it this way and that as he talks. "Do you ever worry about whether they're like their profile?"

"Totally. That's called a catfish—when people lie and use photos that don't belong to them."

"Ah," he says. "I was wondering what that meant but didn't want to ask."

"You learn something new every day, Grandpa," Wyatt chimes in with all the wisdom of her youth.

I sigh, feeling a twinge of vulnerability creep in. "I think I already have app fatigue."

"What's that?"

"It's burnout. When you're on it too much, or it's not giving the results you want, you burn out." I pick at the food on my plate. "I'm not saying I want to give up, I'm only saying . . . if I see one more man holding a fish, or read one more biography where the guy is searching for his partner in crime, I'm going to explode."

"What's wrong with saying you want a partner in crime?" Dad's fork is suspended in the air. "Your mom is *mine*."

They really are cute.

And close.

Which is one of the reasons it hasn't been easy to find a man who wants to dive in headfirst and commit to me.

"Why can't you meet someone at the grocery store?" Mom finally says, dabbing at the corner of her mouth with the napkin that was on her lap. "I don't understand why you're still single. You're a beautiful girl, Margot. You're funny, you're smart."

I stare at her. "I wish it was that easy." Believe me, I have my eyes on more than the produce when I'm at the store, no stone left unturned and all that.

Not that I've been looking hard the past few years. It's only recently that I've decided to launch myself into the Datingverse.

"What about Ricky Robinson, Paul and Nancy's son?" Mom asks. "He recently got divorced. He's living with them right now, but only because his ex-wife bled him dry."

"Bled him dry? He sounds fun." And just what I'm looking for. A man who lives down the hall from his mom and dad, with a bitter ex.

"Don't be judgmental," Mom scolds me. "He has a good job at a wealth-management firm."

A finance bro?

No thanks.

I don't care who his folks are—I do not need to date the man living in a basement. And despite the inquisition and the frown upon my mother's face, I know my parents and Wyatt are my biggest supporters.

They're always there to lift me up when I need it most and want me to be happy. The problem is, they think that road to happiness includes a man, and that ideology isn't likely to change.

"Pump the brakes on giving him my number."

Mom's lips purse, but she gives me no argument.

"So no dates yet?" Dad attempts to lighten the mood by continuing to pry, as if this were the only available topic of conversation in their Rolodex of topics.

"No dates," I reiterate. "I'm working on it."

He makes a humph sound, head down, focusing on his plate. "How is work going?"

So glad he asked! So glad he changed the subject!

"Great. I lucked out this year—no parents have complained so far. No injuries, no accidents."

Yet.

I love being a first-grade teacher, but occasionally it's not as fun as it sounds, especially when I have a student who cannot seem to behave themselves. Or keep their hands to themselves. Or is prone to crying or getting into scuffles on and off the playground.

This must be my year because so far, so good.

Twenty little angels I am pleased to call my students.

"Well, aren't *you* lucky." Mom smiles. She knows all my work-related business—she's a teacher, too—and although we're not in the same school district, she knows what it's like.

She gets it.

"Can I be excused to use the bathroom?" my daughter asks, napkin set on the table, halfway out of her chair.

I nod. "Yes, of course. Do you know where it is?"

Her head bobs up and down. "Around this wall and toward the back."

Biggest Player

I tilt my cheek so she can bend and give me a smooch. "Don't take long. If you're not back in ten minutes, I'm sending out a search party."

Kidding, *not kidding* . . .

The remaining three of us watch as she bounds off, destination in a spot with low visibility.

Dad clears his throat to gain my attention. "So. Have you heard from Colton?"

I groan.

Of course they would bring him up.

The good news is, they didn't bring up Wyatt's father in front of her.

"No, I haven't heard from him." Nor do I expect to.

I was seventeen when we met.

I wouldn't call us high school sweethearts, though. We didn't start dating until we ran into each other at a fraternity party my sophomore year while attending the same university. I was in school for elementary education, and Colt was getting his bachelor's in business, and one drunken night during Greek formal . . .

Wyatt was conceived.

The thing is, we were never a couple.

We dated here and there, but it wasn't serious—and so, Colton is in her life, but it's the sort of strained relationship between two people sharing a common bond and not much else.

Our child is our bond.

Did we try to make it work? Sure, of course. Why wouldn't we?

No one wants to be an unwed mother.

But it didn't take us long to realize we weren't meant to be, and now Colton has Wyatt every other weekend and his holidays and takes her on his family vacation once a year.

"How is he doing?" Mom asks.

"Fine." I look down at my plate. "The same. The usual."

Just dandy. Kind of a dick, to be honest, but dandy.

"Is he still with Gretchen?"

"Yup."

Gretchen is Colton's girlfriend. They've been together for about a year, and from what Wyatt tells me, they talk every so often about moving in together.

Which is his business—unless it affects our daughter.

"How did they meet?" Dad wants to know, though we've been over this before. "I forgot."

"Dating app."

"Ahh." He leans back in his seat, satisfied with that answer. "Shouldn't be too difficult for you then, hey?"

I pretend to ponder the question for a moment, tapping my chin thoughtfully. "If you don't count the guy who tried to impress me with the number of vintage boxed action figures he has in his spare bedroom."

My father smiles. "Nothing wrong with having hobbies."

He's referring to his collection of sports memorabilia, of course—*the collection that costs thousands and thousands of dollars.*

"That's true." I nod solemnly. "Where would I be without all my holiday decorations?"

I have dozens of totes of ornaments, baubles, lights, garlands—anything and everything to make the house festive in winter, spring, and fall.

Glancing around, I see no sign of Wyatt reemerging from the direction in which she went. I crane my neck to look for her.

"How long has Wy been gone?" I ask my parents, taking the napkin off my lap, ready to rise.

"She's fine, Margot. What trouble could she possibly get into? The exit is on the opposite side of the room." Dad gives me a patronizing grin.

True.

But there is such a thing as stranger danger; the world is full of creeps, and therefore, "I'm going to check on her."

I need an escape from this conversation.

My parents nod when I stand, and resume eating as I excuse myself to see about my daughter.

I stop short when I round the corner and find her chatting it up with a glamorous couple several tables away from the powder rooms, bantering and tossing her head back, giggling as if she's known the man all her life. As if he's said the funniest thing *ever*.

"Wyatt Hazel St. John!" I gasp, horrified. "I was about to send out a search party for you!" I chastise, heart racing like a bullet train, about to thump right out of my chest.

I put my hands on my daughter's shoulders.

"I am so sorry."

Stop speaking.

Stare at the man who just two seconds ago was giggling with my kid.

I don't recognize the voice, but I definitely recognize the face.

The hair at the back of my neck rises as I study him.

The man turns his head in my direction, catching my gaze.

"No. Way." Is there sound coming out of my mouth? "It can't be."

There is no way.

But it is him. Has to be, there is no mistaking it.

The guy from the dating app—the one I got into an argument with because I implied he was a catfish.

Idiot.

Asshole.

Narrowing my eyes, I direct my glare at his face and give him my haughtiest tone.

"You. What are you doing with my daughter?"

Chapter 5
Dex

What are you doing with my daughter?

I don't recognize the voice, but I sure do recognize the face. When I tell you I'm about to be in a world of trouble, I'm not exaggerating.

Actually.

Pause.

Let me rewind and tell you how I got into this mess in the first place. Bear with me, would ya? It's a long ride.

Remember Madisson? The young woman on the dating app with two *s*'s in her name that I said was annoying? Yeah, that one.

Well. I swiped on her.

I know, I know. I shouldn't have done it, but I felt bored and she's smokin' hot, and sure, maybe it isn't the smartest thing I've done this week—especially coming off that bad date with Claire. All I wanted was a little redemption in the dating department, something to fill my time—maybe get a decent meal and a good drink—and Madisson felt like the easy, fun solution.

So I created a new profile.

Harlow said that's what I needed to do since, technically, you're not able to update or change pertinent information on Kissmet once you create your account.

Hence, a new bio was born. Even added some photos of myself from college and none with my current team or of myself in a football uniform. Nothing about my career, nothing about my famous friends.

I was all business this time around.

Instant match.

Instant fun.

Except . . .

This date isn't going as smoothly as I was expecting it to, not by a long shot. In fact, it's taking the same kind of turn the date with Claire did but in a completely different way, and I'm about to get to that.

Be patient.

Catering primarily to older couples, groups of pompous gentlemen, and golfers at the bar for happy hour, Dickson's is posh—the kind of restaurant with outdated velvet wallpaper and cherrywood paneling. The kind of restaurant with an attendant in the bathroom who gives you a warm towelette once you've finished washing your hands. I'd bet money that they have a cigar-smoking lounge too.

Classy.

Impressive.

When the server asked what we'd like to drink, Madison tried to order a bottle of their most expensive wine. An entire bottle, for herself.

The server's brows raised, and he glanced at me for approval. "Ma'am, the most expensive wine is fifteen hundred."

My date squealed in delight, clapping her hands, smiling brightly.

It was that moment I thought to myself, *Self, how the fuck do you find these women?*

I shake my head. No way am I paying fifteen hundo for a bottle of alcohol for a woman I've known ten minutes.

"She'll have something by the glass."

Pouting, Madison crosses her arms—crosses her legs—bouncing her knee like a petulant child.

"Are you angry I didn't order you an entire bottle of wine? 'Cause for the record, I'm having beer."

Her chin tilts up in the air. Sniffle. "It's fine."

Bounce, bounce goes her knee . . .

My eyes, damn them, choose that moment to trail over her smooth, tan legs, stopping short at the strap on her ankle—the black box there has me doing a double take.

Please tell me that's not what I think it is.

It can't be.

Madisson uncrosses her leg, the black anklet disappearing from my view.

Nosy, I pull back, tilting my large body for a better vantage point beneath the table so I can see for myself, one way or another.

The box on her leg does indeed appear to be what I think it is.

Shit.

"Not to get personal, but are you wearing an ankle monitor?"

Madisson's petite frame shrugs, nonplussed. "Yes."

I'm not entirely sure how I feel about that. At a loss for words, I let my mouth drop open. "Uh. Why?"

"I'm on probation." Duh. "House arrest."

No idea what to say to that.

Correct me if I'm wrong, but aren't ankle monitors sometimes used to monitor alcohol consumption? One of my buddies was on probation in college; he had to wear one, too, and I remember him saying the bracelet utilized transdermal testing to detect liquor through the skin, using whatever crazy science-technology shit they use.

Or something.

If Madisson has a drink of wine, it will surely buzz.

I narrow my eyes at her across the table. "Are you supposed to be drinking?"

"Who's going to tell my probation officer?" Her eyes sparkle, and her red lips curve into a sultry smile, especially when the server sets down our drinks. *"You?"*

Jesus Christ.

I cannot be seen with . . . with a *felon*. "Have you been convicted, or are you awaiting trial?"

I've seen enough teammates who've had run-ins with the law to know how this shit works, especially rookies.

"It was a minor offense," Madisson scoffs as she bites on her thumbnail, ignoring my hard gaze. "Chill out, I'm not a danger to the community."

Chill out.

Those words rear their ugly head, coming back to haunt me at the most inopportune time, because I said the exact same ones to someone else only a short time ago.

Now I understand why Margot got so pissed off hearing them.

Chill out?

I don't think so.

I lift my beer and take a drink so I have something to do with my hands other than pick at my napkin.

"What was the offense?" I blurt out. "If you don't mind my asking."

Again, my date shrugs, the red sequin dress making a slow descent down her arm.

"Accidentally showing up at someone's workplace." She hesitates. "But, like—it was a total misunderstanding, and I only went there 'cause I had been drinking."

"A drunken, accidental stalking?" I feel myself blinking rapidly. "Of who?"

"Some girl."

She's being deliberately vague. "What girl specifically?"

Her red pouty lips form the words. "My ex-boyfriend's new skank of a girlfriend. Then him. But they're full of crap. Why would I give a shit about either of them? She is a total downgrade."

I mean—Madisson is attractive, no doubt about that.

But her behavior is as ugly as it gets.

And apparently she's a criminal. They don't strap ankle monitors on anyone and everyone for funsies—there is a reason the court ordered her to wear it, and I want no part of that.

I shiver—not because I'm cold; I shiver because my brain is unable to process this new information. None of this is in my wheelhouse, and not to mention, the sight of that monitor has my dick shriveling three sizes.

"Will you excuse me? I think I have to take a shit," I announce, wipe my mouth with a napkin, though there was no food on my face, and toss it on my chair before stalking away from the table.

This date was foolish, and I knew that before it began, but did that stop me?

No.

I should have left Madisson in the category of Absolutely Not, the way I had done while using my *other* profile. The real me, professional-football-player me.

"You're a fucking idiot," I mumble to myself, once again stuck in a situation I want no part of.

Think with your head next time, not with your cock. I chastise myself as I navigate through the dimly lit restaurant, grateful for the short trip to the toilets, though I must weave between tables with my massive body.

I have to admit, this is a real romantic place, adorned with flickering candles, dark wallpaper, and hushed conversations.

Glancing up at the glowing chandelier, I let its light guide me to the elegant restroom tucked away in a corner, two mahogany doors placed side by side.

Toilets.

Nice.

I push through the door on the left.

Stepping inside, I peer around cautiously for a bathroom attendant. I'm in no mood to smile and chat politely to a stranger, even one stationed here solely to do a job that includes handing me a paper towel.

Phew. All clear.

Instead of a human I'm greeted by the soft scent of fragrance, the misting machine in the corner giving off a low hum as it gently sprays the room. Surrounding me is the quiet beat of classical music.

Marble countertops gleam under dim lighting, so very similar to the atmosphere outside.

I crouch down, searching for feet beneath the stalls.

"Sweet, I'm alone."

Letting out a sigh of relief, I stand at the sink. Turn on the cold water, splashing it on my face.

"You are the biggest fucking idiot." I steal a glance at my reflection in the mirror, frowning. "Do better next time."

How do I get out of this mess?

Madisson and I have only ordered drinks so far, no food, but let's be real, this isn't the kind of place you come for *just* drinks. Not if you're seated in the main dining room. This is the kind of place you come for an *entire* meal: starter and entrée, followed by dessert—and by *dessert* I *do not* mean Madisson naked in my bed with my face between her legs.

Which reminds me: Know what would be so cool right now?

Escaping through a window the same way they do in the movies.

I've always wanted to do that. It would be some real serious spy-thriller, action-movie shit.

I've always fancied myself an action-movie star if I'm being honest—perhaps I'll cross that bridge when I retire from football.

Looking at myself in the mirror, my eyes scan the room behind me, landing on a frosted-glass window above one of the stalls. From my vantage point, it looks too small—would barely be large enough to fit my ass through, let alone my whole body.

What would it take to squeeze through?

There's no realistic way I would fit.

Not a chance.

Still, I go into the corner stall. Survey the window's dimensions, mentally measuring the inches. Climb onto the toilet seat and peer through the glass, gauging the distance from the bottom of the sill to the ground below.

"Yeah, not happening." My escape will have to wait for another day.

I return to the sink and wash my hands as I contemplate my options:

Return to the table and rush through dinner.

Return to the table, make my apologies, and exit early.

Invent an emergency. I can text Landon right now and tell him to call me, pretending he's my brother who needs me, like, immediately.

Pay for the drinks at the front, ditch her. Block her.

And when I say block her, I mean block the shit out of her.

Problem is, she knows my true identity because she is a jersey chaser. The last thing I need is for her to go to the media. The last thing I need is her selling a story.

Note to self: *do not let her take a photo of us or let someone else take our photo.*

"Why are you being such a pussy about this? You are a fucking legend. Grown men want to be you; women want to sleep with you." I crack a smile, remembering what a badass I truly am. "Get out there and take control of the situation. Tell her you're leaving."

I square my shoulders.

Drop them. "Ugh. Don't be such a goddamn chicken!"

Dumping someone mid-date is the worst kind of dick move, even I know that. And I may be an asshole, but I'm not entirely insensitive—I care about people's feelings 80 percent of the time but still . . .

I need to get out of here.

Hope lost for a subterfuge escape, I pull the exit open and step back into the dining room, the noise hitting me at an unwelcome decibel.

At the same time, I feel someone smash into me.

Two things register in my brain at once:

1. The person is not an adult.
2. It's a young girl.

She springs back, an apologetic expression written on her scrunched-up face. "Oh my gosh. Sir, I am so sorry!"

Her little hand is pressed to her chest.

I notice that her fingernails are bright blue.

"Sir? Kid, I'm only twenty-five." Then. "Random question—did you happen to notice if there's a window in the women's bathroom?"

"I don't think so?" She pauses, tilting her head. "Why? Were you planning to climb out of it?"

"Yes," I answer honestly. "I can't find one I'd fit through."

The young girl laughs. "Who are you trying to get away from? A bad date?"

I'm surprised by how perceptive she is. "Yes."

"Hmmm," she hums. "You know, if you paid me, I could help you run her off."

My ears perk up.

It's that easy? All I have to do is pay her?

"Really?"

This kid is fucking brilliant! I like her. I like her a lot.

"Really. I'm having dinner with my family, and they're boring." She yawns. "My grandma is hounding my mom about her love life, and who wants to sit and listen to that?"

Sounds good to me! "You scratch my back, I'll scratch yours."

She nods. "Cool."

I pull the leather designer wallet out of my back pocket and unfold it, glancing down at the money tucked inside.

I remove a twenty and hold it out to her. "This oughta do it."

The kid has the audacity to fold her scrawny little arms across her chest. "Twenty bucks?" She snorts. "Don't insult me."

I stare her down. "But how old are you? Like, eight?"

She pulls a face. It looks like she's sucked on a sour lemon. "I'm not eight—I'm ten."

Great.

A preteenager, probably in middle school.

"You're not supposed to ask people their ages, unless you're an ageist," she announces with authority.

"What's an ageist?" This is a new term for me.

"When you discriminate based on age."

I shift on my heels. "I'm not discriminating. I was making an observation."

"You were trying to take advantage because you thought I was a kid."

I mean—she is a kid. But I'm not stupid enough to say that out loud so she can give me another set down.

"What's your name?" she asks.

"Dex."

The kid lets out a low whistle. "Yikes."

I refuse to feel insulted by someone not even five feet tall.

"What's yours?"

"Wyatt."

I nod appreciatively. "That's a pretty badass name."

"I know." She flips her hair.

"Okay, Wyatt—how much is it going to take to get you to help me out?"

Wyatt rubs her chin, deep in thought. "Well. The LEGO kit I want is a hundred and fifty bucks."

My eyes bulge. They're charging that much money for bricks these days?

I pat at my pockets and come up empty. "I don't have a LEGO kit on me right now. Sorry."

Wyatt rolls her eyes. "I know you don't have a LEGO kit—but you can give me the cash and I'll buy it. I'll beg my mom to take me to the mall."

I narrow my eyes. "Are you shaking me down right now?"

'Cause this feels like extortion.

"Shaking you down?" She narrows hers back at me. "I don't know what that means."

Not sure if I believe her; she seems really smart. I begrudgingly remove a crisp one-hundred-dollar bill from my wallet, plus another twenty to sweeten the deal, and make the amount a cool one forty.

"This should cover the LEGO set."

She plucks the bills out of my hand. Counts them like a banker—then counts them again—and slides them into the pocket of her conservative floral dress.

"Not one fifty?"

"Sorry, kid. It's all I have—unless you take credit cards."
"Fine." She looks around. "So what's the plan?"
No idea.
"*You're* the mastermind here."
Wyatt nods in agreement. "That's true. I am. No offense, Dex, but you don't seem like the kind of guy who's quick on his feet."
My mouth drops open. Never have I ever had anyone say that to my face, and if any of my teammates or friends overheard her—specifically that twat Landon—they would drop dead laughing.
Not quick on my feet?
Wyatt is a little shit, that's what she is.
But also: she's not wrong.
She doesn't give me time to reply, asking, "Do you have kids?"
I shake my head. "No."
"Did you tell your date that you don't have kids?"
I shake my head again. "I might have mentioned it?"
Wyatt snaps her fingers. "Oh! I have an idea—why don't I walk up while you're at the table and pretend you're my dad? I'll really lay it on thick. She'll think you're a huge liar and get mad."
Hmm. Solid plan—but I still have my doubts. "What if it doesn't work?"
She smiles up at me. "Satisfaction guaranteed or your money back!"
"Good enough for me." I have total confidence in this short person I bumped into by fate. "So . . . now what?"
Wyatt gives me a none-too-gentle shove, pushing me in the direction of the open dining area. "You go back to your date and let me handle this. Pretend to act normal."
Obediently, I walk back to my table the way Wyatt has instructed me to, Madisson watching me with a curious stare as I approach. When I pull out my chair and reseat myself, I give her a nervous smile.
Remember to lay the napkin back in my lap.
Can she sense that I'm up to no good?
"Hey, babe." She leans over to kiss me. "What took you so long?"
Babe?

That's a no from me.

Do not pass go. We have known one another fifteen whole minutes, twenty tops.

"What took me so long?" I frown. "Uh. There was a line."

She purses her lips unsympathetically. "Pfft. Try being in line for the bathroom at a concert."

I inwardly scoff. Any occasion I'm at a sporting event, I'm either on the field playing or I'm in one of the suites watching from the VIP section. Ergo, I never stand in line or fight for urinal time.

My parents didn't teach me much etiquette when it comes to being fancy, but what they did teach me was that when I'm eating out at a nice restaurant, I shouldn't keep my elbows on the table, and I should sit with my back straight.

Just as I'm reaching for my beer, Wyatt appears around the corner, feigning shock when she sees me sitting at the table.

"Dad?"

Oh shit.

"Hey!" I stumble, unprepared for her to be such an enthusiastic actor. "Kiddo."

"Oh my God, Daddy! Why didn't you tell me you were going to be here?" The girl bounds over, bubbly as ever, wrapping her puny arms around my neck and squeezing. "Daddy, I missed you so much."

"Did she just call you *Dad*?" Madisson leans back in her chair, folding her arms. Stares across the table. "You didn't tell me you have kids."

"Oh—there are so many of us," Wyatt informs her, voice booming, arms squeezing the life out of my neck. "I'm one of eleven." She enunciates the number eleven. "Technically most of them are half siblings. I'm only blood related to three of them."

My jaw drops open.

Madisson's jaw drops open, too, red lips agape. "Eleven?"

Wyatt nods with authority. "I know, right? Can you imagine what that costs him every month in child support payments?" She lets out a low whistle. "Yikes."

Jesus Christ.

I want to get rid of my date—not have her running to the media with fake news about my dozens of illegitimate children!

I tamp the air with the palm of my hand.

"Okay, simmer down—she doesn't need to know all the skeletons in my closet." I grit my teeth, prying Wyatt's arms off me and returning them to her sides. "Who are you here with?"

"Grammy and Pop Pop," she tells us, directing her gaze at my date and squinting. "You're so much older than his usual type."

Oh my God. She did not just say that.

When I said I wanted to run my date off, I didn't mean I wanted to embarrass her to the point that *I* felt like crawling under the table.

"How old are you?" Wyatt asks Madisson. "Like, forty?"

Madisson has no idea what to say, managing a low, irritated "Twenty-four."

"Dang." My "daughter" grimaces. "You look way older. I was being nice."

I can see the range of emotions changing Madisson's face—she wants to say something rude to my "child" but also doesn't want to be rude to my child.

It's a touchy spot to be in, except I don't sympathize. She misrepresented herself the same way she thinks I did. Unlike in her profile, she has that ankle thing on and also clearly comes off as a gold digger, only interested in a relationship for clout.

"Hey, Dad, did you order that rat for me yet?" she loudly asks.

"Rat?" Madisson's eyes go wide.

"Yeah. I love rats so much. My last one got loose in the house, and now he's living in the wall, so Dad said he'd buy me a new one." She lets out a long, loud sigh, then boasts, "Our house has a reptile room. One of my *many* brothers has a snake collection."

"Snakes?"

Wyatt nods enthusiastically. "Do you like snakes? Ricky has some big ones." She laughs. "Bob is my favorite—except for the times he escapes and gets into my bed. He loves beds."

My date shakes her head. "No. I don't like snakes."

"That's too bad. Dad lets us keep some of the aquariums in the living room."

I am genuinely amazed at the words coming out of this kid's mouth—and dare I say she is one of the best improv artists of her generation.

Give this kid an Oscar!

For real.

I am so impressed with her performance I'm tempted to slip her another hundred bucks.

My lips part, ready to reply to her snake comment, when a gasp has my attention.

"Wyatt Hazel St. John! I was about to send out a search party for you."

A woman who can only be identified as Wyatt's mother is standing next to the table, her hands going to my fake daughter's shoulders.

"I am so sorry." The woman begins her apology tour.

Stops speaking.

Stares me dead in the eyes as if she can see into my black soul, as if she knows me.

And this is where it all starts making sense, my friends—this is where it all catches up to me, shit hitting the fan as my sweaty brain zips along a mile a minute, details clicking into place. Click.

Click.

Click.

Now you know the full story of how we got here, so can we all chill the fuck out and move on?

Yeah. *That's what I thought.*

"You." She's glaring at me harder than anyone has ever glared. "What are you doing with my daughter?"

"Mom," Wyatt begins. "Why didn't you tell me Dad was going to be here tonight? You know I wanted to show him the rash on my arm."

Oh shit. The kid is method acting, caught up in the little drama she's spun out of her ass.

The woman looks understandably confused, but before she can say another word, my date cuts in.

"Jesus. Is this your ex-wife?"

Wyatt nods. "One of them."

Her mother looks back and forth from me to Madisson, to me to Madisson, to—

"Wrapping children up in your web of lies, I see?" She clicks her tongue.

I barely notice my date sitting at the table, puzzlement marring her pretty face.

"I'm sorry—do I know you?" I already know the answer but stall for time, no idea what to say that will make any of this better.

It's a fucking mess.

"We have not met in person." Wyatt's mother looks down at her daughter. "Wyatt, sweetie, you know better than to talk to strangers."

Ah. There it is.

"I wasn't talking to a stranger. I bumped into Dad." Wyatt pauses. "Don't you recognize him? Where are your glasses?"

Her mother rolls her eyes, taking her by the hand. "Enough out of you, young lady."

Feisty firecrackers, both of them.

Damn, I like this kid.

She reminds me of me.

"You know what?" Madisson announces, pushing back her chair and standing, tossing her napkin to the tabletop. "This is way too much drama, even for me." She snatches up her purse. "I can see now that this wasn't worth the trouble I'm going to be in with my parole officer."

And with that, she storms off toward the exit, the three of us staring after her.

Chapter 6

Margot

What.

The.

Actual. Hell.

Is going on.

Am I losing my hearing or did his date just say, *I can see now that this wasn't worth the trouble I'm going to be in with my parole officer.*

Parole officer?

"What the hell is going on here?" I glare at the idiot from the dating app. He is a man I literally just deleted. "What the hell are you, some kind of creep?"

Dex from the dating app holds his hands up as if in surrender, and I can't help but stare at them. They're big hands.

Huge.

"This isn't what it looks like."

I snort. "Oh really? What do I think this looks like? Please, be my guest and tell me."

Because what it looks like is he has my daughter in some sort of situation I can't wrap my brain around. Whatever this is isn't just a friendly conversation—they're up to something. It's confusing, and I know for a fact she referred to him as Dad when I walked up.

My ears were not playing tricks on me.

This is sus.

Not only that, I know my daughter well enough to know she's prone to mischief—this has Wyatt shenanigans written all over it.

"It's fine, Mom—he *paid* me," my angel-baby child informs me proudly, pulling a wad of cash from her pocket and thrusting it in my direction like a prize trophy. "It's LEGO cash."

LEGO cash?

"What? Where did you get that?" I feel my eyes bugging. "I left Grandma and Grandpa sitting at the table because you've been gone so long—and I find you here, taking money from perfect strangers? Wyatt Hazel!"

"I just told you—he gave it to me. I was playing a role."

Dex stands from the table, straightening to his full height, and his napkin falls to the floor from his lap. Somewhat impressed, I watch as he bends to retrieve it.

At least he knows table etiquette.

"You know, it truly is a crime that her middle name is Hazel. The two names don't go together." He winks stupidly down at my daughter as if they are in on some inside joke.

She rolls her eyes. "Tell me about it."

"Excuse me!" I stammer. "Do I need to call the police? Someone better explain what's going on!"

"I needed her help for five minutes." His hands go up in mock surrender, finally appearing chagrined. "That's all. It worked out fine." He pauses, grinning. "Ma'am."

I ignore his jab.

He's being a dick.

"Do you think I'm going to fall for your stupid smile, asshole? Think again." My chin notches up. "And do a better job explaining—this whole thing is weird."

I still have my hand on Wyatt's and give her a nudge with my hip. "Wyatt, give the man back his money."

"I'd rather not." Wyatt shakes her head back and forth slowly. "I held up my end of the bargain. We had a deal."

If looks could kill, my child would be on the ground *withering*, but she doesn't budge, grinning up at her new buddy, and I still have no clue what they're talking about.

I recognize the look in my daughter's eyes. It says, "You are not going to win this battle."

"Wyatt, sweetie, can you go back by Grandma and Grandpa?"

My darling child has the audacity to disagree. "Nah. I'd rather stay here and listen to you argue—Grandma and Grandpa are boring."

That's certainly true. They *can* be pretty boring.

Still.

"This is an adult matter." I give her another look, needing her to listen for once in her life. "And don't think we won't be discussing this later. Tell Grandma I'll be right there, that I had to use the ladies' room."

Begrudgingly, my kid slithers off, but not without watching us over her shoulder the entire way. I'm shocked she doesn't crash into any other tables, her gaze directed solely on me.

Nosy little shit.

I raise my brows at her before looking at Dex.

"So?"

He plops back down in his chair. "So the story is—I had to get rid of my date and your daughter offered to help."

Oh I bet she did. "How did the two of you meet?"

"I was coming out of the men's room, and she was coming out of the women's room, and I made an offhand comment about my date being shitty, and she leaped at the chance to help."

"Leaped at the chance?" Sounds about right. Wyatt lives for adventure. "How much did you pay her?"

He shrugs. "I don't remember."

"Don't you dare lie to me."

He stuffs his hands in the pockets of his jeans, probably the only dude in this place wearing denim.

"Enough to buy a LEGO set."

Dang. Those can be expensive.

He must have been desperate. "Was your date so terrible that you had to hire a child to do your dirty work?"

Dex shrugs. "I'm sure other people have had worse, but the ankle monitor was throwing me off."

Ankle monitor?

Welp, now I have a million questions.

I'm dying for details but don't want to give him the satisfaction of knowing I want to know details.

"And you paid Wyatt to . . ." My voice trails off so he can fill in the blanks.

"Ruin the date."

"And she ruined it by . . . doing what?"

"By pretending to be one of my eleven illegitimate children." He punctuates the sentence with a hard eye roll.

If I had a glass of water or wine held up to my lips, I would have spit it out with those last words.

"Did you say eleven illegitimate children?"

He laughs, tipping back his head. "She was calling me Dad and told my date about how she had ten siblings and has a reptile room at my house." Laughs some more. "Snakes make me vomit, by the way—she was pulling things out of her ass." He continues chuckling. "Classic Wyatt."

Yeah. Classic Wyatt, I guess.

My eyes go wide. "You have a reptile room at your house?"

"No, she was making things up as she went along." He leans back in his chair. "She's a great actress. You should put her in classes."

I feel my eyebrows rise. "You think she needs to learn how to be better at making shit up? No thank you, we're not paying for the privilege when she could teach the class." I hesitate, knowing I should get back to my parents and my cold entrée. "Why would you bring a first date to a place like this?"

"Because I'm a fucking moron?"

"That sounds accurate."

"Gee, thanks." His mouth is set in a grim line.

I tilt my head to the side, studying him. He looks exactly the way he did in those photos, the ones I'd accused him of faking.

Shit.

Even so, I don't mention the dating app. I don't tell him we matched. I don't tell him I accused him of being a fraud. He doesn't need to know I'm the woman who argued with him over petty bullshit in the Kissmet app.

Not worth it.

This man is an Adonis, and I saw the woman he was with. No way is a mousy elementary teacher his type.

"Well. Good luck to you, then. I should get back to my family."

"Thanks for reminding me I don't have one."

My jaw drops open. "Are you serious? You're such a dick!"

He chuckles. "Sorry. Couldn't resist."

My nostrils flare; I am so ready to depart. "Have a good night."

"I doubt that, but thanks."

Chapter 7

The chapter in which two opposing sides swipe on one another again, *despite the heated argument they had last time they matched in the app.*

Dex:
> Why didn't you tell me that was you?

Margot:
> Why did you swipe on me again?

Dex:
> Why did YOU swipe on ME again?!

Margot:
> Because. I wanted to see if you had the AUDACITY to swipe right on me again after I deleted you from my matches.

Dex:
You deleted me from your matches? Weird. I hadn't noticed

Margot:
LOL you are so full of shit.

Margot:
Question

Dex:
Hit me.

Margot:
Did you recognize me at the restaurant?

Dex:
Not at first. I knew you looked familiar though—I couldn't figure out why. My brain wasn't exactly operating at full capacity during that date. Things were slow to click into place.

Dex:
Did you recognize ME?

Margot:
Almost immediately, believe it or not...

Dex:
How???

Margot:
I mean, you have very distinctive features.

Dex:
Such as?

Margot:
I'm not getting into that with you right now—I'm not here to feed your ego.

Dex:
Why? Are you pissed at me about something?

Margot:
Gee, what could I possibly be pissed about? << sarcasm

Dex:
The fact that I didn't recognize you right away.

Margot:
No. I just assumed you weren't that bright to begin with.

Margot:
OMG was that rude? I am so sorry!!!

Margot:
Seriously. I am so sorry, that wasn't nice.

Dex:
A single tear is sliding down my cheek... Want to come wipe it off for me?

Margot:
LOL absolutely not. Asshole.

Dex:
How many times in one night can you call a man an asshole?

Margot:
> Do I keep doing that?? I'm SORRY! For real.

Dex:
> What was that? Say it again into my good ear.

Margot:
> I'm not repeating that again. I've already said it, what—3 times.

Dex:
> No worries. I'll take a screenshot and keep it in my photo gallery for a rainy day. Way better than a spank bank.

Margot:
> You will not. You won't need it.

Dex:
> Who says?

Margot:
> Me.

Dex:
Why wouldn't I need it?

Margot:
Because. We're never going to meet.

Dex:
But we did meet.

Margot:
You know what I meant; we're never going to meet AGAIN.

Dex:
Why not?

Margot:
We don't like each other, remember? I have a CHILD.

Dex:
Oh shit—that's right. You do have a kid.

Margot:
Ha

Dex:
Forgot about my rule about not dating women with kids.

Margot:
It's an actual RULE?

Dex:
Nah, I just made it up. But it makes sense to have a rule, considering I don't wanna be a dad.

Margot:
Wow.

Margot:
Do you have any single guy friends that don't mind kids? ISO a decent dude who's not a creep, and it has not been easy. I'm beginning to lose hope in mankind.

Dex:
I have no single friends that I would set you up with.

Margot:
Not a SINGLE single friend?

Dex:
Of course I have single friends. But they're douchebags and I wouldn't set you up with them.

Margot:
You're kind of a douchebag too.

Dex:
See? You made my point.

Dex:
Switching gears: how did you find me on the dating app the second time? I didn't think anyone would recognize me using old photos

Margot:
Yes, I noticed. And your name is different . . . is Declan actually your name?

Dex:
Yup. Dex is short for Declan.

Margot:
Huh. Would not have guessed. I would have gone with Dexter

Dex:
Yeah, that's a pretty common guess.

Margot:
Well to answer your earlier question, I recognized parts of the pictures you used last time—you CROPPED them, but I still knew it was you somehow. If that makes sense? And your name change isn't all that different.

Dex:
I doubt many people would have put the clues together.

Margot:
Probably not. I'm pretty smart **hair flip**

Dex:
That must be where your kid gets it from ;)

Margot:
Like mother, like daughter.

Dex:
She's a cool kid. I was taking aback by her. Is that a phrase? Taking aback?

Margot:
It's actually TAKEN aback, but yes. That's a phrase. And yeah, Wyatt surprises me on the daily. She's too smart for her own good. I have to be one step ahead of her at all times, which sometimes feels impossible.

Dex:
Well she helped me out a lot. So thanks.

Margot:
Don't be thanking me! I didn't give you permission LOL

Dex:
It was DEFCON 5! This was an urgent mission!

Margot:
Newsflash!!!!! Maybe vet women better BEFORE you invite them on dates. And also: don't invite them to places like Dickson's for a first

> date unless you mean it. That place gives off "I really like you" vibes.

Dex:
> That's kind of what Wyatt told me LOL

Margot:
> Oh I bet she did and PS: she is NOT available for future engagements. Or dates. Do better next time.

Dex:
> OUCH. Also, very funny.

Margot:
> I CANNOT believe how much you paid Wyatt, by the way! Are you out of your mind?!?! She is 10!

Dex:
> Listen, she helped me out, and 140 was our agreed upon price. She said you'd take her to the mall.

Margot:
> We were there this afternoon; she dragged me straight to the Lego store. I'm happy to report

> my spawn is already hard at work, building her new set.

Dex:
> What set is she working on?

Margot:
> It's an apartment building—it's pastel rainbow colored. Pretty cute, actually. Hopefully she doesn't finish it too quickly, those things are hella expensive. I can't be buying new sets every few days.

Dex:
> Apparently so

Dex:
> What did you tell your parents when you got back to the table? That's who you were with, yeah?

Margot:
> Yes. We were with my folks—Wyatt had already filled them in on the excitement by the time I sat back down. That child loves to be the bearer of the tea.

Dex:
That sounds accurate. She was more than willing to jump into the fray when she saw me loitering outside the men's bathroom. Hasn't your kid ever heard of stranger danger?

Margot:
YES. But apparently we have more work to do because LORD, she didn't hesitate to meddle in your business.

Dex:
She's freakishly good at lying.

Margot:
That's terrifying.

Dex:
Good luck with that...

Margot:
Ha ha. Thanks

Dex:
Where's her dad at?

Margot:
> He's in the picture he just travels a lot for work.

Dex:
> What's "a lot?"

Margot:
> He usually only sees her every other weekend—it's the same custody schedule people had in the 50s. Translation: I have her a majority of the time.

Dex:
> That sucks

Margot:
> LOL tell me how you really feel.

Dex:
> Shit, was that a rude thing to say? I meant: sucks that you have your kid all the time and don't have time to yourself.

Margot:
Uh—I mean, it was a bit rude, yes. But nothing you say any more surprises me. It's like you can't help yourself.

Dex:
Was that a compliment? It's hard to tell.

Margot:
No, that was not a compliment.

Margot:
It's probably a good thing that you only date women who are younger than you.

Dex:
What's that supposed to mean?

Margot:
I mean—they're probably more likely to put up with your shit.

Dex:
My shit?

Margot:
You know, let you say and do whatever you want because of the God complex.

Dex:
GOD complex???

Margot:
Oh please, admit it, you think your shit doesn't stink.

Dex:
I don't think my shit doesn't stink—I can be humble.

Margot:
Sure. Okay, if you say so.

Dex:
I do say so

Margot:
Okay.

Dex:
STOP DOING THAT

Margot:
Doing what?!

Dex:
Agreeing with me. It's annoying

Margot:
LOL

Margot:
I will say this: it's so refreshing that I can say whatever is on my mind because I don't care about impressing you.

Dex:
Now I'm insulted.

Margot:
Why?? You wouldn't want to date me anyway. I have a kid, remember?

Dex:
Uh, yeah, I do remember—who could forget a kid like Wyatt?

Margot:
Aw, see? Now that was nice.

Dex:
Was that a compliment?

Margot:
OMG. Were you speaking about my CHILD and using SARCASM?!?! What kind of an asshole are you?!

Dex:
LOL calm down, that wasn't sarcasm. I was being sincere.

Margot:
I seriously cannot with you. Unbelievable. This is why you're having bad luck with women.

Dex:
Is it? I hadn't noticed. Usually women fall into my lap and I don't have to make any effort.

Margot:
See? That's another one of your problems. You're so full of yourself?

Dex:
Am I??

Margot:
STOP DOING THAT!

Dex:
DOING WHAT?! I'm being HONEST

Margot:
I have no idea what to even say to you right now. My mind is blown.

Dex:
Hey. I have an idea.

Margot:
Don't tell me what it is, I don't think I want to know.

Dex:
What do you say about having a drink? You can tell me all the things you think I'm doing wrong and help me step up my game.

Margot:
Isn't there someone else who can be your dating coach? Don't you have any buddies?

Dex:
I have lots of buddies. But they're either A: fuck boys or B: busy with their families. Also, most of the ones I know met their partners in college or high school and don't have the same problems I do.

Margot:
Are you telling me there is NO ONE they're willing to set you up with??

Dex:
Hey, all I'm suggesting is a drink. It's the least I can do after paying your daughter to lie for me.

Margot:
> I mean, in your defense, you DID pay her.

Dex:
> True. And can I point out again that it WAS her idea . . .

Margot:
> I'll allow it.

Dex:
> So, drinks? You can tell me all the things that are wrong with me, and then we can go our separate ways.

Margot:
> Gee. What girl can resist an offer like that?

Chapter 8

Dex

"Take her for a drink, they said. It will be fun, they said," I mumble, disgruntled.

"First of all, I can hear you." Margot laughs, perched on the barstool next to me. "Second, this was *your* idea. I tried to weasel my way out of it, but you insisted."

She lifts her cocktail glass to her lips and sips.

Obviously, I watch.

I've been watching her a lot since we sat down at the bar of an old tavern on the outskirts of the city, closer to where she lives than I do—for the first time I tried to be a gentleman, seeing as she's doing me a favor and all.

"When did you try to weasel your way out of coming tonight?"

Margot rolls her eyes at me over the brim of her glass. "Remember when I asked if you had friends who could help you instead of me?" She swirls the crystal glass, studying the amber liquid and the big square ice cube before taking another sip. "I reckon if you sit here long enough by yourself, some lonely woman will find you."

I feel my entire forehead wrinkle. "Some lonely woman would find me? What am I, a charity case?"

My anti-date snorts. "Hardly. That wasn't my point. What I meant was, all you have to do is sit here and look pretty."

"Aww, you think I'm pretty?" I flutter my eyelashes as I lift my glass of beer. It's cold and in a frosted mug, just the way I like it.

Margot sighs long and loud. "You're lucky Wyatt had a slumber party tonight, or I would have canceled on you."

I'm not sure how to translate what she means by that. "What are you saying? That you can't get babysitters?"

She shrugs. "Sure, I can get babysitters. I just don't like wasting them on pointless"—she pauses, searching for the words—"efforts."

"You think this is pointless?" And what does she mean by efforts? Margot is confusing the fuck out of me.

She turns on the wooden stool, leveling me with a stare. "Yes. This isn't a date. You felt guilty about being an assbag, so you're buying me a drink, and I haven't had the chance to wear my new jeans out of the house, so I said yes."

New jeans?

*Ass*bag?

I'm trying to follow her logic. "You agreed to drinks so you could wear your new jeans?"

She nods, letting out a satisfied *ahhh* after her drink. "Yup. I don't like wasting them on the grocery store."

Margot slides off the stool, sets her glass on the bar top, and skims her palms over the front of her dark denim jeans. She postures and poses, jutting out her hip. For someone who hasn't spent more than a few minutes in my company, she certainly isn't shy.

It's as if she doesn't care what I think of her.

Tucked into the high waist of her pants is a black silk blouse—it's covered with small bright-blue lightning bolts.

The top three buttons are unbuttoned.

It's flirty.

Cute.

Big gold hoop earrings.

If she's trying to keep this evening casual, she's doing a remarkably shitty job because I haven't been able to stop staring down her shirt since we got here, and I sure as hell want to reach over and touch her hair, feel if it's as soft as it looks.

Instead, I set down my beer and crack my knuckles.

"Cute" is what I manage to say.

"Cute," she mimics, hopping back on her stool. "The thing every grown woman wants to be called."

"I don't know what you're getting annoyed about. If I had said those jeans make your ass look amazing, you would be insulted by that too."

Her head shakes. "Not true. These days, I'm willing to take whatever compliments I can get."

Margot laughs, looking adorable and fun and sexy, and in the back of my brain I wonder if anyone has taken our photo and whether or not a picture of us will appear online tomorrow. Or tonight.

One never knows.

I couldn't care less, but I imagine that as a teacher Margot would care a whole lot.

It's a weird, foreign feeling sitting next to a woman who doesn't seem to be interested in me romantically. Financially. Physically.

I should check her temperature; maybe she's coming down with an illness . . .

She plucks up a menu, studies it a few seconds before snapping it closed when the bartender walks over to wipe down the counter—whether he's trying to listen to our conversation or he's ready to take our order, I do not know.

"I find it so fascinating you're on a dating app." She resumes sipping her cocktail. "Is this your first go-round?"

I assume she's asking if I've been on dating apps before. "Yes, it's my first time. My, *uh*—friend's girlfriend created Kissmet."

Margot blinks at me.

Blinks again.

"Are you kidding me right now?" Smacks me on the shoulder as if I were her bro, eyes wide with delight. "Shut the front door! She did not."

I nod. "It's true."

"Stop it—that is so cool! Did she actually?"

I nod again. "Yeah. Her name is Harlow."

"That is so cool," she whispers again in an awe-filled voice. "What's it like knowing someone who created something so useful?"

She sounds so impressed. More impressed than she sounded when she discovered I am a bona fide, real-life professional athlete, my face and name scattered on billboards and products all over the country. All over the world.

My ego bruises a fraction.

I clear my throat. "Harlow is awesome."

"That's so neat," she gushes. "I can't wait to tell Wyatt."

I humph, shoulders slouching.

Perk up when the bartender returns with a basket of chips and another beer for me. Margot digs in immediately, chomping down on a chip. Moans as if it's the best thing she's had all week.

"What made you decide to start dating? Or go on an app, I mean. I bet you have women throwing themselves at you left and right."

I nod. "My friends are dropping like flies, and I was getting jealous of hearing about it." I laugh. "Once my friend Landon moved to a city to play football and to be with his girlfriend, I . . ."

She waits for me to finish, swirling her glass and staring down into it.

"It's about time to grow up," I say, jerking my head at the end of my sentence as if to say period point blank.

"But you don't want a family." Margot is about to pop another chip in her mouth.

"Nah, too busy for one."

"But you want a girlfriend?" Her nose is wrinkled up now, which tells me one thing: I said the wrong thing.

"Sure."

She chews.

Swallows.

Then.

"*Why?*"

"Why do I want a girlfriend?"

A nod. "Yes. You just said you were too busy for a family—wouldn't that same rule apply for a partner? Wouldn't that make you too busy for a relationship?"

"No, dude—a girlfriend can travel with me."

"So while you're working, she can follow you around the United States, waiting for you to get done with your games?"

I sigh with relief. She totally gets it!

"Exactly!"

Margot laughs. "That is the *stupidest* freaking thing I've ever heard."

It is? "Why?"

She shrugs. "For so many reasons, but you know what? It doesn't matter what I think because your dating life is none of my business. What *is* my business is your dragging my daughter into your dating drama, knowingly or not—she's done nothing but plot and plan more money-building schemes to involve you in since she met you."

"She is not." I chuckle. "And if I may be so bold to point out, she earned that money through hard work."

I hope she isn't going to beat this subject into the ground—I already explained why I paid her kid. We had a deal, and I honored it.

"We're not here to talk about what I should or shouldn't do with my money; we're here because you were going to give me some advice." We're also here because: why not. We connected on the app, shared some barbs, pissed each other off, and now we have one thing in common: we're both single and ready to commiserate.

She could have easily given me dating tips within the app, but after meeting her in person at the restaurant, this seemed like much more fun.

"It sounds like you know what you're looking for," she says after a time, crunching on more chips since the bartender hasn't brought the appetizer she ordered. "I think as long as you're honest from the beginning about what you want—which you have been—you'll find someone." Margot pauses. "There's someone for everyone."

She sounds altruistic, spewing do-gooder, motivational bullshit.

"Do you actually believe that?"

"Of course I do." She swirls her glass some more. "I have to."

My forehead creases. "I can't imagine you'll have a problem finding someone to date."

She is so fucking cute.

And funny.

And men aren't as picky as women are, if you don't count me among those ranks. I'm picky as hell.

"Uh, if you think it's easy for me because I'm a female, think again. You said so yourself—you don't want to date anyone with kids. Trust me, there are plenty of men like you, men who want nothing to do with a woman with children, even if it's only one."

Those men are fucking idiots. It's on the tip of my tongue to say. I stop myself, realizing it makes me sound incredibly hypocritical, even though I am being hypocritical.

It doesn't hurt that I've met her now.

And I've met her daughter.

That changes my mind a little, just slightly.

"How many dates have you been on?" I ask, watching as the bartender sets down a basket of fries and a basket of fried calamari, dipping sauces on the side.

Yum.

Margot smacks my hand away when I reach for one of the fries. "You said you didn't want to eat—this is just drinks."

Eh? "Why do you get to eat and I don't?"

"'Cause. I can sit here after you leave and continue to feast. I am in no rush."

That's not fair.

Not fair at all.

I reach for the basket again, and this time she allows me to steal three fries from it.

"How many dates have I been on?" She brings the conversation back around to my question. "Since downloading the app?" She pulls a sour face, thinking. "Eh, this one? Which doesn't count, obviously."

Obviously.

"Should I be offended that you don't consider this a date?"

"Why would you be offended? We clearly have one another in the friend zone."

"We have? Since when?" I steal a calamari, dipping it in red sauce and popping the entire piece in my mouth.

"Are you being serious?" Her mouth falls open. "You have no romantic interest in me."

Says who?

My brain might be saying no, but my dick is saying yes—why do we need to decide right this second who the winner will be?

"Would you like me to have romantic interest?" I ask her, to be clear. I already know she thinks I'm an asshole; she's told me to my face and in writing numerous times.

Margot nibbles on a fry. "I think that . . . had things not gotten off on the wrong foot, things might be different."

"Are you talking about the whole 'bribing your kid' thing?" 'Cause that was an accident.

"No. I'm talking about me getting salty about you being a catfish and you changing your profile because of it."

"But I'm not a catfish. I'm me."

She leans back on the barstool. "Right. And now I have no idea what to do with that information. A teacher cannot date a professional football player—it just wouldn't work." She shrugs, stuffing the entire fry in her mouth before reaching for another one. "Opposites might attract but not when someone is this opposite. It's so extreme."

She laughs.

"How do you know how opposite we are? You don't know me."

Margot rolls her eyes, looking very much like her daughter. "Fine. Give me some of your hobbies."

"I love the outdoors."

"See? I don't."

"I don't believe you," I scoff. "Do you like sledding? Or skiing? Or snowmobiles?"

"Who doesn't like sledding?" she reluctantly allows.

"Do you like secluded cabins in the woods?"

Her eyebrows go up. "For murder?"

That makes me laugh. "No, not for murder. For roaring fireplaces and hot chocolate and watching the snow fall through the windows."

She watches me, a blank expression on her face. "Did you suddenly become a poet?"

I laugh again. "Only trying to prove a point."

She huffs a sigh, crossing her arms. "Fine. I like the outdoors; I was just trying to be difficult."

No comment. "What about you?" I steal more appetizers.

"I like to read."

Was that a challenge?

"Same."

Her head tilts. "Oh, is that so. What kind of books?"

I crack my knuckles, pleased I have an answer to this to fire off. "Mostly audio. Easy to listen to on a flight and in the car."

"Like murder podcasts and such?"

I can't keep the smile off my lips. "What is it with you and trying to weasel a confession out of me that I'm a killer, you weirdo."

When Margot laughs, I study her. Head tipped back, hair falling down her back in waves, tits jiggling in her silk shirt—a dimple suddenly appearing in her cheek. *What'sthisnow?* A dimple?

Stop it right fucking now.

I want to put my finger in her cheek and poke it. How did I not notice this before? Oh yeah, I know how—she's been pissed at me until this very moment.

Dimples are my kryptonite.

A game changer.

It must only appear when she finds something really funny. This new indicator of my humor has activated a launch sequence. Must. Make. Her. Laugh.

Unfortunately, I'm more handsome than funny.

"I don't think you're a killer. Promise." She holds a hand to her heart. "But I am going to give you shit about it—that's a real concern for women in the dating world, so I'm sure you'll hear it again."

I hope not.

"Am I that intimidating?"

Margot has the nerve to laugh in my face. "No! God no. Why, do people tell you that?"

Uh.

Yes?

Literally all the time?

Have I mentioned my football stats? I'm a beefy six foot four, graduated from a Big Ten university with decent grades, sport a bushy beard sporadically, have wide linebacker shoulders, and eat three cheeseburgers in one sitting.

Not to brag.

"Oh my God." Margot cackles harder. "They do tell you that, don't they."

"Stop laughing at me." I spread my arms wide, beer in my left paw. "Do I not look like I could mud wrestle a bear?"

She laughs harder still, damn her. Is she being fucking serious? Why is this so funny? WHAT IS SHE LAUGHING AT?

"Mud wrestle? That is *so* specific."

"You're a brat," I finally say, much to her amusement.

"No, no—by all means, tell me how you're going to wrestle a bear, in the mud, and win. I want to hear it." Margot waves a hand aimlessly in the air, all the while mocking me.

I glare, a thousand retorts in the back of my brain and not a single one that's intelligent.

Chapter 9
Margot

I can do nothing but stare back at him.

He is at a loss for words, but I can see his brain racking for something witty to say. We've only spent a short bit of time in each other's company, but I feel as if I already know him well enough.

Dex is beyond irritated, which makes this all the more hilarious.

Aww. *Poor guy.*

He wants to have a clever comeback, but he doesn't know how.

I'm not doing his ego any favors by giggling at him uncontrollably, but c'est la vie.

It is what it is.

He's staring at me, eyes scanning my face. What does he see?

Not one of those women he chooses to date, the young, carefree kind who are able to give him the time he clearly desires. Someone who can be at his beck and call. Someone without responsibilities.

Dex is younger than I am by several years.

Yes, he has an insane profession. The deep dive I did on him after seeing him in person, at the restaurant, revealed an impressive NFL career—one that intimidates me, despite me telling him to his face that I am not intimidated by him. His job does, not the man himself.

The two feelings are not mutually exclusive.

"Tell me how you're going to wrestle a bear, in the mud, and win," I tease. "I want to hear it."

"I didn't mean literally," he says at last, thieving yet another one of my fries. At this rate I won't have any left; he is consuming them two or three at a time, the basket dwindling at a rapid pace as he jams them into his piehole.

And what a piehole it is.

I avert my eyes so he doesn't catch me gawking at him. Dex isn't my usual type, but who can resist a man built like him? Big. Broody. Good looking and rugged in an in-your-face kind of way. No doubt he has slept with dozens of women; no doubt he was irresistible in college.

I am a grade school teacher.

What am I doing sitting here with a man like this?

"So, besides the outdoors and audiobooks, what else are you into?"

We can't possibly have any more in common, and I'm determined to prove it.

"I love pizza," he blurts out.

My head cocks to the side. "Can pizza be considered a hobby?"

"Sure. I'm making it my mission in life to find the best slice."

Of course he is. *Why wouldn't he be?* "All right, fine. Pizza is your hobby."

"What foods do you love?" He asks me in kind. "Like, what food would you travel the world for?"

"Um—if I could travel the world to find my favorite food, I wouldn't be sitting here right now. I'd be in France." I let a chuckle escape my throat.

"That doesn't answer the question." He chews on a fried calamari, double-dipping in the sauces, first marinara, then the ranch, making a mess out of both containers.

Ugh, this guy.

"I'm not sure—I love pasta." But who doesn't? "So maybe pasta. Or." I nibble on my bottom lip as I ponder. "The world's best risotto."

Dex groans loud enough to wake the dead. "I love risotto!"

"Damn straight."

"You haven't had risotto until you've had Gordon Ramsay cook it for you." He mentions one of the most famous chefs in the world as if he hadn't just dropped a bomb into the conversation, following his comment with a swig of beer.

Waiting for him to come up for air, I watch as his Adam's apple bobs. He sets the glass on the counter. "What? What's the look for?"

"You just casually mentioned that Gordon Ramsay has prepared you risotto."

Dex shrugs his massive shoulders. "I mean, we were playing a game in London and he fed us."

Playing a game in London.

What that life must be like.

I clear my throat. "So yeah. Risotto." I have no idea what more to say. "Love it."

"Oh!" he exclaims. "I love Christmas!"

I perk up. "You do?"

"Totally. I start decorating in November." He gnaws on one of my fries.

I also start decorating in November.

"Do you actually have time to decorate yourself? Isn't November football season?"

I know enough about football to know the season runs through the holidays. My brother is a die-hard fan; he wears his jersey to Thanksgiving dinner and usually leaves the meal early to catch the rest of the game at home. "In peace," he'll say.

"Here's how I do it," Dex begins. "Yes, I have help putting up the decorations in the house, but the trees? Those I do myself."

"Trees? Plural?"

"Yeah, I have at least three. My living room is huge."

Oh.

Okay.

Wow.

This is a surprising factoid about him. Never would have guessed he would be a guy with a forest full of trees, but I cannot say I'd push him out of bed.

"How many trees do *you* have?" he asks me.

"Um. *One.*" Like a normal person. "I don't have a ton of room in my house for more than that."

Dex nods. "Makes sense."

"Are you only into the decorating, or are you into other holiday festivities too?"

"Like what?"

"Like . . ." I consider the holiday festivities one might partake in. "Shopping. Or going to see a play. Holiday concerts. Ice-skating."

"I don't have lots of time for anything else, but I enjoy looking at lights and shit." Dex clears his throat. "There's a competition show on TV that I watch where the contestants compete to see who can decorate their yards with the best and most lights, and the show picks one winner."

Interesting. "I'll have to look for that in the fall."

He makes a humming sound. "When I was younger, my grandma used to drive us around looking at holiday lights around town—that's probably why I get into it so much."

I can relate. "My grandma used to decorate her tree to the hilt. Garland and tinsel—tons and tons of tinsel—the whole nine yards." I love tinsel and would roll around in it if I could.

Sigh.

I wish I had more room, but I do have a bunch of my grandma's ornaments; I inherited them when she died.

I sure do miss her, and now I wish it were the holidays so I could decorate!

"I like most holidays, except Halloween, if I'm being honest." Dex takes the last calamari from the basket and holds it out toward me. "Want the last one?"

I shake my head. "All you."

"People can argue that Valentine's Day is too commercialized, but I like it anyway," he goes on, chewing. "Any excuse to do something fun, eh?"

I grin; I can't stop myself. "What I'm hearing is that you're kind of romantic."

He shrugs. "Don't know about that, but I do try. No reason not to." Dex sighs, rubbing his fingers on the napkin to clean up the oil from the appetizers. "We didn't have much growing up—my parents spent most of their money on stupid shit, and all they did was fight. So once I got older, I just . . ." He adjusts himself in his seat, shifting his ass. "I had a girlfriend my freshman year of college who was big into celebrating absolutely everything. She kind of changed my mind about it."

This perks me up.

The fact he was open minded about celebrating things simply because his girlfriend was into it says a lot about him. It tells me he's easygoing and open to new ideas. It tells me he's willing to compromise when someone he likes wants to do something he might not have been interested in doing.

Huh.

Who would have thunk?

"How long were the two of you dating?" Curious minds want to know what his past relationship status was like.

"Probably a year? Maybe less, I can't remember, we were young." He pushes the empty baskets away so the bartender can collect them, signaling for another round. "Do you want anything?"

My drink is half-full, but the ice has started to melt and dilute it, so I nod. Why not?

We're having fun, aren't we? No reason to rush home; no one is there.

I watch as Dex speaks to the guy behind the bar. Their easy conversation has them both grinning.

Perhaps Dex isn't the giant asshole I pegged him to be the first time we matched on Kissmet. Perhaps I misjudged him. *Or maybe you went at him so hard and aggressively he was automatically on defense.*

Yup. There's that...

Guilty as charged.

Was I the asshole in this situation?

I gulp, reaching for the water glass that has been on the counter in front of me this whole time, the condensation making a watery mess of my hands.

I sip from it, debating. Maybe I should say something about my bad attitude a few days ago? I mean, it's water under the bridge at this point. I don't get the sense he is holding a grudge. He seems like a decent dude.

Dex is actually...

Great.

Deep voice. Ridiculously large hands.

He definitely smells incredible. I've been tempted to lean over and give his neck a whiff the entire time we've been sitting here.

Shit. *Do not start fantasizing about him, Margot—he's not into you.* Well, maybe he is—it's hard to tell—but the fact is, he made it clear he does not want to date someone with kids, and getting involved with a guy (and by *involved* I mean have sex with) who has made his boundaries clear would be a mistake.

Your mistake, not his.

Honestly, Dex is hard to read.

He's friendly to everyone. Charming. Personable.

He's chatty. Willing to share information.

He's asking questions and answering them back.

Shit.

He is so damn good looking...

I lean forward to take the drink from the bartender's hand when he walks it over, smiling and thanking him, at the same time sneaking a sniff of Dex.

He smirks. "Did you just smell me?"

"Pfft. No!" I do not sound convincing.

"I think you did." He moves toward me. "Go ahead. Take another whiff."

"Knock it off." I shoo him away, scoffing, but my heart beats a little faster, betraying me and my good sense. "I wasn't smelling you."

Still.

Flirting isn't a crime, and I could sure use the practice.

"You're such a liar." He grins, taking a swig from his new glass of beer. "It's Blue Steel." He tells me. "I'm their spokesperson."

"Why does that not surprise me," I droll, watching as he pulls his phone out of his back pocket and begins scrolling through the gallery.

"See?" Dex holds it toward me, forcing my eyes to the screen.

Forcing my eyes on the bare-chested photos of him, surrounded by a dark background, dim lighting, glistening skin.

Of course, he's wearing boxer shorts.

He's tan.

He's . . . he's . . .

Jesus. He's perfect.

I swallow.

"Nice" is the best I can do, not wanting to gush or blush or make a fuss.

"I felt like a pig they were oiling up." He laughs, tucking the phone away. "But I have a lifetime supply of cologne. And I bought my childhood best bud a condo with the money."

A little pit forms in my stomach.

"That was very sweet of you."

Dex takes another drink of beer, bobbing his head in a nod. "Yeah. Dude has been with me through thick and thin. He's like the only family I have, besides Landon and a few other guys."

I almost make an *Aww* sound. I almost simper.

Almost.

'Cause the truth is, Dex is making my heart beat faster and my palms begin to sweat and my brain feel a bit addled.

Damn him.

Damn him for being a great guy.

A small part of me wishes he was the asshole he was when we first started talking on the app, so I would have a reason to push him away.

"So." His tongue peeps out of his mouth, running along his upper lip, licking the beer foam. "What's your story?"

"What do you mean?"

"I mean—what's the deal with Wyatt's dad? Or is that too personal?"

"He's around," I tell Dex. "In the picture, I mean. We got pregnant young, but we didn't want to get married or stay in a relationship just because I was having a baby, so we broke up when I was around six months."

Dex's mouth moves. "Ah. So he pulled a Tom Brady."

I don't know what that means but go with it. "Sure."

"No drama?"

"Nah, not really. I've only dated a few people in the last few years and no one that my family has met, so there hasn't been an opportunity." I take a sip of my cocktail. "I have no idea how he'd act if I had a boyfriend."

"Huh. Interesting." He pauses. "Is he seeing someone?"

"Yes, he has a girlfriend."

"How do they get along with your kid?"

"Fine. Obviously I worry, but—what can I do? I can't control his household; I can only control mine. And things are great, I'm just missing that one thing."

"Regular boning?"

I choke on my cocktail, shocked by his words.

No—shocked isn't the right word. Amused? Surprised?

"You went straight for it, didn't you?"

"It's one of my favorite words for sex besides the word *sex*." He laughs.

"Well, that's not the one thing that's missing—there's always a vibrator for that." Ha ha. "You know I meant a relationship. I would love to . . ."

Not be alone.

Have a partner.

Not have to rely on myself for everything.

"I would love to have someone other than my mother on my emergency-contact list," I finally say, hoping he'll find it funny.

And he does.

Dex gives me a chuckle, eyeing me over the rim of his glass. "I get it. My emergency contact is my agent." He rolls his eyes. "How fucking lame is that? My agent and Landon Burke. Like, what the fuck are they gonna do if I break my neck or tear a ligament?"

I blink. "Break your neck? Isn't that a bit extreme?"

"Hey. Out on that field anything can happen."

"Jesus," I breathe. "Your health insurance must be wild."

Dex's snicker is low and deep.

I pry my eyes away from his lips. His mouth.

I lift them to his eyes, only to find him staring at me.

"You're funny," he says at last.

I pause.

"Thanks."

Chapter 10

UNKNOWN NUMBER:
Aren't you glad you gave me your number at the end of that date?

Margot:
I'm sorry, who is this?

Dex:
It's me—your new best friend, Dex.

Margot:
Ahh, sorry, I wasn't expecting to hear from you.

Dex:
Why? We had fun, didn't we, or was I hallucinating?

Margot:

We totally had fun. But you're not looking for a new friend and I'm not looking for any new friends.

Dex:

We can always use more friends.

Margot:

I'm so sure the next woman you meet will LOVE the fact that you're collecting random women on your dating apps.

Dex:

You're not a random woman. You're Wyatt's mom.

Margot:

Ahh yes, forever known as Wyatt's mom . . . mostly in school circles but real life works too. So sexy.

Dex:

Hey, don't get sensitive, I was joking.

Margot:
I'm not! I was joking too.

Dex:
Hard to tell over a damn text message, yk?

Margot:
100%

Margot:
Are you texting me because you're so bored you have nothing else going on? I find that hard to believe.

Dex:
Nah, just wondering what you were up to.

Margot:
he he

Dex:
Having any luck? Any new dates?

Margot:
Yeah, I've been talking to this guy named Paul, but I have mixed feelings about it.

Dex:
Why—'cause his name is PAUL?

Margot:
What's wrong with the name Paul??

Dex:
Nothing. If you like nerds.

Margot:
LOLOLOL omg stop it, how do you know he's a nerd? He could be a professional football player in disguise.

Dex:
Please, no professional football players are on these apps.

Margot:
OH MY GOD.

Dex:
It's just me up in here.

Margot:
That's probably true. Although there is this one guy who says he plays baseball? But he's way too tall so I swiped left.

Dex:
What's "TOO TALL?" if you don't mind my asking.

Margot:
I don't know, I think it said he was 6'5"?

Dex:
Dude, I'm 6'4"

Margot:
Yeah, but that one extra inch is pushing it.

Dex:
You are really something else . . .

Margot:
blushes Awww thank you

Dex:
So what are you doing, it's like—almost bedtime, why you still up?

Margot:
I was writing this week's lesson plans.

Dex:
What does that mean?

Margot:
It means I'm going over the week, day by day, and planning what to teach the children. LOL

Dex:
That is so fucking adorable.

Margot:
Um. Thanks?

Dex:
I'd give my left nut to sit at the back of a classroom and watch you teach little people.

Margot:
Just the left nut? Not both??

Dex:
LOL

Margot:
Have you been drinking?

Dex:
No. Why? Have you?

Margot:
No, but you're being goofy so one has to wonder.

Dex:
I'm always goofy.

Margot:
What are you up to right now? As you said, it's getting kind of late. Or are you a night owl?

Dex:
Definitely a night owl, depending. There's nothing to watch on TV, and I can't get into a new book and the house just feels really quiet, so I figured I'd see what you were doing.

Dex:
Are you a night owl or a morning person?

Margot:
Both, I guess? I feel like I don't need much sleep to be peppy, but who knows. I wake up early during the week because I have to get to school and stuff.

Dex:
Yeah, same. Also depends on the season. If we're knee-deep in the shit, I go to bed at like, 7PM, if we don't have an evening game. I sleep a lot sometimes LOL

Margot:
That makes sense.

Dex:
So what is it like being a teacher and molding young minds and shit?

Margot:
LOL "molding young minds and shit"—no one has ever put it that way. I've always wanted to be a teacher, so I really love my job, even when you have a difficult parent.

Dex:
How are parents difficult?

Margot:
You know—the parents who think Little Morgan is perfect and not the classroom bully when in fact Little Morgan is out stealing toys and pulling hair and scribbling on someone else's paper to be a dickhead. The level of denial can be frustrating.

Dex:
Do you actually have a kid named Morgan?

Margot:
That's your takeaway from that paragraph?

Dex:
Yeah. I'm a detail-oriented person.

Margot:
Yes, I have a kid named Morgan, but that's confidential. Don't repeat what I just told you.

Dex:
My lips are sealed.

Margot:
Dammit. Hold on, I heard something. BRB

Dex:
Holding . . .

Dex:
...

Dex:
10 minutes later, still holding . . .

Dex:
Balls shriveling up.

Margot:
Okay, I'm back. What's this about your BALLS shriveling up? Is that something you say to all the girls or am I special?

Dex:
Ha ha.

Dex:
Is everything ok you said you heard something? What's going on?

Margot:
Ugh, I have this faucet in my kitchen that refuses to cooperate. It's been leaky and making these weird sounds, like the entire house

> sounds haunted when all we're trying to do is fill a glass of water. It's become a nightmare.

Dex:
> Well. Get a plumber.

Margot:
> That's easy for you to say, you probably have 150 bucks to throw at some guy JUST to show up on your doorstep and then another few hundred to fix whatever the problem is. My house is haunted, let's be real.

Dex:
> First of all, I can fix a pipe or a leak. How hard can it be?

Margot:
> Dear Lord, do you dabble in plumbing on the weekends?

Dex:
> No, but I know enough, and there are videos on the internet that show you exactly what needs to be done.

Margot:
> Are you volunteering to come fix my pipes?

Dex:
> Yes. Where in Scottsdale are you?

Margot:
> I'd say it's closer to the outskirts, in the older part. You?

Dex:
> Oh. Definitely the part they refer to as Snottsdale. Ha. It's like we're neighbors.

Margot:
> Er, not even a little . . .

Dex:
> But this is the city, so everyone is nearby.

Dex:
> I can come and look at your shit, it's not a big deal. I have some time, preseason isn't until August.

Margot:
Is that why you have all this free time to date?

Dex:
Yeah, pretty much.

Margot:
K. If you think you can fix my problem, have at it . . .

Chapter 11

Dex

I'm not a plumber, but I can damn well pretend to be one.

I hoist the toolbox out of my sports car, the toolbox I borrowed from a buddy's buddy who is a plumber. It was a massive pain in the ass to meet him, pick up the tools, explain the situation, and then listen to his insistence that he could easily drop in himself as a favor.

Should I have let him? Sure.

Would it have saved me a shit ton of time and a headache? Absolutely.

But I didn't, because I never listen. Not even to my own inner voice, which honestly wasn't talking that loud. Besides, I don't need some other dude, down on his knees, eyeballing Margot's leaky plumbing.

I give the door of her condo a few quick knocks, ignoring the doorbell that's glowing at me—something about ringing an *actual* doorbell gives me anxiety. Like, it's such an aggressive way to announce your arrival, and I don't see a camera, so I can't make a face at one.

I step back, waiting.

Nothing.

"Is she leaving me out here on purpose? She's expecting me," I grumble, knowing *full well* that Margot could in fact be purposely leaving me on her porch to suffer. I don't know her well, but this seems like something she would do to get a rise out of me.

Minutes later, the door opens and she stands there, somewhat out of breath as she regards me through the crack as if she weren't expecting me.

"Oh!" she declares. "How long have you been waiting? I was on the treadmill and didn't hear you knock."

Treadmill my ass.

She isn't wearing workout clothes, and she sure isn't wearing sneakers.

Margot pulls the door all the way open and sidesteps, allowing me room so I can enter her place; the small foyer is cute and cozy. Her condo is larger than it looks from the outside, with high ceilings and tall doorframes.

It's modern and chic.

Huh.

My head is on a swivel as I walk toward the kitchen. She has an open layout, and I can see the sink from the door, taking in the light-gray couch, the dark-gray tile surrounding the fireplace, the shiplap accent wall, and dark beams across the ceiling.

The backsplash in her kitchen is dark gray too. Stainless steel appliances.

The place is spotless.

"Wanna show me what the problem is, ma'am?" I tease, setting the toolbox on the stone counter.

"You're going to just jump right into it?" She laughs. "No foreplay? No 'How have you been?'"

I didn't realize she wanted niceties, but if she wants to chat before I try to fix her plumbing, who am I to argue?

"How have you been?" I ask, because she told me to, grinning when she giggles.

"I could use a drink."

"Same."

Margot nods, going around to the other side of the counter and pulling open a cabinet. It has a crisp white door, and inside are white plates, stacked neatly above cut-crystal drinking glasses.

She takes out two and sets them on the counter.

"What'll it be?"

"Got any beer?" That's an easy enough request, yeah?

She pulls a face. "Er. Not really, but I can make you something? I have Coke and vodka." She scratches her head. "Rum. And wine? That's all I have, sorry. Maybe once I start dating someone, I'll stock up."

I almost say "Ouch," but then I remember—she and I are not dating. She and I are not flirting. We are not looking for the same things.

"I'll do wine, thanks."

She hesitates. "Uh—is it okay if I put it in this glass?"

"You don't have wineglasses?" I ask critically. "Everyone has wineglasses."

She shrugs. "I don't sit around drinking wine, so I'm not about to run out and spend money on something I don't need."

Fair enough.

I watch as she removes a bottle of white wine from a different cabinet, then watch as she hands it over to me.

I peel off the metal wrapping, then twist off the top, pulling out the cork.

"Thanks." She smiles, pouring as I ease onto a barstool, gazing at her as I would a bartender. "You're so strong."

I blink at her.

Then,

"Don't be an asshole—you could totally have gotten that off yourself."

"Obviously." Margot laughs as she slides the glass across the center island toward my waiting hand. "But you're here to help me, and I figured we should start right away."

Is she flirting with me?

Hard to say.

I chug the wine in my glass because wine ain't shit and does nothing for me. I could drink the entire bottle before I felt buzzed. She watches me wide eyed as I down the glass.

"I don't know if you noticed, but I'm a big dude."

"I've noticed."

"You have?" I tease, genuinely curious about her feelings for me. Other than being disgusted by the fact that I don't want to date a woman with kids, I don't actually know—if I hadn't said it... would she go out with me?

She's tough to read.

"Of course I have. I'm a teacher, it's my job to notice stuff."

Ahh. "Are you saying I act like a kid?"

Margot leans toward me, wine bottle in hand, pouring more into my glass as she says, "Did I say you act like a kid?"

No.

No she did not. But still, the implication that I'm like a kid clenches my butt cheeks a bit.

I want her to tell me more about how I'm a big dude, and how she's noticed how big I am, and whether or not I'm her type. She did swipe on me after all...

I take more time sipping the second glass she served me. The flavor is rich and full, and as a man who usually only drinks beer, I'm digging it.

Margot rests on her elbows as she leans against the counter, and damn if I don't notice her cleavage, or the outline of her bra beneath her plain white shirt, or her tan collarbone.

A thin gold chain hangs around her neck with a tiny letter *W*.

It shimmers and winks at me, and I pull my eyes away so it doesn't look like I'm staring at her tits.

Which I am.

I'm trying to determine how big they are without having any information. Would they fit in my hand? Is she wearing a push-up bra?

Admittedly I am an ass-and-tits guy.

Can't help myself.

Margot, unfortunately, is wearing jeans—the slouchy kind they call boyfriend jeans—with rips and tears. They hang down past her hips, so I can't get a look at her backside.

Bare feet.

Hair down.

It's brown and long and in waves.

Little to no makeup.

"I like your freckles," I tell her, drinking half the glass of wine.

Her hand goes up, two fingers touching her skin. Nose. Cheeks. "I used to hate them growing up."

I didn't notice them at the restaurant, and I hadn't noticed them in her photos.

"Do you cover them with makeup?"

She nods. "Sometimes. Depends."

Hmm. "That's a shame."

I kind of want to lick them.

I kind of want to lick her all over, down the middle of her chest, down her stomach, see what's beneath that white shirt.

"Are you okay?" Margot asks. "You look weird."

"Huh?" I give my head a shake. "Sorry. I was just daydreaming." *About what you might look like with no clothes on.* Hey, just 'cause we're not going to have a relationship doesn't mean we can't have fun—does it?

I wonder if she'd be up for a friends-with-benefits situation or if she has her heart set on meeting someone for the long term.

She sips.

I sip.

Finish the second glass and push it forward; the little buzz I begin to feel surprises the shit out of me.

I stand, pushing the stool back in. "I should get to work, eh? I don't want to take up your entire night."

"Sure." She nods. "Yeah, I get it."

"Where's the issue?" I come around to her side of the counter to get to the sink.

Margot pulls the cabinet open and bends to peer beneath. "It's in there."

"It's in there?" I laugh, arm brushing hers.

She doesn't move to give me more space, which I take as a good sign. She's not apprehensive of me, and she doesn't need to create distance.

"Have a flashlight? I'm going to have to get down in there." To be on the safe side I add, "And maybe a towel or two." If anything I'll need one for my head, to get comfortable.

"You're actually going to crawl down under the cabinet?" She appears skeptical. "Are you going to fit?"

She wouldn't believe the places I can fit myself, *if you catch my drift.* Ha!

I don't say it out loud—I don't need her thinking I'm a pig.

As I get down on my hands and knees to look below her sink, she hands me a flashlight that materializes out of nowhere. I click it on, pointing it at her pipes.

"Yup, it's leaking," I announce as if I've just solved her problem—a problem she was well aware of. She knew there was a leak and did not need me to remind her.

The thing is, I have no goddamn idea how to fix a leak, and we both know it. We also both know I'm never going to freely admit being incompetent.

No.

What I'm going to do is get down under this sink and get inside her cabinet and make a bigger mess than she already has.

Chapter 12

Margot

Question: *Why do I get the feeling that Dex has no freaking clue what he's doing?*
Answer: *Because it's obvious he has no idea what he's doing.*
For all his grunting, it doesn't seem as if he's done much of anything, short of asking whether I have duct tape handy . . . and other items one should never need while repairing things at home.

"What do you need duct tape for?"

I'm bending over his body, doing my best not to ogle his bare midriff, but my eyes linger far too long on his torso. His flat stomach. The happy trail disappearing beneath the waistband of his jeans, which are a tad too big.

He has an innie belly button.

A cherry birthmark just above it.

His broad shoulders are lodged in my dinky cabinet, and the coif he walked in with, which was perfectly styled, has been a chaotic mess the few times he's lifted his head to address me.

Deep frown lines are etched across his forehead.

"Are you *sure* you know what you're doing?" I ask for what has to be the third time, and not to sound doubtful—'cause I have absolute faith that he does not in fact know what he's doing. I make a half-assed attempt to keep the laughter out of my voice.

"Absolutely," he grunts, hand fumbling around in front of him, reaching for another tool from those that have been scattered on the floor. "I've watched a bunch of tutorials, plus my buddy's buddy told me how. How hard can it be?"

How hard can it be, indeed . . .

Famous last words.

I shift my weight as I hover, enjoying the sight of him out of his element. From what I know about him, Dex is confident, somewhat arrogant, and in control.

Seeing him like this—struggling and flailing—not only has me giggling at him but also has butterflies wakening in the pit of my stomach.

"Let me know if you need anything. I'm right here."

His legs shift as he makes room for his huge body.

A loud clunk echoes from the sink, followed by a muttered curse. "Are you sure everything's okay down there?"

Everything is not okay down there, and I need for him to admit it before the faucet or pipes explode.

I nibble on my thumbnail nervously.

"Yep, I think this is what my buddy said to do." His deep voice mutters with strain, though he will not admit defeat. I hear him twist a wrench, watch as his biceps flex under his T-shirt as he cranks. "Lefty loosey, righty tighty."

"This isn't the worst view," I mumble to myself, unable to stop staring at his midriff. I mean, the man is harmless while he's under my sink; I can ogle him all I want, yeah? Once he's standing in front of me, though, that's a whole other story.

I only pretend to be brave and put on a happy face, but deep down inside I'm a confused, mushy mess when it comes to men.

I take the glass of wine from the counter and down a mouthful, admiring Dex's handiwork. And his stomach.

"Maybe you should take a break," I suggest, after he utters yet another curse. "It's not too late to call a professional." It's not too late for his plumber friend to come by and fix what Dex obviously cannot.

He adjusts himself inside my cabinet, leaning on his elbows so he can look up at me, blue eyes filled with determination. "No way am I calling a professional. Winners don't quit."

Winners don't quit?

Oh Jesus.

"This isn't football."

Dex grunts.

Returns to his back, determined to figure this out on his own.

I raise a brow but decide not to say another peep about the time he's been below the sink. Shouldn't he have a grasp on this by now? Shouldn't he kind of already have this figured out?

I press my lips together.

Actually, now that I think about it . . . maybe I should be filming him. So when everything does inevitably implode, I have it on my phone for posterity and I can watch it again and again. Or show Wyatt. She would think it's hilarious.

Or maybe my time is better served going to the bathroom and grabbing a stack of towels. Just in case.

It's endearing, this desire he has to fix my problem.

Me, a practical stranger.

Me, a random woman he met on a dating app and has no interest in dating.

Makes him seem human, not this larger-than-life figure I had to read about on the internet.

Minutes tick by, and he is still grunting and making a big stink beneath the counter.

I can't *see* his frustration, but I can *feel* it simmering. I can hear it with every turn of a wrench or screwdriver or whatever tools he's using that I can't see because it's dark down there.

I'm too scared to look, honestly.

He wipes his hands on a dingy rag I handed him earlier.

"Everything all right?"

"Just fine," Dex grumbles, his tone far less confident than it was before. "Almost there."

Sure it is.

I stifle a giggle, my attraction for him growing. His determination is charming, even if it is slightly misguided.

Don't quit your day job, Dex.

"Okay, I definitely think I've got it now," he declares triumphantly, beginning the slow shimmy out of his spot. He uncurls himself, emerging at last from under the sink, his hair tousled, face flushed.

He doesn't look any less hot than he did when he got here.

More so, if I'm being honest.

"Moment of truth. Let's test it out." He reaches to turn the faucet, and my breath hitches, caught in my throat.

Nothing.

For a brief, glorious second, *nothing* happens. Nothing at all.

No water, no gush, no explosion.

My shoulders relax, thinking maybe he has actually managed to fix the—

A burst of air emerges from the faucet.

Whoosh!

Water shoots out of the faucet like a geyser. I don't know how, but it arches through the air, drenching Dex and me and spraying water all over the kitchen. This way, that way—all the ways!

Water is everywhere.

I scream, "Oh my God!"

Frantically fumbling for a towel, I toss it over the nozzle to stop the outpour of water from spraying everything in sight. "Holy shit!"

Holy shit, holy shit, holy shit!

We are both soaked.

Water covers me from head to toe, my white T-shirt drenched.

My clothes cling to me as I stand here, dripping water onto the tile floor, shivering as Dex stares at me, wide eyed and horrified, droplets of water dribbling from his hair.

"Dex!" I sputter. "I . . . this . . ." I have no words.

"Oh my dude, I'm so sorry!" He scrambles to turn the water off, but that only seems to make the spray worse if that were possible.

"What is happening!" I shout with a laugh, the situation too ridiculous to do anything but. If I don't laugh, I may cry.

This was inevitable; let's be real here. Dex is a pretty football star, not a handyman.

Side by side we stand in stunned silence, the hissing of my pipes the only sound in the air. That and the mini waterfall cascading down the front of my cabinet, pooling on the floor.

"That was not supposed to happen."

"Ya think?" I move, water at my feet dripping from the countertops. What a freaking mess!

A knot forms in my stomach, nerves and hysteria creating a bubble that rises in my throat and threatens to erupt like my pipes.

I burst out laughing.

"This isn't funny!" he protests, though a smile tugs at the corners of his mouth.

"No, it's not. It's a mess. But also, it kind of is." I wipe water from my eyes, almost positive I'm crying too. "I told you we should have called a pro."

"I am a pro."

"Do not compare yourself to a skilled tradesman. You play sports." Not even close to being the same thing.

He shakes his wet head. "All right, fine. You were right—we should have called my buddy."

I grab another nearby towel and hand it to him, still chuckling. "I think it's safe to say you need to retire your borrowed tool belt."

He sighs, using the towel to wipe his face. "You didn't happen to film that, did you?" He looks so sheepish, standing there dripping wet, that I feel a pang of sympathy.

"No. But I thought about it," I admit, stepping closer and putting a hand on his arm. "I appreciate you trying. Really. It means a lot to me."

He glances down at me, eyes roaming down the center of my chest. "Are you wearing one of those nipple bras?"

"What? No!" I laugh, batting at him. "Why would you say that?"

"'Cause I can totally see your nips through your shirt."

I look down. Sure enough, not only are my areolas on full display because of the cheap, threadbare bra I'm wearing, but my nipples are determined to escape.

"Oh shit." I cross my arms. "I feel like I've entered a wet T-shirt contest I have no business entering."

Dex reaches forward, his big hands unfolding my arms and holding them out so he can look at me. "What the hell are you talking about? Look at these boobs. They're amazing."

I feel myself blushing despite the fact that I'm cold.

"Aw, gosh. I'm flattered you th-think so," I stutter. It's been ages since a grown man has blatantly gawked at my tits, T-shirt impeding his view or not.

"You're the cutest fucking thing I've ever seen, all soaked to the skin and dripping wet."

I'll never forget the way he said *and dripping wet* . . .

Dumbly, I nod.

Let him walk me backward until my ass bumps the cabinets.

His hands on my hips—I have no protest, only curiosity. What's he going to do with me once he has me where he wants me?

Chapter 13

Dex

I have her where I want her.

The best part is, she's already dripping wet.

Not for me, but still.

Wet is wet.

I put my mouth on the side of her neck, inhaling that perfume I like so much, its musky scent mingling with her damp skin, and when I put my lips there, she tilts her neck.

Margot is shorter than I am—who isn't?

I have to bend a bit at the knees to accommodate her, or better yet, why don't I lift her onto the counter to make things easier?

Damn good idea, Dex.

I do what I've been wanting to do since she sassed me in the restaurant—I kiss her on her pouty mouth, savoring the surprise and the hands that are now sliding up my spine.

Margot tastes delicious.

She doesn't hold back either. No hesitation, no shy bone.

I move so I'm standing between her legs, pressing against her and the cabinet front, dick straining to say hello to her. He's eager to play—as usual.

Ignoring the mess that is being made, we kiss—and damned if I don't begin exploring the wet T-shirt clinging so seductively to Margot's body, her boobs now in my palms.

Yes, both of them.

It's electric, a kiss that makes me forget the chaos around us and the giant mess I made because I was trying to look cool.

Margot doesn't seem to give a shit, pulling me closer instead of pushing me away, her fingers tangling in my mussed-up hair, her soft lips warm. It's a contrast to the cold water dripping from my hair. Hers. The sink.

Drip.

Drip.

Drip.

It feels like we're in our own bubble, untouchable and invincible, lost in each other, and I swear, I could eat her up.

I could spread her legs, kneel in front of her, and—

The sudden sound of a door opening jolts us back to reality.

We break apart, breathless, and turn to see Wyatt standing in the doorway of the kitchen, frozen in place, eyes wide and her mouth slightly open in shock.

"Mom? What the . . . ?" Her eyes are everywhere, taking in the scene.

The floor. Her mom and me.

The floor.

The ceiling.

"What on earth is going on here?" Wyatt's voice is a mix of surprise and amusement, though there's an undeniable edge of her disapproval there too. "Mother!"

Yikes. *Not the preteen disapproval . . .*

Margot gives me a little shove so she can hop down off the counter, her face turning a deep shade of red. She pulls at her T-shirt so it's not clinging to her stomach, or her boobs.

Damn shame.

"Wyatt!" Her voice is high pitched in the way that screams GUILTY. "Hey, sweetie! What, um—are you doing home?"

She's still pulling at her top so it doesn't stick to her frame.

Wyatt has her eyes locked on my face, the unflinching little shit.

"I forgot my face stuff and my blanket, so Grandma and I decided it would be easier if I slept here tonight." Her face is stone-cold sober. A veritable mask of judgment. "What were the two of you doing?"

"Kid, I think it's obvious what we were doing," I'm tempted to say, though it's not the right time, and I don't want to risk getting nudged in the gut.

"I had a little . . . problem with the faucet, and um, Dex came over to fix it. You remember Dex, don't you? From dinner?"

Wyatt's gaze shifts between us, taking in our soaked clothes and the puddles spread across the kitchen floor. "Yeah, I can see you had a problem with the faucet." Her hands are on her hips now. "Looks like you had more than *just* an accident with the faucet."

Her eyebrow arches in that knowing, sarcastic way only a preteen can manage.

Honestly, she's scaring me.

I clear my throat, trying to regain some semblance of composure. "I thought I'd be helping her out."

"Yeah, I sure bet you wanted to help." Wyatt smirks, crossing her skinny arms and leaning against the doorframe. "This is definitely not awkward at all."

Margot attempts to smooth her wet hair, failing to look anything other than flustered. "Wyatt, sweetie, it really *was* just a plumbing disaster. We, uh—I was just helping him clean up."

"Sure, Mom. Whatever you say." Wyatt rolls her eyes. "Next time, maybe you guys could try not to flood the kitchen while sucking each other's faces off."

Sucking each other's faces off. That's a new one.

I file it away for later, stifling a laugh, impressed by Wyatt's boldness—but also acutely aware of how embarrassing this must be for Margot.

Me? Not so much.

"Your mom was thanking me for flooding the kitchen."

Margot smacks me in the ribs. "Would you shut up?"

"Ha. Better you than me!" Wyatt's knowing smirk brings me right back to when we met in the restaurant; she was totally in her element and the one giving me direction, not the other way around. Balls of steel, this one.

"It's not as bad as it looks." Margot tries to lighten the situation with a lie, still yanking at her shirt.

"Seriously, Mom, this kitchen is a mess. I should have stayed with Grandma. *Ugh.*"

Margot nods. "We're going to start cleaning up."

Her daughter's brows rise. "Need help?"

Another nod. "Sure. If you can bring me all the towels from the bathroom, that would be amazing."

The kid disappears, but *not* before shooting me a glance over her shoulder with narrowed eyes.

Shit.

She doesn't trust me.

She must know I'm not a huge fan of kids.

"She won't be gone long. I have a feeling she's going to lurk around the corner somewhere and eavesdrop."

"Ya think?" Although there aren't many places to hide in this tiny place, there's no doubt that Wyatt will feel the need to spy. Probably nothing more exciting than catching your mom making out with the dude who paid you to lie for him.

The kid seems like she's always up for the next adventure, and while she looked protective just now, she didn't look pissed.

"I guess I owe you." I manage to sound abashed.

"Owe me what?"

"Well. First off, I owe you an actual plumber. I'll call my buddy and have someone here tomorrow—promise. Secondly, I owe you an actual night out." I feel like the worst, biggest fucking idiot, and an asshole.

Margot gives her head a little shake. "You don't owe me a plumber—and you don't owe me a night out." She laughs, her boobs jiggling in the sexiest way.

She pushes the hair out of her face. It looked so damn pretty when I first arrived, and now she looks like a cute drowned rat.

"Sure I do."

"You're going to send someone to fix this and *feed* me?"

I shrug. "I mean, maybe we don't go to eat first. Maybe we do an activity, like golf."

"Whoa." She walks to a small closet in the kitchen and removes a mop. "Slow your roll."

She hands it to me, and as we start sopping up the water, Wyatt returns with the towels, taking charge of her mother and me with surprising efficiency, directing us on what to do next as if she were a tiny drill sergeant. Eventually the awkwardness of the moment starts to fade, replaced by a sense of camaraderie.

The three of us working together.

A team.

Above Wyatt's head, Margot and I share a few amused glances, silently acknowledging the absurdity of the entire situation.

"So wait." I stop mopping, leaning against the mop handle. "You don't want to golf with me?"

How am I supposed to show her how good I am at everything if she doesn't want to hang out with me? Golf, pickleball, rugby—you name it, I can play it. And playing with her would surely be pretty damn fun.

"You know, for a guy who doesn't want to *date* me, it sure does seem like you're trying to date me."

"I thought we were friends," I point out. "Friends hang out."

"Do friends make out too?"

Some of them do!

I roll my eyes and go back to mopping. "That kiss lasted less than two minutes."

"And I would have ended it regardless of Wyatt busting us."

"Hey!" Wyatt says. "I'm literally standing right here."

That makes us laugh, and I throw my head back, more entertained by her than I'm willing to admit out loud.

"Wyatt, your mom is so full of shit." I look at Margot. "You would have kissed me all night if she hadn't walked in, admit it."

She shrugs, resuming her task as I move the mophead around the floor. "Guess you'll never know."

Guess not.

"So what do you say? Let me make it up to you, and then I'll leave you alone."

She snorts. "You keep telling me that. And yet, here you are, in my house, not leaving me alone."

"Hey. You can say no."

"True. But I'm a single mom with a limited budget—it's not a crime to try and weasel free plumbing out of you. Or free food."

∼

I'm home and I'm dry.

And I'm strolling through the bedroom with a towel wrapped around my waist when my agent calls, his name lighting up the screen of my cell later than usual.

Huh.

Weird.

I hit accept, put the phone on speaker, and toss it to the bed so I can continue getting dressed.

"Hey."

"How you been?"

"Fine." I pull on a T-shirt. "What's up?"

Cut to the chase, dude.

I wish he'd get to the point; this small talk makes me fidgety. If he has bad news, I need him to fucking say it.

Trent laughs.

He's new to me—I signed with him less than a year ago, and although he's a ballbuster who does not put up with shit, he's also up in my business. Always wants to know how I'm doing, where I'm at in life, if I'm in touch with my feelings.

That kind of bullshit.

"Is something wrong?" I can't take the suspense.

"No, man." I hear rustling in the background and wonder why he's still working this late at night. "Just had some free time and thought I would check in."

I pause in front of the mirror, staring at my reflection.

Damn, I'm handsome.

Damn, I'm hungry.

I pull on some shorts, grab my phone, and head toward the kitchen in search of pizza—or a sandwich.

"So what's been going on with your love life? Landon said you were on a dating app?" He doesn't waste a single second digging for the dirt, does he? Can't figure out why he'd even care.

"Yeah. But it's not as easy as I thought it was going to be."

"Really? How so?"

"First of all, I had originally gone on the apps as myself, Dex the football player, and that only served in attracting gold diggers." I yank open the fridge to inspect the snacks Carrie hopefully prepared. "Then Landon told me I was being a fucking twat and I shouldn't be on the app as myself. So I created a fake profile with fake-ish information and—lo and behold—attracted a woman who hates my guts."

"How can a woman you haven't met hate your guts?"

"'Cause. We had words when I was being myself."

There is a long pause on his end of the line. So long I have to ask, "Dude. Are you there?"

"I'm here. I'm just trying to figure out what the hell you're talking about."

I give my head a shake, tucking my phone under my chin so I can remove a few containers from the shelves. "Doesn't matter. The point is, she hated me and now we're friends."

"Who is this person?"

I don't have time to keep explaining this shit to him. I mean, I technically do, but why would I want to? He should learn to pay more attention.

"Some mom I met on the app."

"A mom?" It sounds like his eyes just bugged out of his skull. "You're dating a single mom?"

Does he have to say it like that, in that tone? Rude.

"No, I'm not dating a single mom," I scoff. "Honestly, though, her daughter is pretty fucking cool."

"You met the daughter?" I can hear his brows go up into his receding hairline and his blood pressure rise.

Dude needs to chill. "Can we not get into it? I'm hungry."

"So you are dating her or not dating her?"

"Not."

Trent is quiet a few seconds as he considers all this new information. "Why?"

"Why am I not dating her?" I crack open a container and stare inside. Sniff it for good measure. "I just told you—she has a daughter."

"Ah," Trent breathes. "Gotcha."

I don't say more. It's not like I need to explain what my boundaries are and why, when it comes to my personal life, because before this week, I had *none*.

"She's a teacher—it's not like she has time to babysit me."

My agent lets out a low whistle on the other end of the phone, and it's really fucking polarizing. "A first-grade teacher and a single mom? Man, that's, like, the holy grail."

Holy grail? I slap some mayo on a piece of bread with a butter knife and take the chicken from the storage container and plop it on top of the bread, too, half listening.

"What the hell are you even talking about? How do you know she teaches first grade?" I don't remember giving him specifics.

I stuff the cold sandwich into my mouth and chew while he explains, but he ignores my questions and drones on as if I hadn't asked them.

"Think about it. The public would eat that shit up. You, dating a first-grade teacher and a single mom?"

I stop chewing long enough to say, "What are you getting at?"

"Nothing. I'm just saying it would be great for your image."

"My image doesn't need helping."

"Doesn't it?" he mutters, quite rudely I might add.

I'm America's Sweetheart, I can do no wrong! Why would my image need shining up?

"Everyone's image could use a little PR," Trent explains. "You've been known as a playboy for a really long time. It wouldn't kill your reputation to be seen with a woman who isn't a model for a change. Your fans would love it."

I would never do that to Margot.

And besides, she'd junk punch me if she thought for one second I was only interested in her because it would be good for my public persona.

"*Think about it. That's all I'm saying . . .*"

Chapter 14

MARGOT

You don't think it's weird that a man who said he didn't want to date a mom is taking you on a date?

I know.

I found it odd, too, when Dex started using the words *date* and *see where this can lead* in his messages to me but shrugged off the niggling in my stomach because as friends have said, *You can't sit around waiting for men to come to you—you have to get out of the house.*

Okay, but what if the man doesn't actually want to be in a relationship? Should I waste time hanging out with him?

Wyatt is with her dad this weekend, so it's not as if I didn't have time to spare. No other men on the apps have asked to meet, and I haven't asked to meet them, so here I am, with only the sage advice of Wyatt's and my friends' words ringing in my ears.

As I push through the heavy glass doors of Glam Golf USA, a rush of cool air hits my face. It's one of those indoor and outdoor places—bars and food inside, golf turf outside—the perfect combination for people who may not be golf enthusiasts.

People such as myself.

I step inside, and the soft whacking of golf balls and loud chatter create an electric backdrop for a day that started off partly cloudy.

Maybe this is going to be fun, I think, despite the doubt in my gut.

My heart races a little faster than usual. After all, this isn't just any outing, it's a second date, and I haven't been on one of those in what feels like forever.

My eyes scan the room, taking in the scene. Flat-screen television sets are everywhere, showing the turf, targets, and games that players are here to play. There's an actual golf tournament on others. Baseball too.

I walk farther in, my sneakers making no sound against the polished concrete floor. I'm feeling a bit out of place in my casual yet carefully chosen outfit.

Black capri leggings.

Black cropped quarter zip.

Black ball cap.

I'm wearing more makeup than usual, simply because I wanted to dress up and look cute, and this activity didn't give me the opportunity to wear anything else.

I didn't want to golf in jeans, though now that I'm glancing around, plenty of people are wearing them.

Dammit!

I walk all the way into the lobby, my confusion growing.

Where is Dex?

Am I the first one here?

I half expected him to be waiting near the entrance—or maybe in the parking lot—but there is no sign of him.

I dig my cell out of my cross-body bag, checking our message exchange once again to make sure I hadn't gotten the time wrong.

Huh.

I'm on time, if not a few minutes late.

A flicker of doubt hits me. *Did Dex change his mind?*

Determined not to let my nervousness show, I approach the reception desk, where two cheerful young women greet me. "Welcome to Glam Golf USA! Do you have a reservation?"

"Hi." I sound more confident than I am. "I'm supposed to meet someone here. His name is Dex? He might have reserved a booth or whatever?"

So. Confident.

She taps at her keyboard, then looks up at me with a reassuring nod. "Yes, I see a reservation for a Dex—looks like he checked in. Simulator 202, up on the second floor, second spot on the left."

"Thanks."

I'm breathing heavy by the time I make it up two flights of stairs, and to my relief I find Dex already practicing his swing as if he weren't expecting company.

He raises his head as I approach, broad smile spreading across his handsome face. "Hey! You made it!"

"I made it." I grin at him, waving my arms so he can see I'm in one piece. "Wouldn't miss it."

Then he does something that shocks the hell out of me. He bends down and envelops me in a hug. Squeezes. Smells the top of my hair, even.

Is he drunk?

I didn't realize he was a hugger.

"I was starting to think you might have changed your mind."

Me, change my mind? I was worried he was going to change his!

"Not a chance. I don't have Wyatt this weekend, so I didn't have a lot going on." I laugh, hoping that doesn't sound like an insult. "Though I was worried I might have walked into the wrong place for a second there."

"Nope, you're exactly where you need to be." He pauses. "And don't you look adorable. Ready to show off your skills?"

Skills? Hardly. "I'm more likely to show off my ability to make a fool of myself."

But that's not what happens.

Turns out, I'm shockingly good at hitting targets on a turf golf course, especially after I've consumed an entire Twisted Lemonade.

I wiggle my ass during my turn, glancing over my shoulder to see if he's actually watching my ass, disappointed when he smiles, eyes nowhere near my bum.

Darn.

I may not be trying to reel him in, but it never hurts to be consensually ogled.

Squeezing one eye shut, I survey the landscape down in front of me, then check the monitor to make sure I'm aiming at the spot giving me the highest number of points. Because this is a game, and so far I'm kind of kicking his ass.

Dex may be bigger and stronger and more *arrogant*, but that's where it ends when it comes to skill level.

He's biting the green weenie, and he's making no secret that he's getting frustrated.

When it's his turn—after I score yet another whopping thousand points—he struts to the little square piece of grass designated for swinging, stretching and making a show. I lean on the table where we have our drinks and snacks, trying my best not to laugh out loud.

He's taking this way more seriously, and perhaps that's his problem?

"You're trying too hard," I tell him with authority, as the lead scorer. "Do you want me to show you how to swing the putter?"

He gawks at me. "This is a 9 iron."

Potato, po-tah-to.

"Whatever." I can't flip my hair because I'm wearing a ball cap, but I would if I could, *just to be a brat*. "You're holding the club all wrong."

I don't believe half of what I'm saying, inwardly giggling at my own audacity.

"You're an expert on golf now?"

"Trust me." I grin, taking the club from his giant hands. "First, you need to loosen up a bit. You're as stiff as a board. Go like this."

I shake my body like I have the wiggles, feeling slightly ridiculous, arms and legs jiggling. It pays off when he tips his head back and laughs, copying my movements.

"I feel so stupid." He laughs again.

"Don't. It'll make you a better player."

Then.

I position myself behind him, wrapping my arms around his waist, but because he's so much taller than I am, guiding his hands is a fail in the most hilarious way. Our heights are so mismatched, I can't see what I'm directing him to do.

The proximity sends a shiver down my spine.

"Like this," I speak to his back.

"This?" he asks, amusement in his voice. "Are you sure?"

"Exactly like that," I murmur, even though I can't actually see around his body to know what he's doing with his hands. "Now, relax your shoulders."

The tension in his muscles eases slightly, my arms still around him. I feel for his hands, making a show of adjusting his grip, fingers brushing his.

His hands are warm. Large. And electric.

The *touch* is electric, sending tiny jolts of excitement coursing through my sleepy veins, and instead of adjusting his grip, I want to wrap my arms around him in a hug and squeeze, relishing the weight and feel of him.

He's like a burly mountain man, and *ugh, it feels so good.*

"Now swing," I tell him, giving his neck a little push with my fingers so he bends his head. "But keep your head down."

He swings, and the club slices through the air with surprising grace.

The ball? Soars up and over.

Over some more, to the right . . .

Too far to the right.

Like, way *way* too far.

"Yikes," I mutter as it hits the mesh barrier that stops balls from flying into the land next to Glam Golf USA. "You may have put too much man power into that."

"Maybe it was the coaching."

"Nah." I shake my head. "You're too strong. You should relax a bit."

Dex laughs. "Listen to you, giving me instructions."

"Somebody has to. I feel like you've been running amok for too long."

I realize two things:

The words are probably true.

He knows it and is suddenly aware of it.

Dex steps away, moving toward the outdoor furniture arranged in our pod, then sits on one of the couches. He pats the spot beside him, still holding the club in his other hand.

"Let's chill for a second."

I nod, joining him on the sofa, sinking in next to him cross-legged.

I look at him, so casual and cool—meanwhile, my traitorous heart is racing far faster than it freaking should be, considering how casual this "date" is supposed to be. We're here because he is going to wine me and dine me for the simple fact that he fucked up my kitchen sink.

"Everything work out with Dan?"

Dan is the guy who actually knew what he was doing, the one who came and put everything to rights with a few twists of the wrench. Took him under ten minutes. Also, Dan was cute, single, and flirty.

"Everything was *great* with Dan." I stress the word *great*, remembering how he leaned against my counter, smiling broadly when I offered him a glass of wine. We chatted for a while, and he casually tried to find out if I was single, too, only mentioning his divorce four times. "Thanks for sending him over."

Dex looks slightly embarrassed. "No more leak?"

"No more leak, no more noises. Everything is dry. Things are right as rain."

I might also have a date next week!

"That's good." He sets down the golf club and reaches for his drink, a beer he's only drunk half of. "How is Wyatt?"

"Living her best life."

"What's the deal with you and your ex?" he blurts out, taking me by surprise. "You told me you weren't together after you had Wyatt, but you never really said if the two of you get along."

I cock my head to the side. "We get along fine. He's a good dad—spends plenty of time with her."

I leave out the part where Colton is mostly an asshole.

"You were saying he had a girlfriend?"

"He does." I'm shocked that Dex listened. "Honestly, I think he has commitment issues, not that it's any of my business, because they've been together a year and they're barely having the conversation about moving in together." And I know she's pressed for it because my daughter tells me.

He's had several relationships but nothing long term, always ending things around the two-year mark. Then again, who am I to judge? I've never been engaged or married, either, and our daughter is ten!

All I care about is that his home is safe and Wyatt is well taken care of.

"As a momma's girl, Wyatt doesn't always love going to her dad's," I theorize. "But it could just be a mother-daughter thing. Dads are sometimes the odd man out when it comes to girls."

I need to stop babbling; Dex is getting a glazed, far-off look in his eyes.

But also: HE IS THE ONE WHO ASKED!

"What about you? No kids of your own. Any nieces or nephews?"

"No—I have a brother, but we're not close." He takes a sip of beer. "He used to play football, too, but after his freshman year at state, he got cut from the team."

"Is that why you're not close?"

Dex nods, rubbing the scruff on his chin. "I think at first, he tried being happy for me? Like when I was drafted. But my parents made it hard, playing the comparison game, and now none of us talk."

I have so many questions, but I'm filling in the gaps with my imagination, not wanting to be rude.

"I'm sorry. That stinks."

"Yeah. It hits hardest during the holidays, but now I have my friends and shit. If we don't play during the holidays, I usually go with Landon to his parents' in Ohio, but now that he's living with his girlfriend in Green Bay, I might do that this year."

"Already thinking of Christmas?" It's difficult to imagine this big tough dude decking his halls full of decorations.

"You know it." He winks. "I start counting down the days until December twenty-fifth in October."

It's on the tip of my tongue to say "You know who else shares the love of decorations during the holiday? Kids. You should have one or two."

I bet he would make a great dad, although, based on what he's told me about his family, there is some trauma there that could perhaps be preventing him from going that route in his personal life. It's not my place to tell him that just because he has issues with his own parents and brother, he would not have the same issues in his own household.

"Can I ask you a question that might be too personal?"

Slowly, he nods. "Sure."

"Do you want to be married, or do you just want to date someone?"

"I want to be married."

"But you don't want kids?"

"Someday maybe."

This conversation is feeling a tad too deep, and we're trying to have fun, not dive into the deep end—as much as I'd love to pry. I wouldn't call myself nosy, but I do love learning about people. I've never met a professional athlete, and they seem like a breed of their own.

Dex certainly fits the stereotype.

Single. Ready to mingle. Not ready to commit but might want to commit. Can't make up his mind. Lives alone.

"Any pets?"

He shakes his head. "I can't even keep a plant alive."

"What pet would you get if you had to choose?"

"I don't know. A pug? Or one of those French bulldog things."

"So. Something with a mashed-up face?"

He chuckles. "I'd get something with a face only a mother could love."

"Yeah, those are pretty darn cute." I hesitate to bring up my daughter, but "Wyatt has always wanted a dog. She wrote me a letter once, outlining all the reasons why she would make a good dog mom." I smile at the thought, the letter still tucked away in my dresser drawer; the same drawer where I keep letters to the elf and tooth fairy. "I don't doubt that she would take care of one."

"Why not get her a dog then?"

"She's at school most of the day, and I have to work too. And I have a tiny yard." I fumble to explain.

"So? Get a tiny dog."

"You make it sound so simple."

"You're stone cold, aren't you?"

"No—I'm just realistic. If I had some help . . . maybe."

Dex thinks for a few moments; I can actually see his brain working. "Is that why you want a boyfriend?"

I pull back. "Is that what you think?" Although, yes. That's part of it. "Who doesn't want a partner to shoulder some of the heavy lifting? And by *heavy lifting* I mean emotional support." I sigh. "I have good days and bad days, and wouldn't it be nice to come home after a long day and put my head in someone's lap while we watch TV?"

"My head probably weighs at least fifteen pounds."

We laugh.

"What's the average weight of the human head," I tease, feeling more relaxed now. "Like seven pounds?"

"Something like that. Mine looks like a bowling ball."

I cackle. "No it does not. Do not make that comparison—I don't love the visual for you."

"I can't help it, that's the first place my brain went."

"Maybe when you're wearing a helmet it looks like one?"

"For sure." His eyes crinkle at the corners, and I want to reach out and touch him.

Lord help me, do I want to touch him . . .

Chapter 15

Dex

"So I've been giving this some thought . . . I think we should actually date."

I stare at myself in the mirror of the movie-theater bathroom, practicing the lines I've been thinking about since my call with Trent, a niggling guilt rooting itself in my belly.

"You have nothing to feel guilty about," I tell myself out loud as I wash my hands. "You like her. She likes you. It's only dating, you're not proposing." What can it hurt to take her out a few times?

And if we get photographed and a news outlet picks it up . . .

All the better.

"Why are you being such a wuss about this?" I say, pulling a paper towel from the dispenser and drying my hands. "Go out there and—"

"Dude. Are you talking to yourself?"

A kid of about nine years old is staring at me, having just rounded the corner from the bathroom stalls.

"Sorry. I thought I was alone."

He ignores me and comes to the sink to wash his hands too.

"What are you seeing?" I ask him, forgetting all about stranger danger and not talking to random children because it might terrify them, but in my defense, he started the conversation.

He ignores me.

I give him props and ignore him, too, pushing through the bathroom door and back into the theater lobby, where Margot is waiting for me, popcorn and snacks in hand.

I promised her an entire day of fun to make up for the water incident in her kitchen, and I plan to deliver. I even let her pick the movie! Bought her whatever snacks she wanted and a beer too.

She has a blanket folded over one arm because, according to her, she always gets cold when she's in the theater and always has one in the back of her car.

"Ready?"

She nods happily, a pep in her step. "I've been dying to see this movie."

I haven't.

I don't love chick flicks, but this one is a mash-up of action, comedy, and romance—so with any luck, we'll both enjoy it. Usually I'm a fan of sci-fi or movies based on comic books, or even horror, depending on the mood.

Margot and I score seats near the back, in the middle, surrounded by a sea of empty seats.

Perfect.

As the previews for new movies begin, Margot nudges me and offers me the popcorn, her hand already firmly planted inside the big bucket of kernels.

I shake my head, not hungry for it yet.

"I only eat once the movie has started," I whisper, leaning closer.

She stuffs a handful into her mouth.

"I want to see this," she tells me, referring to the preview of a movie releasing in winter, eyes locked on the screen. "Looks so good."

A few minutes later she's pointing at the action unfolding in front of us. "Why do they make so many action movies? Not everyone likes watching this crap. Pass."

Then, "Oh!" She nudges me. "I love Kat Kittson! She's making another rom-com!"

I have no idea who Kat Kittson is, but apparently Margot loves her.

She continues analyzing movie trailers, remarking that it's one of her favorite things about coming to the cinema, enthusiastically giving them a thumbs-up or thumbs-down—until the opening credits roll for the movie we're here to see.

The lights dim.

I turn, studying her profile—the outline of her nose. Chin. The silhouette of her hair.

She's so focused and intent, already laughing at one of the funny one-liners. I know her eyes are crinkling at the corners in the adorable way they do, her dimple on full display, *and now my focus isn't on the film.*

What would she do if she knew about my conversation with Trent? I was so close to spilling the beans today when we were golfing but lost the courage. I honestly don't want her to think I'm a piece of shit, but I also want to be direct with her. What better time to start?

I mean, look at us.

Friends.

But there's no fucking way she wants to keep it like that. She originally swiped on me because she wanted to date me, yeah? Or to bust me because she thought I was a catfish, but that's a minor detail. She may pretend we're not attracted to each other and that she wants to keep me at arm's length, but she can't fool me.

I see the way she blushes when she catches me looking at her, and I felt her breathing get heavier when she wrapped her arms around me at Glam Golf USA. Not to brag, but I've met enough women to know when they're hot and bothered, and Margot was hot.

And bothered.

Is it my imagination, or does Margot lean in a little closer each time she offers me a snack?

I glance at her again, drinking in the sight as she watches the screen, as if she were a teenager, and my mind wanders. I made out in a movie theater once when I was a teen, always horny, always putting the moves on people first.

Speaking of horny . . .

Why is the blanket across her lap drawing my eyes to it? Why do I want to slide my hand beneath it and run my palm along her inner thigh? *The blanket feels like a barrier and an invitation all at once.*

Wonder what she'd do if . . .

Should I, you know, put my hand under it?

Regardless of our relationship status, what better way to springboard to the next level than with a little foreplay.

Am I right or am I right?

Talk is cheap; fooling around is forever.

I yawn.

Reach across the back of her seat, stretching as if I were exhausted, and yawn again—the way they do it in the movies. Lay my hand on the back of her chair, touching her hair before letting my hand slide to her shoulders, *real cool and nonchalant like.*

She looks over at me, brows raised. "Wow. That's your move?"

Yes, that is my move. Not the best move, but a move nonetheless . . .

"Why do you have to call me out like this?" I laugh. "Pretend we're on a date."

Definitely don't feel as smooth as I thought I was.

"A date?" She shivers. "If you say so."

Every time Margot laughs at a clever line from the characters on screen—or pretends to fan herself at the sight of the hunky male lead, with his handsome face and his great hair—I feel a flutter of excitement.

She's so fucking cute. I can't wait to get my hands on her . . .

I want to kiss her again.

That short-lived and interrupted kiss in her kitchen was too quick to register in my brain as memorable, and I wouldn't mind trying it again to see if sparks fly this time. It's been fucking with my mind ever since.

She shifts in her big red leather chair, the warmth of her leg pressing against mine. Impossible to ignore.

I'm not into this movie.

Barely paying attention, which we all knew was going to happen, too busy am I as I contemplate how best to make my next move.

With deliberate slowness, I slide my hand under the blanket, feeling the soft fabric of her leggings glide against the tips of my fingers and palm. Brush them over her knee, letting it rest there.

Her mouth curves into a smile.

I lean over, kissing her neck. Jawline. The spot below her ear.

"Are you trying to kiss me?"

"Do you want me to?"

She nods, setting the popcorn in the seat next to her.

My palm is still on her thigh when our mouths meet, bodies now turned to face one another, the cup holder that had once separated us now pushed out of the way.

Our tongues dance, the sweet taste of soda and the salt from her popcorn—buttery delicious—flirt with my senses as my fingers inch toward the center of her thighs. Light. Teasing.

She moans against my mouth, wiggling in her seat.

Encouraged by her excitement, I continue, my fingertips trailing along her inner thigh, feeling the heat of her skin through the thin layer of fabric.

Her lips curve into a small wicked smile. "You're trouble, you know that?"

She's breathless.

I grin, trailing kisses along her jaw. "You love it."

We both do.

How often do we get to feel like . . .

We're young again?

Not that we're not young. Shit, I barely just turned twenty-five.

Her hand moves to my forearm, fingers curling around my wrist—but instead of pushing me away, the little minx guides me higher. The silent encouragement sends a thrill through me, and I wonder if being pleasured in public is something she's done before.

I let my hand slide farther up her thigh, the intimacy of the moment electrifying.

The movie plays on, the romantic scene unfolding in the background barely a blip on our radar, our attention on each other. At least, mine is on her since I'm the one doing all the touching . . .

Margot's breathing grows heavier, her chest rising and falling in a rhythm that tells me she's getting turned on.

"How's this?" I whisper, hand teasing.

She nods, biting down on her lower lip from the anticipation. "Perfect."

I continue my slow, tantalizing caresses—at least, that's the vibe I'm going for—feeling the tension and desire building between us. Her soft sighs and tiny moans are sweeter than the sound of my chef announcing that dinner is being served, and that's saying a lot because I fucking love to eat.

Seriously love it.

My hand moves with more confidence now, fingers tracing patterns on her thigh, venturing closer to her most sensitive spots, only holding back to make her squirm.

"You're going to drive me crazy," she murmurs just loud enough for me to hear, her voice a mix of frustration and pleasure. Whining. Pouting.

I chuckle, savoring the power and intimacy of the moment, but what she has yet to realize is that she holds all the power. All of it.

"That's the idea."

My fingers reach the apex of her thighs.

Once again, she shivers.

I take pleasure in knowing she feels pleasure, 'cause why the hell else would she be shivering? *I bet her thighs would quake if I was kneeling between her legs* . . . but that's a pipe dream to save for another day. Or another outing.

Ha.

Like a good girl—or a bad girl, depending on how you look at it—Margot parts her legs to grant me better access, breath now coming in shallow, uneven gasps.

Naughty, naughty . . .

The vixen likes it.

And so, beneath the delicate fabric my fingers go and find her wet and ready. So wet. So ready.

Even though it's been ages since I've gotten anyone off like this—usually we're in a bed or at least somewhere private. Oh—and naked. I begin to move my fingers in languid, deliberate strokes, feeling her body respond to my touch. Margot's hand covers mine under the blanket, her grip tightening with each passing moment.

My fingers travel with practiced ease, finding a rhythm that makes her breath catch and her body tremble beneath the lap blanket.

I am driving her wild.

Margot leans her head back against the leather theater seat, eyes fluttering closed as I work my magic, getting her off like a goddamn boss, the hands I get paid so much money for doing double duty.

I am a triple threat.

Football, good looks, and foreplay. *Bam!*

Margot's quiet moans are almost drowned out by the sounds of the film, but I know she's making them—I can tell by her parted lips and half-closed eyelids. It's an expression that's driving me wild too.

I lean in, pressing a kiss to her neck, and take pleasure when I feel the pulse racing beneath my lips.

"This is so fucking hot," I whisper, my voice rough with desire.

God I wish we could fuck.

Or at least I wish I could properly go down on her, and I doubt she'd want to do it in the back of my car, though it's on the tip of my tongue to ask.

"Don't stop," she begs.

Up on the giant cinema screen there's an explosion.

It's timed perfectly with Margot's, her body tense, hand still covering mine, not wanting me to stop. Breath coming in sharp, ragged gasps, and holy shit, who knew it would be this easy to make her come?

She shudders.

Obviously she does, because like I said, I'm so fucking good at this. The quiet cry escaping her lips sounds like a five-star review that I want to rave about online.

I did this.

I made her come at the movies.

In public.

In an awkward position.

With only one hand.

Fuck. Yeah.

We sit for a moment, pretending to watch the movie while her body finishes racking with spasms, the blanket covering her lap and covering up our shared secret.

I withdraw my hand, triumph filling my gut as Margot turns to look at me, her eyes sparkling with satisfaction. Desire.

"Well," she says at long last. "That was interesting."

Interesting?

What the hell is that supposed to mean? "Is that a good thing or a bad thing?"

Her head gives a tentative shake. "It's . . . it means we probably have to have a conversation."

A conversation?

Shit. About what?

That cannot be good . . .

Chapter 16

Margot

"It's not a bad thing."

We're walking out of the theater; then we stop when we get to my car, the blanket that was covering my lap during the movie draped over my arm—it is now going to be a forever reminder that I let him diddle me during half of it.

A blush creeps up my face as I open the back door to my car and toss the thing in the back seat, slamming the door quickly so I don't have to look at it.

I am lighting that thing on fire the second I get home . . .

"Anytime anyone says they want to talk, believe me, it's never good."

I love egging him on. "Stop being so dramatic."

"I've never been dramatic in my entire life," he announces, leaning against my driver's side door, pulling me in until I'm standing between his spread legs.

He's so big.

So much taller.

"So you're only being theatrical for my benefit? Gotcha."

"That's not what I . . ." He's looking down at me, and I'm looking up at him—and obviously the only logical thing to do right at this moment is kiss him.

All I have to do is go up on my toes and plant one on him . . .

Still.

I don't.

On the one hand: we did what we did. On the other: I don't want to feel used. Or needy. Or greedy.

I don't want him to have the upper hand or feel like he's driving this train wreck.

It's me.

I'm the captain and *I* say when.

"You want to kiss me," he says. "I can tell."

As a response I roll my eyes. He's cocky enough, he doesn't need me feeding his ego by confirming his suspicions. Unlike some people, I can contain my primal urges.

Er.

Recent events notwithstanding.

Movie second base does not count.

"Stop trying to distract me," I tell him, adding a little bit of salt to my tone just to let him know who's boss.

"Distract you from what?"

He is too handsome for his own good, and my God the man knows how to use his hands . . .

No wonder he gets paid so much.

Raw, unbridled talent in those fingers . . .

"From the talk." I sigh, knowing that the next words out of my mouth are absolutely necessary. "Listen, Dex. You're a really nice guy and—"

His loud groan cuts me off. "Are you breaking up with me?"

Huh? "No. We'd have to be dating for me to break up with you." Dumbass.

"Oh." He grins down at me.

"Can I continue?"

He nods.

"Listen, Dex. You're a really nice guy, and I have a lot of fun with you. But I have a daughter to consider, and what I'm looking for is a relationship—not a new friend." I hesitate. "Pretend you're normal and you start dating me, then you find out Dex Lansing is my buddy. You wouldn't be thrilled."

"But you're not dating anyone."

I run a hand through my hair, distracted again when his hands go to my waist and pull me closer.

Dammit!

I'm trying to lay down the law here!

"That's not the point. I want to be dating someone."

"Um. Should I be insulted?" he wants to know, not looking insulted in the least.

I tilt my head. What is he talking about? "Why would you be insulted? You let it be known from the second we swiped on one another that you didn't want to date a woman who has a kid, and now here we are, talking in circles."

"What if I changed my mind?"

"Did you?"

It takes him a few seconds to respond.

Then slowly, he nods. "Yeah. I think I did change my mind."

Shut up. He cannot be serious right now.

"You changed your mind, and now you want to date. Me. Specifically."

Another nod.

His hands roam up my rib cage, and when his fingers brush the sides of my breasts, I swat at him. "Stop it, Dex, this is serious."

"This *is* serious."

"Stop repeating me."

"I'm not repeating you."

Oh my God.

I adjust my stance, giving his chest a poke with the tip of my finger.

"So you're telling me that you woke up this morning and suddenly you feel differently? Because I will tell you right now—you do *not* date a single mother if you don't mean it."

His mouth falls open as if he's going to say more, but then it closes, as if he can't decide *what* to say.

Dex swallows, Adam's apple bobbing. "I mean it."

Such conviction.

"Why?"

I need to know his reasons before I can decide if this is a good idea. I cannot let him in if I don't believe his intentions are pure, but honestly, if sex is the only thing he's after, he can get that anywhere.

Can't he?

As far as professional athletes are concerned—especially really hot, handsome ones—women must be tripping over themselves to bang him. I know I would be if it was just me.

But it's not.

I have Wyatt, and we are a package deal.

"You actually need me to tell you why I think you're amazing?"

No. But it's always nice to hear.

"Yes, please."

Sue me for wanting compliments and flattering words about myself.

Dex takes a deep breath, his eyes locking on to mine with an intensity that makes my heart skip a beat. I asked him to take this conversation seriously but didn't really think he could be this intense—but here he is, bringing the heat.

"Where do I start?" He exhales, hands still on my hips. "You're strong. You've been through so much but haven't given up looking for love. Still smiling, even though you frown at me a lot and yell. You're an amazing mother to Wyatt. I can hear it when you talk about her. She's incredible because you are incredible."

His words start to melt me like buttuh—and I didn't think I was the kind of woman who could be so easily swayed.

Dammit!

"And you're smart," he goes on. "You're funny. You make me want to be a better person just by being around you." *Ah, shucks.* "I've dated plenty of women, sure, but none of them have made me feel the way you do. None of them have made me want to settle down, to build something real."

I blink, trying to process his words. "And you just realized this *today?*"

He shakes his head. "No, it's been on my mind a few times and today, well. Today, I just . . . couldn't ignore it anymore. I couldn't keep pretending that what we have is casual when it's anything but, and I honestly don't want to be friends."

He doesn't want to be friends.

He wants . . .

I take in a gulp of air, images of us in bed passing through my brain—the part of me who hasn't had sex in months making some of these decisions for me. If I were a man, this would be the part where I'm thinking with my dick.

My heart is pounding.

I can feel the tears starting to prick at the corners of my eyes. Ugh, not in the parking lot of a movie theater! How inconvenient.

See, the thing is . . . I want to believe Dex, I really do. But it's hard. It's so hard to trust when you've been let down before. Wyatt's dad let me down, and sure, he's there for his child, but I will never, ever, forget how he left me when I was pregnant rather than standing beside me and supporting me.

Dex is not your ex.

Dex is not a boy the way Colton was.

"Dex, I have to protect Wyatt. I know she's already met you, but I cannot bring someone into her life who's not going to stick around." I pull back so I can look him dead in the eyes. "She might be bubbly and outgoing, but trust me, she gets attached quickly."

"I get that," he says. "No matter what, we're friends. What's the harm in dating and doing things together? Just don't fall in love with me," he jokes.

I roll my eyes. "You're the one who's going to fall in love with me."

His eyes darken. His lips press together with an unspoken . . . something.

I swallow hard, my throat tight with emotions. "This isn't about me. Wyatt comes first, always."

"What does that mean? You're going to cancel on me if she has her period?"

"She doesn't get her period because she is ten, but yes, if she's sick and we have plans, I would cancel on you. That's what moms do."

I can see that he's fighting for some patience but give him some slack since this is new to him and not something he originally wanted to sign up for.

Such a bad idea.

My girlfriends are always warning me about red flags, only I have no idea if he's a walking red flag or just a regular one?

I take a deep breath, trying to steady my racing thoughts. "Okay. This probably isn't going to be that easy. Being with me means accepting all of it—the good, the bad, the ugly. It means understanding that sometimes I'm going to be tired and stressed because my students are going to make me bonkers from time to time and I'll come home and not be the easiest person to be around."

"The good news is, we don't live together, so I won't have to put up with that."

I stare. "Seriously?"

"Was that the wrong thing to say?" He clearly has no idea.

"Kind of," I say finally. "We can try this, but . . . if you hurt us, I swear to God I will—"

"I won't." He puts his hands up in surrender. "I promise you, I won't."

He pulls me into his arms, wrapping me in a hug, and for the first time in a long time, I let myself believe that we can have a future together. A future where Wyatt and I aren't alone, where we have someone who loves us both and wants to be part of our lives.

Plus, he's so hot.

Shit.

Stop focusing on how good looking he is, Margot!

Okay, but he is...

Then, in the parking lot of the movie theater—where the streetlamps above us are starting to go on, one by one—he pushes my back against my car, sliding his hands to my ass. Squeezes my cheeks in his massive palms before lifting me, pressing his lips on mine.

The cool night air contrasts with the heat of his hands, searing my skin through my thin leggings, making my skin tingle.

We seal our deal with a kiss, one that's rough and sexy and has the asphalt beneath my feet disappearing.

So sexy...

My arms loop around his neck, pulling him closer, fingers digging into his shoulders.

The car door stabs into my back, but I don't care—all I can focus on is him. His hands are so big and strong and confident, holding me up as if I weigh nothing. His lips, urgent and demanding, claiming mine with a passion that leaves me breathless.

Yes, Dex, yes...

As we make out like teenagers, the little seed of doubt slips further to the back of my brain, and my hands—the ones that were on his shoulders—slide into his hair.

Fingers crossed.

Chapter 17

Dex

"What the hell did you just say?"

I hate kissing and telling, so the last thing I want to do is repeat myself. But this is Landon and he's my BFF, and I need someone to talk to besides Trent, for real.

"You heard me." I don't have the guts to repeat myself, which is the reason I'm being deliberately coy.

"What I thought I heard you say was that you jerked your date off at the movies and now you're going to date her?" Landon chuckles into the phone, multitasking in his kitchen. "But that can't be right because this is the woman with the kid."

"I said what I said." The look on Landon's face when I say those words makes me laugh.

It's one kid, not seven. I can handle that.

"You said you didn't want to date someone with kids."

I know what I said! Everyone keeps reminding me! Do I have to get it stamped across my forehead, jeez!

"Am I not entitled to change my mind?" I grind out the words, agitated, not wanting to explain myself. Again. It was bad enough rambling on like a fucking idiot in the movie-theater parking lot. Never have I ever spewed such nonsense.

No, I said. *It's been on my mind a few times and today, well. Today, I just . . . couldn't ignore it anymore. I couldn't keep pretending that what we have is casual when it's anything but, and I honestly don't want to be friends.*

Jesus Christ.

I sounded like a moron and can't believe she bought it.

Not that I don't *like* Margot, but it goes against the boundaries I set for myself and told her on replay, and now I look fucking wishy-washy changing my mind.

Thanks to Trent.

In the camera's view, I can see Landon hesitating and his dog, Kevin—a cowboy corgi—in the background, sniffing the floor beneath one of their pristine white cabinets, looking for crumbs.

Honestly, I'm a bit shocked by the fact that Landon hasn't yet bought a bigger house since he signed to play for this new team, in a new city, but instead moved in with his girlfriend.

I guess time will tell.

Maybe bigger, better houses aren't his thing.

My eyes go to the ceiling of my own kitchen, and I eyeball the shiny, glistening monster of a modern chandelier hanging above the round table.

"Are you entitled to change your mind? Of course you are." He pauses. "But did you actually? You're cool with kids, now?"

I mean . . .

"Eh."

"Eh? What the hell does that mean?"

And here we are at a crossroads. I can either go left and tell him the truth, or I can go right—and lie.

It's now or never.

"Dude. What I'm about to say you *cannot* repeat."

The tone of my voice has Landon stopping what he's doing to give me his full attention.

"Oh shit." He's staring at me now, a carrot in his hand. "What?"

Biggest Player

Let's see, how do I say this without sounding like a world-class asshole?
"It was an accident."
Shoot. Not what I meant to say.
I try again as I watch Landon take a bite of carrot. "What I meant was—my intention wasn't to date her at all. But then I was having a chat, and the subject came up about how dating a single mom might actually be good for my reputation? Not that I'm a complete shithead, you know? Just that teams like someone family friendly, and I date models."
My buddy stops chewing. "Dude, no."
I nod. Yes.
"Dude, stop fucking around, this isn't funny."
"In my defense, I tried bringing it up to her first to see how she'd feel about it."
He narrows his eyes. "Did you?"
Not really. I wanted to but didn't have the balls.
There's a long pause before Landon curses. "You really are a dumbass, do you know that? A real fucking dumbass."
Like I need him reminding me?
"She knows we're just friends," I lie. "We've been hanging out anyway, which is basically like dating—why not let the public think it's more than that?"
"Because. She has a kid, that's why."
"I know. But we don't have to hang out with it."
It.
I feel instant guilt in the pit of my stomach, speaking about Wyatt that way.
I sound like a fucking jerk.
"Are you listening to yourself?" Landon is shooting veritable daggers at me through the phone, and it's a look he hasn't given me before. "Whose dumb idea was this? It couldn't have been yours—you're not *that* coldhearted."

"Was that a compliment?" 'Cause he's not wrong about that; I'm not actually this cunning. "Trent may have mentioned fake dating her when we had our call last week."

The words taste like chalk in my mouth, and my friend's sigh is loud enough to hear all the way from here to Green Bay.

"Not to be rude, sometimes it's not always in your best interest for you to take his advice. It's just his opinion. Do you get what I'm saying?"

The whole situation is now completely fucked, and it's my own damn fault.

Margot and I were having so much fucking fun, and I went and ruined it by asking her if she wanted to actually date me, even though I don't actually want to date her. But since meeting her, all the fun has been taken out of swiping on dating apps—this connection that we have may not be . . . *sexual*, but it feels . . .

Stable.

Special.

Now there's a word guys don't think about when they're imagining boning a chick.

Have I been imagining boning her?

Yes. Yes, I have. And the more I get to know her, the more attracted to her I become.

Shit, fuck, shit.

"What are your options?" Landon asks me. "How are we going to get you out of this mess? You can't take the words back."

We.

I love that he phrases it like that; I don't feel so alone.

I pick at the homemade pasta Carrie left me, kind of wishing she were around—although she would go batshit on my ass if she knew about the shitstorm I created.

"Why are you saying it like that?" I furrow my brow. "When you started dating Harlow, you lied to her too. You didn't tell her who you actually were. You let her think you were some dude who hung out with his parents on the weekends and was going through job interviews."

"This isn't about me—this is about you." My best friend points at me through the small screen of his phone. "Harlow will be the first person to tell you it freaked her out when she found out who I was." I hear him open a door and close it. "I don't know, man. You may have fucked this up beyond repair."

"How?"

"'Cause. You either have to tell her what you just told me—about Trent telling you it would be good publicity to date her—or cut her off completely and never see her again." He tosses a ball for the dog. "Those are your options."

"I don't like those options."

He sighs. "Then you should have thought this through before letting your dick lead the way."

"I didn't let my dick lead the way. She hasn't even seen my dick."

Another sigh from Landon. "You know what I mean. You don't blurt shit out to someone on a whim, not single moms. You don't mess with them unless you mean it."

"Funny, that's what she said."

Landon's expression softens slightly, but his eyes remain stern. "It's not funny, Dex. She's not just some girl you walk away from. She has a kid. She has responsibilities. If you hurt her, you hurt her kid too."

Damn. Since when is he the voice of reason?

Since you decided to tell him your problems, that's when.

I glance down at the pasta. "I genuinely like her. And Wyatt—that's her daughter's name. She's seriously something else."

I didn't expect to feel this way. Or this guilty.

"Feelings aren't enough. You have to be honest with her. She deserves that."

I run a hand through my hair, frustration bubbling up. "But if I tell her the truth, she might never forgive me. And if I cut her off, I'm just another guy who let her down."

Landon nods, understanding the dilemma. "That's the risk you take when you get involved with someone who has more to lose than you do. You need to decide if you're willing to put in the effort to make it right."

I think about the moments I've shared with Margot and Wyatt. The laughter, the late-night talks, the way Wyatt's face lights up when I see her. I know I can't just walk away.

"I want to make it right," I say quietly. "But I don't know how."

"Start by telling her the truth. It's going to hurt, but she deserves to know. Then, show her that you're serious about being there for both of them. Actions speak louder than words."

I nod, a sense of determination settling in my chest. "You're right. I owe her the truth."

Maybe.

Maybe not.

Not now, at least . . .

No fucking way am I ready to let her go.

Chapter 18

Margot

I, Margot Mahoney, am dating a professional football player.
"I am dating someone."
Wow.
Sounds so weird to say.
Granted, we haven't been on any dates yet since Dex made his little pronouncement, but we've been texting a lot. Although last night, he invited me along with him for a signing event. I didn't have plans today, so I agreed.
A signing event.
I'm not sure what that is, but I'm assuming we're going to go somewhere people can meet Dex in person and get stuff signed?
My friend Cora, a teacher who works with me at the elementary school, is meeting me for lunch today in the teachers' lounge. Our little gatherings are a highlight of my day when we can coordinate them. She teaches fifth grade to my first, and we started at Scottsdale's private Sage Brush Elementary at the same time, becoming fast friends.
And since we never have enough time to gossip in between class, when I mention I'm seeing someone, she literally spits out some of her tuna sandwich—which is disgusting all by itself, let alone the fact that some of it is sitting in small chunks on the table.

Gross.

"Dating someone? Say that *one* more time without smiling."

"I . . . am dating. A guy."

"You cannot drop the words casually like that when I ask, 'So what's new with you?'" Cora's sandwich falls to the table. "I do not have time for you to play games with my anxiety levels."

"I'm not!" I swear.

"So spill! Details, girl! Who is it?"

I play coy. "Someone I met on the Kissmet app."

"Wait. Why am I only hearing about this now?" She takes a bite of sandwich and chews. "What else are you holding out on me?"

"Nothing." *Some things.* "I wanted to make sure that he wasn't going to flake on me."

She groans. "Don't be the friend that starts ghosting because she met someone."

"I haven't been ghosting you! It's just . . . been a whirlwind." Total understatement.

Cora's sandwich is suspended halfway to her mouth. It sags in her hand as she studies me. "Why has dating some guy been a whirlwind?"

Let's see: How do I put this?

"I met him on a dating app, but he's . . . kind of well known?" I give her a toothy Cheshire cat grin she cannot quite decipher.

"Well known? How?"

I explain how it went down when I first matched with Dex—how I thought he was a catfish; he had used all those professional football photos, nothing in his bio felt personal.

I assumed it was fake.

"I swiped on his profile so I could call him a liar and accuse him of being a catfish."

"And . . . ?"

"He's not. He's the real deal."

Cora leans forward and glances around the break room, lowering her voice to make sure no one else is listening. "Shut the fuck up. Are you serious?" She almost never curses.

"Yeah." I'm trying my best to sound chill, as if I deliver this sort of news all the time. *Fake it till you make it and all that...*

"Who is it?"

"His name is Dex."

"Dex, Dex..." She sets down her sandwich and wipes the crumbs from her palms. "Why does that name sound familiar?"

I don't know if she's a football fan, but I know her boyfriend is. I've listened to countless hours of her complaining about him ignoring her while he watches the games, so it's not *impossible* that she would recognize the name.

"Um. He's very popular—or so he says."

"Oh my God, Margot. How are you sitting here casually teaching first grade like there isn't some big hunky football guy falling at your feet?" She smacks the tabletop. "This is like every girl's dream!"

"Surely not every girl's dream."

Eh. It's certainly not mine.

The reality is, I have no desire to be surrounded by chaos and Goliath men, or women who chase those men. Not to mention Dex has flip-flopped about his feelings more than once. We haven't committed to each other yet, but we are giving it a chance.

"The selfish part of me was curious to know what dating someone like that is like." Not that I want to compare it to a science experiment, because that makes me sound like a selfish jerk. "He really is larger than life."

Large, as in huge.

I'm picking at the slices of the apple I'm not craving, mulling over the idea of Dex while my friend drones on and on. Eventually she notices I'm not paying attention and gives the tabletop a few raps of her knuckles, the way we do with our classes to get their attention.

"You are so lucky." She sighs. "I bet he's so romantic. I thought Mark was so exciting when we started dating." Another sigh. "Now he farts in front of me and scratches his nuts, and all the mystery is gone."

Ew.

I don't love that for her.

"You're right—he's not like anyone I've ever met." Or dated. Or been in a relationship with.

Shit. He's not even like anyone I've been in the same room with!

He's the total opposite of Colton, who by comparison is conservative, buttoned up, and opinionated. A real turd.

Not that Dex isn't opinionated . . . if he weren't, he may have been more open minded to dating a single mom when we first matched.

Still, here we are.

Cora and I continue eating (only ten minutes left of recess!), chatting about students, which parents have emailed or called to complain, and upcoming lesson plans. But every few minutes Cora brings the conversation back to Dex.

"Are you going to tell me his last name, or do I have to drag it out of you?" My friend has her phone out.

"Why?"

"So I can stalk him."

I snort. "At least you're honest."

"Listen," she deadpans. "Mark will be on one end of the couch watching some stupid comic book movie when I get home—then I'll plop down on the other end and play on my phone. At least give me something to google while we're ignoring each other tonight. Some eye candy."

My brows raise. "How do you know he's eye candy?"

"He plays football, *obviously* he's eye candy."

I titter. "His last name is Lansing. But can you do me a huge favor and not turn this into a full-blown investigation? Don't go liking and double tapping all his stuff. If he notices and pokes back on you, he's going to see me on your profile page, and then what am I going to tell him? My friends are creeps?"

Cora isn't convinced. "Who cares? He's a guy. They don't give a shit about things like that, and besides, I bet he pays someone to do his social media."

That sounds likely.

He mentioned a chef, so I'm sure he has a cleaning lady—all the things I would kill for if I had the money.

Le sigh.

Must be nice.

"What's this date you have tonight?"

"I have no idea," I admit, stealing one of her potato chips. "He gave me one hint, and it was: there will be lines."

"Pause. I can't believe I'm about to say this, but I wouldn't be doing my duty if I didn't ask. Have the two of you fooled around yet?" She wiggles her eyebrows.

"Sort of but not really."

Cora pulls a face. "What the heck does that mean?"

"It means no, we haven't slept together—if that's what you meant."

She claps, delighted. "Girl, why? I slept with Mark on the first date. I was so hard up, and he smelled like cheap drugstore cologne, but I didn't care." Cora laughs.

"Gawd. The first time we were alone together was at my house, and he destroyed my pipes. The second time was the movies, and we ended up talking in the parking lot."

I don't tell her about him fingering me; I don't have time to relive the entire story, not with the clock ticking. Not with the sixth-grade science teacher shooting us glances because Cora can't keep her voice down.

"Are you planning on dragging this out like you're saving yourself for someone special?"

I roll my eyes. "We're not rushing anything."

Cora snorts. "You're allowed to have a life, Margot. If you want to get laid, get laid. He is probably filled with so much testosterone. I bet he'd screw your brains out every chance he got."

My face turns red; I can feel it.

"Maybe. But this is not just about me. Plus, if I'm being perfectly honest, I think I'm a little intimidated by him. He's . . ."

Unlike anyone I've known.

Cora nods along as I talk.

"I need to make sure he's serious. He's already met Wyatt, so I wouldn't be the only one getting crushed if he doesn't want to be in a relationship."

The thing about my friend?

She's only sympathetic to a point.

"Right, right." She's nodding, but it's sarcastic. "You're dating a professional athlete, Margot. If he wasn't serious, why would he waste his time with a single mother? He wouldn't. You haven't had sex, you said so yourself. So why bother, no matter how much of a smokeshow you are."

That has us both laughing.

"Did you just call me a smokeshow?"

Cora stands, collecting her garbage. "Yes. You know you're a MILF."

Pfft. "I don't think my child is old enough for me to be considered a MILF."

"Yes, you are." My friend giggles. "Trust me."

I rise from my chair, too, and follow her to the trash bin. "I'm an elementary school teacher. What the hell business do I have dating a man with fans who line up to meet him for his autograph?"

Cora tosses her chip bag. "Are you freaking kidding me? If you reject this guy, I will hunt you down. I will gather all our friends, and we will ride at dawn."

"At dawn to do *what*?" I laugh.

"To . . . take away your lady card—do not fuck up this opportunity!"

She needs to calm down. "Can you keep your voice down? Ryan is listening." We glance over at him. "Don't get carried away here. Baby steps."

We pause in the doorway of the lounge. "I get that, Margot, I really do." She pauses. "You're smart. You've got a beautiful head on your shoulders, but you tend to overthink things, hey? Just this once don't overthink it. Go for it. The worst thing that can happen is you're disappointed—best thing that can happen is you find the love of your life."

I highly doubt Dex Lansing is the love of my life, but stranger things have happened.

"Thanks, Cora." I give her a little side hug. "You always give the best pep talks."

"It's a gift." She flips her hair dramatically. "Now real quick, tell me more about this date tonight—what are you going to wear? Maybe have your tits out."

She whispers the last part about my tits because now we're in the hall and it's filling with children fresh from recess.

"Jeans and a cute shirt?"

"Jeans and a cute shirt?" Her groan is louder than her speaking voice. "I cannot cosign on a shirt. Don't you have something *sexy*?"

"We're going out in public—I'm not going to have my boobs out!"

"You're dating an athlete. Give him a show."

I laugh. "Literally the only things I have aren't fun. My closet is embarrassing—I also have nothing that shows cleavage." Although I could probably borrow something tight.

"If you don't embrace the fact that you're going out with a sexy sexpot, there is no hope for the rest of us."

I stop at my classroom, smiling sweetly at my students as they file back into the room. Like an angel.

"Why do you always make things about you?" I say through gritted teeth.

"I'm speaking for the committee. The itty-bitty-titty committee."

We lean against my door with a case of the giggles.

"I'll try." I hold my fingers up. Scout's honor. "Don't expect any miracles."

But a miracle sure would be nice.

Seated back at my desk, I give my students some time to unwind and get settled in. Everyone needs a bit of me time, and I am no exception, wanting several moments to process and clear my head from Cora's teasing.

Show off my boobs?

I couldn't.

I wasn't lying when I said there was nothing in my closet to show off the girls around Dex, and I'm not about to run to the store to buy something new.

That would be silly.

I nibble my bottom lip. *Why not? Why* not *go to the store and buy something a little less conservative?* Invest in yourself!

Lord, give me the confidence to enjoy myself tonight.

I don't know what to expect, but I hope I survive a night with Dex Lansing.

Chapter 19

Dex

The place is packed.

Not that I'm surprised, but it's always nice to see a good turnout, especially when you're bringing a date.

A first for me.

It's not *unusual* for my teammates to bring friends or family to these things, but for me? I've never had anyone to bring. Just me, myself, and I.

Which puts me solely in the spotlight, front and center, no wife or kids or girlfriends lingering nearby to draw attention. Occasionally my agent will show up, depending on the city.

This signing event is local.

Obviously we're contractually obligated to be here—the same way we're contractually obligated to do postgame interviews—and in case you're wondering, yes, we get paid for our autographs. It does kind of feel weird taking money from people, but I can't be the only dude at the table not charging fans.

It would piss off my teammates, and the rookies can use the extra cash. They don't always rake in the big bucks unless they're drafted in the first round.

I'm tempted to take her hand when we walk into the building, Margot stepping into place beside me. I catch a whiff of her perfume when the wind kicks up. She looks fantastic and smells better, but also: she looks fantastic.

This is going to be the longest hour.

I regret inviting Margot along because now the only thing I want to do is be alone with her. I want to be in a half-empty theater with my hand under her blanket . . .

That will have to wait.

I introduce Margot as my friend when the event coordinator greets us, and she's given a spot off to the side where she'll be able to easily see the fans and the action.

Me.

I'm the action . . .

There is a long table draped in a black tablecloth where me and two of my Arizona teammates will be seated with stacks of glossy 8 × 10 photos of ourselves, along with glossy team photos. You know the kind—the entire team sitting on the bleachers in the stadium, looking badass and serious? Yeah, those.

Those will be free, but the headshots cost money.

"Oh my God, this is so exciting," Margot says nervously. "I hardly know what to do with myself."

She's not wrong; people are lined up in the lobby, the line flowing down through the venue and probably out the front doors, each person waiting for their moment to meet us.

I pat her on the behind to comfort her.

I notice quite a few kids and teenagers and would have given my left nut when I was younger to meet any of my pro sports heroes.

I also notice I'm placed between Kendrick Hayes and Dominic Rivera, two of the most popular and well-known players on our team besides me, although Dominic is a rookie and doesn't get as much playing time.

We draw a massive crowd.

"This is crazy!" Margot is next to me, pressed into my side as if she doesn't want to lose me.

I turn to look down at the top of her head, watching as she nervously runs a hand over her hair.

She has it down. It falls in long waves over her shoulders, which are bare because of the white top she's wearing. It's not overtly sexy, but it's tight and clings to her breasts.

I can see cleavage from this angle.

They haven't opened the line yet, so there's still a bit of time to chat and tell her how events like this work.

"They don't last long—we've only agreed to be here an hour, so they'll close the door at seven, and anyone who wasn't in line won't be able to meet us."

She nods in understanding. "It seems like something that will go quickly."

"Yeah, they do tend to go quickly."

"Are they always like this?"

"Always like what?"

"You know—full of energy? Loud? Busy?"

It is loud, fans chattering excitedly as they wait, and I can see several of them looking at their watches and phones for the time.

Two more minutes.

I'll have to take my seat in a few seconds.

"Not always but usually," I reply, butterflies in my stomach betraying my cool, even tone. We're part of the hottest team in the league right now, and the fans' enthusiasm is palpable. It never fails to amaze me.

I shake my hands out. "Jeez, who knew I'd be nervous?"

I play in stadiums full of thousands and thousands of people!

"Here. You might need this, then." She rises on her toes to kiss me on the cheek.

"That's all I get?" I flirt, puckering my lips.

Margot rolls her eyes, planting a kiss on my lips before I take my seat.

Behind us is an eight-foot-tall backdrop, twelve feet or so wide, with the team logo in the center. Managers, event coordinators, and building supervisors are among the throng to oversee us. Everyone wants a glimpse. Everyone wants credit.

They move the line-control barriers, and the fans rush forward.

I grin as a young boy clutching a football walks over, his eyes wide as he approaches, clearly in awe of us.

Me.

"Hey, buddy. How are you?"

He stands in front of me, not sure what to do or say. Shy.

"What's your name?"

"Bryce."

"Well, Bryce—do you want me to sign your football?"

He nods, still clutching it.

"Want to hand it over?" I wink, taking the ball in one hand and then signing it with a flourish, black Sharpie now permanently attached to my right hand.

Bryce beams as I hand it back, staring at the signature.

And off he goes . . .

Kendrick's manager does the Lord's work, keeping the line moving, ushering people along. I've met her on several occasions since her office is in downtown Phoenix, and I'm always appreciative of her no-nonsense, no-bullshit attitude, making sure everyone is on task.

If we let everyone have five minutes of our time, we'd be here until midnight.

And speaking of time . . .

With each minute that passes, each interaction becomes a blur—a sea of faces, names, and excited chatter. A sea of autographed photos and posters. Footballs. Some fans come with stories of how we've inspired them in their lives, some come with memorabilia.

All of them want a selfie.

This connection with the fans makes every moment being here worthwhile. This is more than just a contractual obligation; it's a chance to make someone's day—like young Bryce's, who couldn't have been older than twelve—to be a part of something bigger than ourselves. And that, more than the paycheck, is what keeps us coming back to the table.

I want to be me when I grow up.

Ha!

There are no lulls, but Margot appears beside me, resting a hand on one of my shoulders and squeezing. "How we doing? Hungry yet?"

Starving. "Hell yes."

"Twenty more minutes," she whispers in my ear before going back to her spot, her presence somehow reassuring.

Yeah, I'm a big boy. I do this shit for a living.

But it's also . . . nice knowing she's behind me.

Didn't realize I would appreciate it the way I am.

We obviously haven't had the opportunity to speak since I took my seat at the table, but I'm looking forward to grabbing a quick bite on the way back to her place. I can always eat.

It's still early enough.

Twenty more minutes turns to fifteen.

Fifteen turns to ten.

Eight.

Three.

Then,

The event is over.

The event planner is locking the doors to the room where we're seated and reintroducing herself to us as Tracy, asking if there's anything more she can do before we leave.

She shakes our hands.

"Thanks so much for keeping these dipshits in line," I tell her, tossing a thumb over my shoulder at Kendrick and Dominic, who both take offense, though not really. They're faking their outrage.

"Dipshits? The fuck, bro!" Kendrick clutches his heart dramatically, shit-eating grin on his handsome face. *Damn, he's a good-lookin' bastard.*

"You haven't even introduced us to your friend here, and you're throwing us under the damn bus. We want to be invited back. Not cool."

"Tracy knows I'm fucking with you." I wink.

"He's the worst." Margot bumps me with her hip, putting her hand out for an introduction to my friends. "It's my fault for bringing him."

Kendrick takes it, lingering a little too long, his massive frame looming over hers. For a brief second I think he's going to kiss her hand.

I give him a stern glower. "Guys, this is Margot. Margot, these are my teammates—the two dipshits of the apocalypse. Kendrick and Dominic."

"Don't listen to anything this asshole tells you." Dominic laughs. "Unless he tells you I have a massive dick. Then go ahead."

"Dude." I glower some more. "You can't spout off, telling my date you have a massive cock."

Kendrick agrees. "Imagine how disappointed she'll be when she sees yours in comparison."

They laugh.

Idiots.

"Wow. You're like my students."

"Students?"

Margot raises an eyebrow at us. "Yeah, this is nothing. I've dealt with worse than the three of you."

"Dang. Sorry?" Dominic is nosy as fuck, and now that he has a kernel of gossip, he wants the tea.

"I'm a teacher. My daughter will be in middle school next year, so—enough said."

His eyes bug out. "You have *kids*?"

"Well, no. I have *one* kid," she corrects. "But sometimes having one is like having ten, especially when she has friends over."

"Shit." Kendrick lets out a low whistle. "Bro's dating a mommy."

And now the word will spread like wildfire—Kendrick will repeat the information to his agent, his agent will repeat it to a media outlet, and soon it will be in the news.

This is almost too easy.

Satisfied, I slide my arm around her waist. "Her daughter is more mature than I am."

Beside me, she shakes her head. "That's not even a little true. If it was, I wouldn't be able to stand you."

"Are you two the same age?" Dominic is rude enough to ask.

I thought you weren't supposed to ask a woman her age, but here he is, asking Margot her age like a Neanderthal.

"No?" Margot squints. "I think he's, what, three or four years younger?"

I can tell she's trying to do the mental math or genuinely cannot remember our age gap and wants me to chime in. We've never actually discussed it; our ages were only ever shown on the Kissmet app, and we haven't messaged one another there since we met in person.

Doesn't matter.

This is even better tea for the media: Single mother. Older woman.

Boom, internet-troll gold.

And there goes the guilt that keeps punching me in the gut, reminding me what a fucking douchebag I'm being.

I nudge the feelings away and instead grin back at my friends, arm still around Margot, pleased as punch to be standing with her tonight.

"You guys want to come out and grab something with us?" I ask Kendrick and Dominic. They both shake their heads.

"Nah, bro. I'm hitting the gym tomorrow with my sister. She gets my ass up at five," Kendrick says.

"Tomorrow is Saturday," I point out, horrified at the idea of waking up at five o'clock to exercise when I'd rather be sleeping. Or fucking.

"She don't care what day it is."

I rack my brain. His sister is younger, in college, and if my memory serves me correctly, he is her legal guardian.

"She still living with you?"

"Yeah, when she's not in school. Total pain in my ass."

"Aww," Margot chimes in. "It's sweet, though, that you let her boss you around. I love it when younger sisters do that."

He shrugs. "Have to be in the gym anyway, might as well get it over with."

Dominic nods. "I stopped drinking, so I'm gonna head home."

Kendrick smacks him. "Don't lie, bro—you're going home to watch *Love Is Blind*."

"So?"

"So. Don't act like an angel when you just wanna be in bed by eight."

I understand his wanting to be home, where it's quiet. I'm the same most nights, but usually only get that way during the season. Our season hasn't started yet, so I can go crazy and stay out until ten! Ha.

We give one another hugs, say our goodbyes to everyone else. Darkness has arrived by the time Margot and I step outside; it's a stark contrast to how bright it was when we arrived.

"Feel like going out?" I ask, 'cause I'm still hungry and getting hungrier by the second.

"It seems like all we do is eat when we're together," she says sheepishly. "When you're not busy scheming to ruin dates, or breaking things inside my house."

"I broke *one* thing! And I don't even think it was my fault—your pipes were fucked before I even got there. Plus, I'm not a toolman." I could go on defending myself against her accusations.

Is she going to bring this up for the rest of our lives?

Probably.

She's a shithead.

Margot rolls her eyes but can't hide her smile. "What did you have in mind for food? Nothing fancy, I hope. I'm dressed for flirting, not a nice steak house."

I have her covered because I'm not in the mood for fancy either. Hardly ever am—not when a juicy burger is the cure for most ailments.

Or dessert, which is even better. Carrie is the only one keeping me honest. And healthy.

"There's this new place I saw on Instagram with the craziest shit," I say, pointing in a vague direction of the restaurant since we're already in the downtown area. "They have these insane milkshakes. You won't believe what they stick on top of them."

She raises her eyebrows to tease me. "Burgers?"

Dammit, how did she know? She ruined the surprise.

"Yes, but not *just* burgers. Also doughnuts, cookies, pretzels—pretty much everything." Rubber ducks. Candy. Entire pieces of cake.

All depends on which shake you order.

I want one so bad.

"I've seen those." Her eyes widen in horror. "They look like a literal heart attack in a glass."

"Yeah, but they also look fucking delicious." I grab her hand and begin pulling her along. She laughs again, her giggle easily becoming one of my favorite sounds. "There's only one way to find out."

If we can find the place.

With my free hand, I pull up the walking directions, relieved to discover it's not that far from where we're standing, only three city blocks.

Win!

We walk the few blocks, sidewalks still bustling, the neon lights of the Sugar Ice Cream Shack beckoning.

"Shoot." Margot groans as we approach. "There's a line."

Pfft, please. "This is where it comes in handy to be a douchey football player."

The dude at the door spots me when I approach him. I understand his silent message: "You guys want me to let you in?"

I nod, giving Margot a tug. "Come on."

"What are we doing?" She is frantically looking around, hissing, "We can't skip all these people! I won't be able to look anyone in the eye."

We can and we do.

Damn right, we skip the line.

Once we're inside, seated comfortably in a corner booth near a bright, candy-covered bar—one that serves alcohol, of course—we pass the time waiting for our server by people watching, making up ridiculous backstories for everyone around us.

"See that guy with the man bun? Definitely a secret agent." Margot is nodding toward a tall, muscular guy with a suspiciously serious expression who's scrunched at a table with two teenagers, one boy and one girl, both of them ignoring him and playing on their phones. For a man surrounded by ice cream and doughnuts, he sure looks miserable.

"How can he be a secret agent when he's in here eating ice cream?" I don't love that theory; it makes no sense. "I was thinking he's the type of guy that owns his own gym and doubles as a bodyguard on the weekends."

"You think he's that girl's bodyguard? Could be." She shrugs. "Although he's probably a single dad, and this is his weekend with the kids, and he's trying to spend time with them, but they'd rather just play on their phones."

That was going to be my next guess.

"What are you getting?" I ask her, plucking up a menu and opening it. It's absurdly oversize, and we laugh as we try to hold them up and read at the same time, laminated pages bumping and making it difficult.

"I feel like I need a map to navigate this thing." She peeks over the top at me. "It's gargantuan."

"Just close your eyes and point," I suggest. "What's the worst thing that could happen?"

"Why do I get the feeling that you say that a lot?"

"'Cause I say that a lot?" I laugh. "It only fails me fifty percent of the time."

When the server comes to take our order, we both opt for the most ridiculous milkshakes on the menu. They're not cheap, and ordinarily the price tag might make me cringe, but how can anything topped with an entire slice of cheesecake be a bad investment?

Mine? Has a mini doughnut tower precariously perched on top.

In short order both desserts are plopped down in front of us. We stare.

"That looks absolutely . . . revolting," she says, looking from mine to hers to mine. "Seriously. Who came up with this? It's nonsense! This must weigh at least five pounds!"

I steal a cookie from the side of her glass and pop it in my mouth before she can scold me.

"This is . . . wow." She's eyeballing her own concoction. "I have no idea how to start eating this."

There are spoons in a cup holder on the table, and I hand her one, also taking one for myself, plus a half-dozen napkins.

We're going to need them.

"Epic, isn't it?" I say, tentatively sipping my milkshake while trying not to topple the doughnuts.

I love how it looks. So fucking cool. "Do you mind if I take a picture before we eat these?"

Margot rolls her eyes but pushes her glass toward mine so I can snap a photo with my phone.

"Are you going to look at that later?" she teases.

"I might."

She sticks her tongue out at me before plucking a piece of cheesecake off her glass, then taking a careful bite.

"Oh my God, yum."

"Good?"

She moans. "I was wrong. This might be worth a sugar coma."

"Told you," I say smugly, chewing thoughtfully. "I have excellent taste."

"That's what they should name this place. Sugar Coma," she suggests, sucking ice cream through the shake's blue straw, then forking the cheesecake balanced on top.

Soon we're both clutching our guts and moaning, leaning back against the seats. Stuffed.

"I can't take it anymore," she complains.

"Neither can I—and I can usually eat until it's gone."

We sit in silence for a bit.

"Hey," I say after a time. "Thanks for coming out with me. I know we didn't get to spend any actual time together at the signing, but I really liked having you there with me."

"You're welcome." Margot lifts her spoon and licks it. "You're lucky I like food."

"Just the food?"

She looks at me, her expression softening. "No, not just the food. You know it's the company I like even better."

Seriously, the old Dex—the Dex of last week—would have gagged hearing a compliment like that and might have laughed at her. This new Dex is eating her words right up the same way I was lapping up this ice cream.

"Good to know. Because I was thinking . . . maybe next time, we could do something different."

"Like what?"

"I don't know. Something crazy. Something we've never done before."

She tilts her head, considering. "Like skydiving?"

"Jeez, dear God, no." I laugh. "Not that crazy. But we'll figure something out." I pause. "Maybe next time we can do something with Wyatt?"

I'm feeling her out, gauging whether or not she wants to reintroduce me to her daughter—for real this time. Even though I've met Wyatt already, it was in the most unconventional circumstances. I'd rather do it properly.

"I don't think I want 'something crazy' and 'maybe we can do it with Wyatt' in the same sentence." She laughs. "But I get what you're saying."

This perks me up. "Is that a yes?"

Margot leans over and kisses me on the lips. "No. But I'll think about it."

Chapter 20

Dex:
Just wanted to thank you again for coming tonight...

Margot:
Thank you for inviting me—I had a great time. It was unlike anything I've ever seen watching you sign autographs.

Dex:
You've never been to anything like that before?

Margot:
No, never!

Dex:
Then I'm glad your first was with me.

Dex:
What are you up to rn, thinking about going out with me again?

Margot:
I can neither confirm nor deny whether or not I was thinking about going out with you again.

Dex:
So, no to taking Wyatt somewhere fun?

Margot:
I'm thinking about it. I can't decide if it's too soon to bring her into the fold as a full-time player. Ha ha.

Dex:
Yeah, but she already knows who I am. There are no takebacks.

Margot:
True. She does ask about you now . . .

Dex:
She does?!?

Margot:
I mean... she might have done

Dex:
Why am I just now hearing about this?! What sorts of things does she say?

Margot:
LOL you are so nosy

Dex:
Listen, I need all the help I can get. You're not exactly running straight into my arms, you're making me work for it. If I have the kid on my side, my odds just got exponentially better.

Margot:
ALL THE MORE REASON NOT TO LET THE TWO OF YOU IN THE SAME ROOM. I don't need the two of you ganging up on me.

Dex:
Us?! We would never

Margot:
> LOL bullshit. And just 'cause you wouldn't doesn't mean my child wouldn't. Wait. Did that make sense?

Dex:
> No but I got the gist of it.

Dex:
> And you can trust Wyatt and me in a room together. I promise not to fall for any of her master plans.

Margot:
> Hmm. We'll see.

Dex:
> And speaking of skydiving, they have those indoor places . . .

Margot:
> OMG no, I have no desire to be strapped into one of those suits and have a mask on my face in front of you—I'm trying to be cute, not have all my best parts stretched and blown around . . .

Dex:
Trust me, I'd still be attracted to you.

Margot:
Ah so you admit it, you think I'm like really pretty . . .

Dex:
Hot. Cute. Pretty. Sexy.

Margot:
Stop, you're making me blush . . .

Dex:
Blush all over?

Margot:
LOL maybe.

Dex:
This I would like to see . . .

Margot:
Dream on.

Dex:
You wouldn't send me a selfie?

Margot:
Not a sexy one. And besides, I don't take great photos.

Dex:
I don't believe that for a second. You're so fucking cute I can't even stand it anymore.

Margot:
Flattery will get you nowhere.

Dex:
I don't believe that for a second haha

Dex:
You're not even gonna give me a little peek? Not even a cute selfie?

Margot:
Maybe if you ask nicely . . .

Dex:
I thought I was!

Dex:
Please? Pretty please?

Margot:
Hmm, I'll think about it. What about you? How come I'm the only one in the hot seat here, do I get something in return??

Dex:
Fine, twist my arm.

Margot:
Oh God, now I'm nervous

Dex:
No dick pics. Promise. I don't need those all over the internet.

Margot:
Should I be offended by that comment? I would NEVER sell pictures or post them on the internet without your permission. I would be horrified if the roles were reversed.

Dex:
I mean—there are definitely going to be pictures of you on the internet... Comes with the territory.

Margot:
The thought of that makes me ill. Let's not talk about it.

Margot:
** Chooses pic. Hits SEND **

Dex:
Dang. Better than I imagined—and there's even a little boob showing. I totally zoomed in on that

Margot:
I am SO EMBARRASSED. Delete, DELETE

Dex:
Hell no, I'm putting that in my spank bank.

Margot:
You're so romantic.

Dex:
> And you like it

Margot:
> Maybe I do. You're growing on me just a little . . .

Dex:
> Just a LITTLE? Sounds like I have my work cut out for me.

Margot:
> Don't sweat it.

Dex:
> Easy for you to say! You're not easy to impress

Margot:
> Oh stop it—I'm impressed, okay? You have nothing to worry about.

Dex:
> Well then when am I going to see you again? Since skydiving is out, I'll have to think of something else. Hot air balloon ride?

Margot:
How about a picnic?

Dex:
God no.

Margot:
I take back what I said about you being romantic...

Chapter 21

Margot

In the end, I cave.

Actually, that's not true, and it's not fair.

I didn't cave—I gave some serious thought to the dilemma and eventually had a conversation with my daughter. Her opinion matters to me, and she deserves to have input.

So here I am, bringing Dex up to my daughter when I told myself I wasn't going to get her involved in my dating life until I was certain I was going to continue seeing him long term.

"You went on a date with Dex?"

I nod. "Yes. After you shook him down for LEGO money, he took me out . . . sort of as an apology but also to explain himself better. And we ended up having fun."

My daughter smirks, doing a fist pump. "You're welcome."

She's happily walking beside me as we head to the park. "What exactly am I thanking you for?"

"Playing matchmaker."

I give my head a shake but smile. She has no idea I had swiped on Dex before she ran into him, but I don't hold back explaining it to her now, filling her in on the same details I gave Cora.

"So you see? I'd met him—sort of—and you've met him, so now I'm trying to decide if the three of us should . . . hang out."

My child misses nothing. "Don't you like him?"

"I do! I do like him. I just . . . I'm not going to bring someone around my child until it's a serious relationship." That's my rule anyway—I'm not sure what other people do, but it's what I believe.

Wyatt cannot keep the skepticism off her face. "You've never had a serious relationship."

Why must she point out the obvious?

I've dated several different guys for several months but still never wanted to introduce them to my kid, nor did I discuss them around her.

"True," I say slowly. The very fact I'm discussing Dex with her is new, uncharted territory.

"What makes Dex different?" Why does my daughter sound like one of those dating coaches on television? Or someone three times her age.

Lordy.

I pause on the sidewalk, choosing my words carefully, considering that my audience is ten.

"There's something about him that makes me think it could be more than just a few dates. But I don't want to rush into anything." I use the simplest terms to describe how I feel, starting off again toward the park.

Good exercise and a good excuse to talk.

She nods sagely. "I get it. You want to be sure."

"Yes, exactly. I want to be sure for both of us." I hesitate. "I don't want either of us getting attached too soon."

My daughter's face lights up with a mischievous grin. "Well, you should give him a chance and don't future trip about it. You never know unless you try, right?"

"What's future tripping?"

"It's when you worry about things that haven't happened yet. Like you make things up in your brain and freak out about them," my daughter explains. "For example, thinking about how you're going to spend the holiday with someone, and you only went on two dates with them. It's useless to stress."

I laugh, feeling the weight of the decision lighten just a bit. "How did you get to be so wise?"

"I don't know. Are we getting ice cream later?" In true Wyatt fashion she does a complete one-eighty on the topic, so quickly it makes my head want to spin.

"We haven't had dinner yet. Let's not future trip, okay?"

Wyatt rolls her eyes. "That's not the same thing."

Oh.

Shoot.

I realize how uncool I sound because I was trying to sound cool.

"Mom." My kid pokes me in the arm. "If you end up marrying Dex, will I have to call him Dad?"

I nearly choke on my coffee. "Whoa, slow down there, kiddo. We're not even close to that stage."

She shrugs as if she hasn't dropped a bomb into the conversation. "Just checking. I like to be good and prepared."

That she does.

"Good and prepared? You sound like you're planning a mission to Mars."

"Well, dating is kind of like a space mission, isn't it? Lots of unknowns and possible aliens." Wyatt pulls a face, sticking out her tongue and crossing her eyes, wiggling her hands around her head.

I burst out laughing, ruffling her hair. "Yes, and let's hope Dex isn't an alien."

"Or AI," she whispers with wide eyes. "You never know with technology these days."

"If he starts glitching, I'll let you know."

"Oh, I'll know. You won't have to tell me." Wyatt pauses, hopping over a large crack in the sidewalk. "Wouldn't it be cool to have a robot dad?"

"He's not going to be your dad," I remind her. "You have a dad. And speaking of which, how is yours?"

"The same. He works a lot," Wyatt tells me.

"Does he still have two phones?" Colton is a workaholic and always has been. He used to use it as an excuse not to be in a relationship, telling me he wanted to be established first. Well, GUESS WHAT, PAL, WE ALREADY HAVE A DAUGHTER! Cannot get any more established than that...

"He's always telling me I look just like you."

She *does* look like me. Long brown hair, big green eyes, and the same freckles spattered across her nose that I used to count (as a game) when she was little.

I tap her nose with the tip of my finger, booping it. "You're so stinking cute."

She pulls away from me and runs, considering herself too old now for mushy stuff.

"I don't want to talk about dad. He's boring," she shouts at me, jogging backward. "What's Dex like? Does he have a cool job? Any pets?"

I chuckle at her curiosity. "Well, he's a football player, actually."

She stops short, waiting for me to catch up. "Like, real football? With the big stadiums and everything?"

"Yep," I say, nodding. "Not sure what position he plays, though."

"Wow! That's super cool!" Wyatt exclaims. "Do you think he'll teach me how to throw a football?"

"You'd have to ask him that," I reply, smiling at her enthusiasm. "Maybe someday. But first, let's see if Dex is someone who's worth all this excitement."

Wyatt's eyes light up. "Do you think he likes me?"

"He's already mentioned we should all hang out. I'm bringing it up because I felt it was something we needed to discuss and not decide impulsively." I try to pull her in for a hug, but she evades me. "Besides, who wouldn't like you?"

"People who don't like fun, maybe," she retorts with a giggle.

"True," I concede. "But Dex loves fun, so I think you two will get along just fine once you get to know each other better. Baby steps."

"What if we're at a restaurant eating and he tries to ditch us, the way he did with that one date?"

I burst out laughing. "That's a good point. You should ask him."

She shrugs. "I will."

We spend the next few minutes chatting about our potential outing, and as we near the park—kids playing on the swing sets and other equipment that Wyatt considers herself too grown up for—I can't help but feel a mix of excitement and nervousness.

This could be the start of something wonderful, but only time will tell. For now, I'm just grateful that my daughter is mature enough and supportive enough to understand my dilemma.

I love that we can talk.

"Can we get ice cream on the way home?" Wyatt wants to know, always hitting me up for sweets.

"I guess so. But only if you promise not to be a smart-ass when you meet Dex again."

She crosses her heart with a serious expression. "I promise. I'll be nice. But I'll still ask the hard-hitting questions we all want to know."

"Fair enough," I say, finally pulling her into a quick hug. "You're my little detective."

She squirms out of my embrace, still trying to maintain her "too cool for hugs" demeanor. "Yeah, yeah. So, when are we doing this?"

"How about this weekend?" I suggest. "I'll text Dex and see if he's free."

Wyatt's eyes light up. "Awesome! I'll wear my best outfit."

"Which outfit do you consider your best?" I am genuinely curious.

"My white pants and that pink shirt." She says it with a dramatic roll of her eyes. "Or that dress Nana Simpson bought me for Easter."

Nana Simpson is Colton's mom.

"The dress might be a bit much for what we're doing, but I love that you want to look nice."

Dex seems determined to impress my child, and it sounds like she wants to impress him too.

As Wyatt dashes away from me again, I pull out my phone and send a quick text to Dex.

Me:
Just had THE TALK with Wyatt to see how she feels about "US"

Dex:
You did? What's the verdict?

Me:
She's fine with it. We can set something up, I feel like it's safe

Dex:
Safe? Gee, try not to sound so enthused.

Me:
Sorry, but now I'm incredibly nervous...!

Dex:
It'll be fine. I'm great with kids

Me:
> You are?

Huh. Interesting.

Me:
> Which kids?

Dex:
> My friends have kids—give me some credit. They all love Uncle Dex... especially Kalen Baker's son. Loved that drum kit I sent him for Christmas.

Me:
> OMG I would hate you.

Dex:
> Yeah, Kalen hates me all right LOL

I smile at the screen, feeling a flutter of anticipation.

Chapter 22
Dex

I settle on rock climbing.

I figure it will be fun for Wyatt, and also, I get to see Margot's lower half in one of those harnesses you're required to wear.

Plus.

She'll get to see me in one, too, *if you catch my drift*.

We agree to meet at the climbing center. It's crowded, but not everyone is participating in rock climbing—they have miniature golf, too, something she and I have done already in a roundabout way.

I lean against a tall column in the lobby waiting, wondering if I should be outside watching for them, second-guessing myself.

So unlike me.

Stuff my hands in the pockets of my athletic pants, trying my best to look casual.

It's an impossible task.

The last time I felt *casual* and *unaffected* was . . . at a bar, probably. It helps knowing there's no need to exert effort when people approach me, *and by* people, *I mean women*. I do not go to them. Don't have to.

Yeah, yeah, I know what you're thinking—I sound cocky and arrogant and not worthy of a woman like Margot because I'm an immature bag of shit, and to that I say: So what?

I never claimed to be perfect, and I've been up front from the beginning.

Mostly.

The way I see it, I'm up against three things when it comes to Margot and her affection:

She straight up told me to my face *not* to fuck with her unless I was serious. She is a package deal.

I'm fucking with her anyway, even though I'm not in the market for said package.

I'm keeping a secret from her now, and it may or may not fester, depending on how I spin the truth. To myself, or to her.

Time will tell.

Not that she has to find out about my conversation with Trent, but I was an idiot when I told Landon about it because saying the words out loud somehow made it feel sordid?

"We're just friends and she knows it. Deep down inside she knows this isn't the real deal," I mutter to myself.

How could she? I am a grown child!

"Now is not the time to grow a conscience." I shrug off the angel on my shoulder—he has no place here. I haven't done anything wrong.

"Dex!" a voice calls to me, and I see Wyatt flying toward me, braids flapping behind her as she beelines toward the column where I stand.

"Hey, Wyatt." I return her enthusiasm, though it may not quite reach my eyes. Too much on my mind for that.

I try to shake it off . . .

"Hello, Mommy," I say to Margot.

She scowls. "Don't do that."

"Too soon?" I chuckle.

"Uh—yeah." She laughs, though, shooting her gaze at her daughter. Whoops.

Guess I shouldn't be making innuendos in front of the kid. She's too smart. In fact, her beady little gaze is bouncing between her mom and me, back and forth, back and forth until I clear my throat.

Busted.

"Who's ready to have fun?"

Wyatt's arm shoots in the air enthusiastically, as if she were raising her hand at school. She waves it around for good measure.

"I cannot *wait* to climb this wall. There's nothing I want more," Margot deadpans, and I can't decide if she's being sarcastic or not, so I ignore her tone.

I tilt my head.

Goddamn, she's cute even when she's being a shithead.

Margot is dressed in one of those ways chicks dress when they try to look like they made no effort in their appearance but took a ridiculous amount of time to make it look like they made no effort in their appearance.

Leggings. T-shirt with a college logo. Sneakers.

Fanny pack.

My brows go up at *that* choice.

I've taken the liberty of getting us registered and have the waivers ready for Margot to sign. All that's left is introducing ourselves to the climbing instructor, who is so granola he doesn't recognize me, and if he does, he clearly does not give a shit.

He is so. Into. Rock climbing.

Nerd.

"I'm going to run to the bathroom before we get started," Margot announces, giving her daughter one of those looks my mother used to give me when I was young. It says "Behave while I'm gone."

I watch her walk off, sidestepping several people along the way, as the place is moderately busy.

As soon as her mother is out of sight, Wyatt whirls toward me, eyes wide. "You know what we should do?"

She is wasting no time.

I'm terrified by this child, to be honest, and what she could possibly be about to say. She's got an adult brain trapped in a preteen's body, and I can see the wheels spinning.

"No. What should we do?" I haven't the faintest.

"We should have a *hand*shake." She announces it in a conspiratorial whisper, practically giddy at the notion.

"A handshake?" *Thank God that's all she wants to do.* I thought she was going to say something truly horrifying, like: "Why are you such a lying asshole?" Or, "Why are you dating my mother when you have no intention of getting serious?" Or, "Why are we rock-wall climbing when you clearly have no idea what you're doing and your body weight is going to be too heavy for you to hoist up the wall without a fight?"

"Sure." I can do a handshake.

"The kind you have to practice and that we can do when I see you."

I nod. "I know what kind you're referring to."

Wyatt immediately grabs my hand, zero hesitation, bumping my hip with hers, as if attempting to recreate the handshake from *The Parent Trap* remake. The handshake done between the redheaded twin and her fancy butler slash driver.

I can't help but laugh.

Wyatt looks so determined, tongue sticking out between her teeth in concentration.

"Have you actually ever done a handshake?" 'Cause a few things go into one, and one of those things is skill, based on your level. "We can start with something easy. Like this."

I present my fist so she can bump it. Hold out my elbow so she can bump that.

Clap, clap. Bump. Clap.

"Now let's do that again," she tells me, total concentration furrowing her little brow.

We do it again.

Then once more.

So many times that Margot is back from peeing, watching us but not commenting, an amused smile on her face. Arms crossed.

"Are the two of you almost done?" She laughs. "That is your fifth time. Not that I'm in any rush to strap on that . . . belt-bungee-contraption thingy."

"Harness." I correct her terminology. "Which I'm dying to see you in."

She rolls her eyes. "You're so amusing." Not.

"Come on, let's go." Wyatt practically drags me to the wall, hand wrapped around my forearm, little arms and legs working. Pretty strong considering how puny she is.

I let her pull me along, pretending to struggle. "All right, all right, I'm coming. No need to flex those tiny muscles."

"You're just jealous because I'm stronger than I look," she shoots back, her grin wide.

"Sure, let's go with that," I reply, trying to stifle a laugh.

The instructor, some dude named Ben—with a permanent five-o'clock shadow and a smile that suggests he gets a lot of action from this gig—gets us situated with our rappelling gear. Helmets. He has the air of someone who's been scaling walls since birth, and his confidence has Margot smiling openly at him.

I frown.

"All right, guys, listen up," Ben says, his voice carrying easily over the chatter in the cavernous room. "First things first, let's make sure your harnesses are on properly." He walks around, checking each of us. When he reaches me, he gives my harness a quick tug and nods. "Looks good, buddy."

Buddy? *I'm not your buddy, man.*

Wyatt gets the same treatment. "A little tight there, champ. You're not trying to cut off circulation, are you?"

Next, Ben stops in front of Margot. "And you, miss." He gives my date a cheeky once-over, pulling at her straps one too many times, hands lingering at her waist. "Perfect fit."

What a douche.

When we're ready and reach the base of the rock wall, I turn to look up at it. *All* the way up at it, to the top. It's intimidating, but there is no going back. I'll look like a total pussy if I back out now. This was my idea, after all.

"Ready to conquer this beast?" I am all bravado.

Margot groans. "Ready as I'll ever be."

Wyatt stands next to us, looking pretty damn adorable in her gear. "You look like a pro," I tell her to puff up her ego.

"Are you stalling?" She squints up at me.

"Pfft. Me? No." I gesture grandly toward the wall. "Ladies first."

Margot and Wyatt both narrow their eyes at me.

"Oh no," my date announces. "This was your idea—you go first. You're not getting out of this that easily."

"Fine," I grumble, fidgeting with the strap on my helmet. I hate this dumb thing—I look stupid and unsexy. "But if I get stuck, you're coming up to rescue me."

"You're not going to get stuck."

I chuckle, fiddling with my harness straps. It's got my nuts in a vise grip.

Meanwhile, a few feet away, Ben is demonstrating the essential moves and giving basic instructions.

". . . climbing is all about balance and rhythm." I swear he looks at Margot when he says the word *rhythm*. "Keep three points of contact with the wall at all times—two hands and a foot, or two feet and a hand." He winks. "Don't forget to trust your gear."

This fuckin' guy . . .

Margot raises an eyebrow, nodding. "Trust the gear. Right."

"I got you—don't be nervous." Ben grins. "It's natural to be a bit frightened. Just remember, your harness and rope are your lifeline. They're designed to hold much more than your weight." He points at me. "Like him."

Me? Fuck you, dude!

Ben points to the rock wall. "Look for solid footholds and handholds. If you feel stuck, take a moment to regroup. There's no rush."

"No rush," Wyatt repeats, determined.

"Any questions before we start?" Ben goes on, scanning our faces.

Wyatt's hand goes into the air. "What if we fall?"

Ben shakes his head. "That's what the belay is for." He jiggles the harness around his waist. "Trust me, you're not going anywhere."

After a final check of our gear, he claps his hands. "All right, who's ready to climb?"

"Dex, you're going first!" Wyatt reminds me impatiently, nudging me toward the base of the wall. "Go!"

Ben gives me a thumbs-up, that fucker.

With everything securely fastened, I grapple for the first grip hold to start my ascent.

Easy!

I climb up another few feet, moving quicker—and more confidently—up the wall. The rock feels cool beneath my palms, and solid, and I find my rhythm faster than I was expecting. Not too far below, I hear Wyatt and Margot chattering away, their voices carrying up.

"Do you actually think he's going to make it to the top without falling?" Wyatt asks.

"I give him about ten minutes before he slips," Margot replies with a laugh. "He's not built for this."

"Yeah, he *is* pretty big," Wyatt agrees.

"Hey!" I shout down to them, trying to sound indignant. "I can hear you."

"Focus on climbing!" Margot shouts back. "Stop looking down at me."

"I'm not looking at you—I'm looking down your shirt."

She glances down at her shirt; it provides full coverage. Ha! Made her look!

"Could you not say things like that?" She laughs. "Tiny ears are listening."

"Whoops."

I resist the urge to make another smart-ass remark, and I keep moving.

The higher I go, the better the view gets.

Through the massive windows flanking the entire warehouse, I catch sight of the sun beginning to set. It casts a warm glow over everything. It's actually quite beautiful from this vantage point, and for a moment, I forget about the teasing and the banter with Margot and Wyatt and focus on the bell at the top of the wall.

So close.

Closer . . .

Finally, I reach the top. Ring the bell. Haul myself over the edge. Stand with my hands on my hips, gazing down at them triumphantly.

"Made it! Beat that, you two!"

Margot squints up at me, shielding her eyes from the fluorescent lights. "All right, show-off, your turn to watch. And no commentary, we're trying to concentrate."

I grin as she starts her climb. "No promises!"

"Here we come!" Wyatt gives me a thumbs-up. "Let's see if Mom can do it without complaining the whole way up."

Margot turns to her daughter, looking incredulous at her audacity.

"Oh, she'll complain," I call down to them, popping a squat and settling in to watch. "That's half the fun."

Chapter 23

Margot

"I still can't decide if that was fun for me or not."

I'm huffing and puffing when my feet touch the ground again, harness firmly planted up my backside—a.k.a. butt—squeezing and squishing all my bits.

All my nerves are short-circuiting from the sensation.

"Mom, you should see your face." Wyatt laughs, high-fiving Dex in the most aggravating way. The pair have done a special handshake no fewer than a dozen times.

"I don't want to see my face," I tell my child. Honestly, I don't need to see my face to know how red it is. I can feel it burning, not just from exhaustion but from the embarrassment. The last thing I would choose for a date is to have my pants up my ass crack, yet here we are.

"You did great." Dex, for his part, puts one hand around my waist and pulls me in, planting a loud, chaste kiss on top of my head. "And you look adorable."

"I don't feel adorable," I mumble, trying to discreetly adjust the harness and pull fabric out of my rear. Dex laughs, the sound deep and warm, and I can't help but smile despite myself.

"Seriously, Mom, you were awesome!" Wyatt chimes in, her eyes shining with pride. But she's my number one sidekick, so she has to tell me I'm awesome. It's, like, her job. "You climbed that wall like a pro."

"Well, I don't know about that," I say, glancing up at the towering wall I just scaled. "But thanks, Wyatt."

Her encouragement feels like a balm, soothing my frazzled nerves. Most days, she's the sweetest sweetheart.

Other days, she's a total monster, but I won't dwell on that.

Right now I'm focusing on bringing my breathing back to normal and on Dex's massive hand on my hip as if it belongs there.

Feels like it does.

I feel small next to him, tiny.

Safe.

Wyatt giggles, breaking my thoughts. "Dude, I was like a spider monkey up there!"

He chuckles, shaking his head. "A spider monkey? You definitely looked like one, hanging on to those handholds. Are you sure this was your first time rock climbing?"

Wyatt nods. "I totally want to do it again."

Dex laughs. "Well, little spider monkey, how about we cool down with some ice cream? My treat." He glances at me. "If it's okay with your mom."

"You mention ice cream in front of her and expect me to say no? As if there's a choice?"

Rule 1: *Never mention sweets in front of a child and expect to get out of it. Kids never forget anything.*

Rule 2: *I'm the one who looks like an asshole if I say no to ice cream, damn him.*

Wyatt, bless her adorable heart, is already celebrating, bouncing on her toes. "Yes, yes, yes to ice cream."

They high-five.

"Isn't he just the best?" I ask playfully. "He's trying to bribe us into hanging out with him longer than I would normally allow us to be out on a Sunday night."

"Don't be a party pooper." He says it with a grin, holding up his hands in mock surrender to make himself look innocent. "So, what do you say? Want to follow me in your car? There's a place not too far from here."

There always is.

"I have no choice, do I?"

He shakes his head.

Settled in the car, my child grins. "I like him."

I give my daughter side-eye as we pull out of the sporting complex.

"Of course you do, he's your sidekick now, siding with you on everything." I am the odd man out! She finally has someone to hang out with who acts her age. "Plus he bought you those LEGOs."

It would be remiss of me not to remind her.

"That's not the *only* reason I like him," she says. "He's fun. And LEGOs are not toys—they're fuel for my imagination."

Ha. True.

It's also true that Dex *is* fun. But fun isn't what I consider a building block of a good relationship, although it helps.

Baby steps.

When we pull up to the small brightly colored ice cream slash tourist shop, Wyatt is practically vibrating with excitement and frothing at the mouth for something sweet. The sign above the entrance reads **Scoops Ahoy!** and the smell of freshly made waffle cones wafts through the air.

My mouth waters, and we're not even inside yet.

It's a whimsical wonderland of colors, twinkling fairy lights, and a dizzying array of ice cream flavors—not to mention T-shirts, mini cacti, hoodies, postcards, and other Arizona-themed treasures.

Wyatt beelines for the counter, licking her lips as she takes in her options, and I can tell by the look in her eyes she is wishing for and wanting each one of them.

Biggest Player

"Can I get . . . um . . . chocolate chip cookie dough? No, wait! Mint chocolate chip! Or maybe both?" my child babbles, her indecision making Dex laugh—*and me cringe.*

I can handle it when my daughter gets hyper, but he's not used to it. I wonder what he's thinking right now.

"Why not both?" Dex suggests, winking at me over the top of her head. "YOLO, am I right?"

I forget that he's a man who makes a ton of money.

Wyatt's eyes light up. "Really? Thanks, Dex! You're officially my favorite person." She hugs him tight around the waist, squeezing her eyes shut in the process.

"Hey!" I protest, feigning hurt. "What about me?"

She turns to me with a mischievous grin. "You're my favorite too." Pauses. "Obviously."

I raise a brow. "How many favorites do you have?"

Wyatt starts counting out loud. "You, Dad, Mrs. Fletcher, my art teacher. Conrad, the lizard. The guy at the botanical garden who always lets me pick the daisies. Dex."

"Dude, that's a lot of favorites," Dex points out.

My daughter shrugs. "I like a lot of things."

We place our orders. Wyatt does order the double-scoop monstrosity that is her heart's desire, while Dex and I opt for a hot fudge sundae we intend to share.

Wyatt scores us a booth by the window and immediately starts chattering, lacing her fingers together and setting her hands on the table.

"So," she begins. "When are we getting together again?" Her gaze bounces between Dex and me.

"We'll see." We haven't even had dessert yet, and she's already ten steps ahead.

"Don't you think it went well?" my daughter asks, putting me on the spot. "I know *I* had fun."

Fun.

There's that word again . . .

"Of course I think it went well," I say, face flushing when Dex turns to watch me, curious, I'm sure, as to what I'm going to say next.

"Then why wouldn't we get together again?" Wyatt urges. "We can go to San Diego or something."

If I were drinking water, I would choke. "San Diego?"

Fortunately for me, Dex decides to chime in, splaying his hands on the tabletop, mirroring my daughter's pose.

"Easy there, little spider monkey. Let's have ice cream first before we take a road trip—*then* we can hijack all your mom's plans to keep me in the friend zone."

I relax, sighing back into the leather of the booth. "Dex and I will talk *privately* about whether or not we're going to see each other again—and if you'll be invited. Young lady."

I stress the word *privately*, and we all grin when the server brings over our ice cream. He sets the bowls in the center of the table and stands at the foot of it, staring down at Dex.

"You're Dex Lansing."

Dex's grin is wide and friendly. "Sure am."

He looks humble, which surprises me. I kind of expected that the first time I'd see someone approaching him in public—the signing did not count, IMO—he would say something cocky like "The one and only!" But he doesn't. He seems modest and chill and at ease.

Which is great, because when the teenager opens his mouth, all that comes out is an awkward "Um."

He is speechless—a total fan.

"What's your name?" he asks the teen, making him stammer even more.

"Dude."

"Your parents named you Dude?" Wyatt pulls a face. "That is so weird."

"Wyatt." My tone is a warning.

"Gavin," the teen finally says, eking out an "I'm Gavin."

Dex holds out his palm to give the kid's hand a shake. "Good to meet you, my man."

Biggest Player

Eventually the server goes back to the serving counter, and we're able to dig into our treats, Wyatt waving her spoon around. "Anyway, all I'm saying is, I think the two of you have great chemistry—and this date was fun."

"When did you say that?" Because she did in fact say nothing of the sort.

Dex tilts his head, amused, stealing the cherry from the top of our sundae and popping it in his mouth. "How old are you again?"

"Ten. I thought you knew that."

"Well, you sound forty."

My daughter giggles, *loving* the compliment.

"I feel forty," Wyatt announces, spoon buried in her ice cream.

"Being a grown-up can be pretty dull sometimes. Enjoy your youth while it lasts." I pause, thinking about my stance on rock climbing. "Tonight was actually a lot of fun."

Dex takes a bite of our sundae and nods thoughtfully. He swallows. "Except those harnesses. I could have done without those pinching my nads."

"Facts." My daughter nods sagely, as if it were the kind of statement she's used to.

Trying my best not to correct him—he's a grown man, I do not need to scold him for using the word *nads* in front of my kid—I create the perfect bite: ice cream, chocolate, whipped cream, nuts.

Taste it and moan. "Yum. So good."

As we finish our treats, the sun sets outside, casting a warm glow through the parlor's windows. Wyatt's energy starts to wane, and she leans against me, letting out a big yawn.

"Tired, kiddo?" I ask softly.

She nods. "Yeah, kind of. But I had tons of fun."

I smile, then press a kiss to the top of her head. "I did too."

Dex stands, stretching, and gathers up our empty containers. "We should get you home, Wyatt. You've got school tomorrow."

He sounds so responsible.

"Yeah. And I have to take a shower before bed." She holds up her hands. "My palms are still covered in chalk."

Chapter 24

Dex:
So. What did you think?

Margot:
About...??

Dex:
Uh—our date tonight?

Margot:
Aka, hanging out with you?

Dex:
Yeah, hanging out with me. Final thoughts and go.

Margot:
LOL and go?

Dex:
> ... waiting on pins and needles for your assessment.

Margot:
> I'm shocked that you care this much LOL. It was fun—wayyyy better than I was expecting.

Dex:
> Welp, THAT'S a backhanded compliment if I've ever heard one.

Margot:
> No! I didn't mean it that way! I mean, not on purpose hahahahah

Margot:
> I just didn't know what to expect, that's all. It was good!!!

Dex:
> So what I hear you saying is that the date exceeded your expectations... What was your favorite part of the evening, besides my nuts in a vise?

Margot:
> Mostly your nuts in a vise. LOL

Dex:
> Ouch that hurt, and also, it actually did hurt. My balls were KILLLING me softly. Or not softly. Like hell.

Margot:
> LOL omg stop. You keep mentioning your junk. I personally did not have that problem.

Dex:
> Would you mention it though if you had?

Margot:
> Okay, fine. I was struggling a bit—my pants were up my butt. HAPPY NOW?!?!?

Dex:
> Indeed. Now you're on my level.

Margot:
> The good news is I forgot to be nervous.

Dex:
You don't seem like the type who gets nervous about anything.

Margot:
False. Getting to know someone is daunting, you know? Wrangling kids is easy. Wrangling YOU, not so much . . .

Dex:
I can relate. Running a football I could do all day, every day. But making time for a relationship is, like, a full-time job.

Margot:
How so?

Dex:
Cuz. I have to give it more thought. I'm on autopilot with football, been doing it so long I could do it in my sleep.

Margot:
Fair enough. Is it hard sometimes to have people only see that one side of you??

Dex:
Sure—of course. There are days where I wish I could just blend in and not stand out so much. My height doesn't help LOL. Had a run of good luck since I met you—every time we've gone out, people have mostly left me alone, thank God.

Dex:
But enough about me. What about you? What made you decide to become a teacher?

Margot:
I had this amazing teacher in high school who really inspired me, and once I was in college I realized I wanted to teach elementary school, not middle or high school. I just love little kids.

Dex:
Do you want MORE kids?

Margot:
Yes, I think so. And I think Wyatt would love a brother or sister or a brother AND a sister.

Margot:
I'm not going to throw the question back your way, I already know the answer haha

Dex:
Hey, I'm taking the kid thing day by day. Just 'cause I don't want to be a dad right now don't mean I don't never want to be one.

Margot:
The teacher in me is cringing SO HARD at that entire sentence. My eye is literally twitching out of my skull.

Dex:
I did okay in school LOLOLOLOL

Margot:
I see that . . .

Dex:
Okay, so besides the kid stuff, is there anything you want to know about me?

Margot:
> Hmm, let's think **taps chin**
> What's something people would be surprised to learn about you?

Dex:
> Shit, I don't know. Lots of stuff probably. I'd say most people don't know I'm really into cooking. It's my way to unwind.

Margot:
> Seriously?? That's so cool. I love to cook too, but my kitchen is so small I can't go crazy. What's your signature dish?

Dex:
> I'd have to go with my homemade lasagna. It's a family recipe that was passed down from generation to generation.

Margot:
> Wait. Are you Italian???

Dex:
> Um, no. It's just something my grandma used to make.

Biggest Player

Margot:
I freaking LOVE lasagna. It's one of my favorites, and as long as it has plenty of ricotta and MEAT, OMG, sign me up

Dex:
You should try mine then, it's fucking delicious.

Margot:
Well, dang, sounds like I would love to.

Dex:
Put me in your calendar this week, I'm gonna cook for you.

Margot:
Awww. Okay **blushes**

Dex:
Sweet. It's another date.

Margot:
You are seriously stepping up. I'm impressed.

Dex:
I didn't know I had it in me.

Margot:
At least you're honest.

Chapter 25

Dex

Why the hell would I lie and tell her I love to cook in my free time?

First of all, I barely have any fucking free time, and secondly, I wouldn't know a lasagna noodle from my ass or a hole in the wall.

That analogy did not make any sense, but that's only because I am FREAKING THE FUCK OUT.

I feel like I mentioned to her before that I have a chef?

I stand at the counter, googling a recipe on how to make the famous Italian dish: *easy way to make lasagna.*

Lasagna for dummies.

How to make lasagna with basic ingredients.

"Fuck." I'll have to run to the grocery store or have supplies delivered because although Carrie does have the cabinets and fridge well stocked, I haven't found any fat, flat noodles.

"Seriously. How hard could it be?" It's just like pasta and sauce, yeah? In a pan and shit.

"I am a grown man."

Mostly.

Despite the fact that I am capable and smart and have been known to boil up a mean pot of spaghetti noodles, I nonetheless find Carrie in my phone and hit call.

"What's up?" she answers after two rings, skepticism in her voice. I get straight to the point. No time to waste.

"I have an emergency."

"What kind of an emergency? There are six meals in the fridge."

Yes, I saw those, but they will not help me in this case.

Broccoli chicken. Chicken and stuffing. Rice and chicken. Rice and vegetables and beer.

Basic, boring, lean meals.

"Can you come and make me lasagna?" I blurt out, unable to stop the panic from entering my voice.

"Lasagna?" Her voice raises an octave. "*That's* your emergency? Oh my God, Dex, why can't you just eat the meals I made?"

"Because I want lasagna, not another version of your 'chicken surprise.' Come on, Carrie, help a guy out." I pause. "Please."

She sighs heavily on the other end of the line, and I can practically *hear* her rolling her eyes. "Dex, you do realize that I have a life outside of your kitchen, right? I do not work on the weekends."

She isn't telling me anything I do not already know.

Still.

I pester.

"Yes, but is it as fulfilling as making me happy with a delicious, cheesy, gooey lasagna?" Another pause. "With loads of ricotta and meat?"

I hear her closing a door and wonder what room in her apartment she's in. "You're impossible."

"I'm charming, you mean."

"More like exasperating. You should have most of the ingredients for lasagna. All you have to do is grab a few more. I know for a fact you have mozzarella cheese. And canned sauce."

I cannot feed Margot canned sauce, not after the bragging I did about the recipe being passed down from generation to generation.

"What ingredients?" I say cautiously, already having googled the ingredients, but part of me knows that if I sound like a complete idiot who cannot be trusted . . . maybe, *just maybe*, she'll take pity on me and come to my rescue.

"Dex!" She sounds as frustrated as I'm becoming. "Stop being lazy and just order the damn noodles, sauce, cheese, and meat. It's not hard."

I pull open the fridge, staring into its interior. "I have an open jar of sauce and a block of cheese I think is still good."

"Right." She is not impressed.

"How old is this ground beef? Or is this tofu. It's a mystery package." I turn it over, this way and that, trying to read the label.

There's a long pause. "Dex. Order a freaking lasagna from Capitano's, this isn't hard."

"Will they deliver it in, like, a pan?"

"A pan? Lasagna isn't served in a pan."

"But I need it to look like I made it myself."

Carrie groans. "I don't even *want* to know why."

She doesn't want to know why, but I'm going to tell her anyway. "I have a date, and I told her I could cook."

Carrie snorts.

Chokes.

Begins laughing so loud—and so long—I hold my phone away from my ear to wait her out.

"Oh my God, I'm literally dying right now," she gasps. "I can't. You are not that guy."

I am that guy.

"If I don't produce a realistic, homemade-looking pasta dish, she's going to think I lied."

Another cackle and Carrie is lost to me again, laughing her ass off on the other side of town.

"Would you knock it off, this is serious," I sternly tell her, frowning.

"Is it, though? Is it serious?"

"I hate you." Why am I her friend?

"No you don't, you're just pouting because I don't have time to drop everything and race over." She wheezes. "What time is your date coming over?"

"Six."

"Dude, it's already four! You cannot make lasagna in this short amount of time! You're going to have to order it, you have no other option. Unless you want to eat at eight. It takes forever to bake."

Anytime Carrie calls me dude, I know she isn't fucking around.

"Shit."

"Yeah—shit is right. Order it and see what happens. Actually, does your date even eat? Most of them don't."

I scowl. "This one is a normal person, of course she's going to eat."

"A normal person? Like. Normal?"

"Yes. She's a teacher, for your information."

I tilt my chin, bragging to my friend that my date isn't my typical type. Carrie lets out a low whistle. "Wow. Seriously?"

"Yes. And she has kids." Well, she has one kid, but that's like having several.

"Holy shit. You're being serious right now."

Why would she think I wasn't being serious?

"Oddly enough." I laugh. "I'm flattered you find all of this so shocking." I feel like it gives me an edge. Makes me cool.

Carrie hesitates. "Huh. Well. If she's coming at six, you better quit screwing around and order that food before they don't have what you need."

True. "Okay, boss."

"Good luck," she mutters. "You'll probably need it."

Chapter 26

Margot

Holy crap—his house is huge.

I have no idea why I'm surprised.

He is, after all, a superstar athlete.

I keep forgetting that fact because while Dex is larger than life physically—he is literally a giant—he doesn't act like the pompous ass I originally thought him to be.

But his house?

Has gates.

Wyatt would be crapping her pants right now if she saw this house.

I pull through after entering the gate code. They open slowly—automatically—and I ease my car over the pavers, which are brick.

The fact that someone younger than I am can afford a place like this is blowing my freaking mind.

For real.

I put the car in park, checking my reflection in the rearview mirror. Add lip gloss. Smooth a hand over my hair.

I catch sight of a man in a car parked across the street just before the gates slide closed again—it looks like he's taking pictures.

My head shakes.

No, that can't be.

I primp a few more seconds, stomach in knots before I push my car door open, and as I'm about to step out and put one foot onto the driveway, my cell phone begins chiming.

It's Colton.

Dude has the worst timing . . .

He has Wyatt, so the alarm inside my brain goes off, mothering kicking into high gear.

"What's wrong?" I ask as soon as I answer, resting back against the front seat, mindful that Dex could look out his front window at any moment and see me lingering in my car.

"Nothing's wrong. Is this a bad time?"

A bad time? "Kind of, but go ahead."

"What are you up to?"

"I . . ." I swallow. "I have a date, if you really need to know."

He does not need to know.

In fact, Colton rarely inquires about how I'm doing or what I'm up to. He literally does not give a shit.

Sure he cares somewhat because I am the mother of his daughter, but . . .

It's not normal for him to ask, just sayin'.

"A date? Since when do you have a date?" My ex laughs in a way I can tell means he doesn't believe me and in a tone that's mildly insulting. There are times I'm reminded of the reasons he and I did not work out, and this cocky attitude is one of them. Deep down in my soul, I truly think *Colton* believes I'm still single because I harbor feelings for him, which could not be further from the truth.

I want to prove him wrong so badly. "It's someone I've been seeing for a while." I sigh so he knows this conversation is wearing on my nerves. "What was it you said you needed?"

"Wy—she wanted me to ask if it was okay for her to color her hair blue."

Say what now?

"Blue hair?" I exclaim. "Since when?"

Biggest Player

This is news to me. My daughter has never, not once, mentioned wanting brightly colored hair, and if she had, I would certainly be open to it. I am nothing if not open minded . . . yet a part of me wonders if she was afraid to ask me? So she asked her dad instead.

One of the downsides of coparenting.

Sigh . . .

"Just the ends of it. The tips," Colton goes on hastily before I can say no. "And I won't be the one doing it. Gretchen said she's done hair before, so it will be easy."

Ah. Gretchen said.

My butt cheeks clench. "Wyatt has never said she's wanted to dye her hair." It's a perfectly perfect shade of light brown, and never once has she wanted it any other color, let alone blue.

I give myself a glance in the rearview mirror, knowing that the longer I sit here, the more my makeup begins to cake on my face.

Ugh.

"I mean, if this is what *she* wants and you're only doing the ends . . ." I bite my bottom lip. "Just the ends—there's a school policy about the whole head."

"Got it."

"This is so random," I say out loud because THIS IS SO RANDOM. On one hand, I seriously want to speak to my daughter; on the other, I don't want to micromanage. Coparenting sucks so hard, and this is one of those days.

"I know. That's why I called." Colton laughs again.

"Noted." I feel my nostrils flaring. "Anything else?"

"You're in that big of a rush to get rid of me, hey?"

I roll my eyes. "I'm sitting in my car, in my date's driveway. Yes, I'm in a rush to get rid of you."

"Ouch," my ex drawls out, sounding hurt.

"Why would that hurt you? Stop being dramatic." I tap my toe on the rubber mat beneath my feet. "Welp. Let me know how it goes. And send pictures if you go through with it."

"Will do." He hesitates. It sounds like he wants to say more, but eventually we end the call.

I stare at my phone a few moments, regrouping. My brain could go down so many paths, but instead I will myself to get it together.

"Focus."

I angle the rearview so I can get one last look at my face before grabbing my purse from the passenger seat, quickly debate whether or not to leave the keys in the ignition, then jam them inside my bag.

Stiffen my spine and give myself a pep talk.

"You are not here to have sex with the man. He is feeding you dinner, do you understand?" *He is feeding me dinner because he was bragging about what a good cook he is and wants to prove it to me, nothing more.*

Right.

Dinner.

Is that what we're calling it these days?

Taking a deep breath, I step out fully and shut the door behind me. The driveway is long and flanked by manicured hedges, leading up to a house that looks straight out of a lifestyle magazine. As I walk toward the entrance, I have to remind myself to put one foot in front of the other so I don't fall on my face.

I am not used to these shoes.

Hobbling slightly, I reach the front door, raising my hand to knock—it swings open before my fist makes contact.

And there he stands . . .

. . . looking effortlessly handsome in a casual shirt and jeans. Bare feet. Freshly shaved. His smile is warm, but there's a glint of mischief in his eyes that makes my heart skip a beat.

Dammit, I was not prepared for this kind of hotness.

"Hey, you made it—and you look so fucking cute," he says, stepping aside to let me in, but then he pulls me in for a quick kiss on the lips I wasn't expecting. "Come on in. Dinner's almost ready."

I step inside, and the interior of the house is just as impressive as the exterior. Modern yet cozy, with tasteful artwork on the walls and soft lighting that creates a welcoming ambiance. We're in Arizona, so the sun is always out and it's always bright, but some houses are dark and gloomy despite that.

Dex's is not.

High ceilings, rounded doorways.

It's beautiful.

I follow him to the kitchen, where mouthwatering smells waft toward my nose and greet me. An exquisite dining table is laid with charger plates and dishes and more silverware than I can count. Everything looks like it came from the pages of a magazine.

"Wow," I say, genuinely impressed as I glance around taking it all in. "I thought you were lying when you said you were a good cook." I hardly know where to focus my attention, eyes bouncing to every surface within their range.

He's a good decorator too.

Beside me Dex laughs, a deep, rich sound that makes me shiver to my core. "I told you. But you haven't tasted it yet, maybe it tastes like shit. Who knows, maybe it's total shit." He jokes. "Come sit."

I settle myself on a stool at the counter and watch as he pours us each a glass of red wine.

"So," I begin, pointing over my shoulder toward his front door. "I'm not sure if it was my imagination, but I think I saw someone suspicious out front."

Dex nods. "Paparazzi maybe?"

Oh.

I guess it makes sense that paps watch his house, but it still feels weird. "Do they sit outside like that a lot?"

He shrugs, taking a sip from his wineglass. "Sometimes." He hesitates. "I think they caught wind that I'm dating someone."

Is he talking about . . . "Me?"

He grins. "Yeah you."

We clink glasses, and I take my first sip, giving him a furtive glance over the brim.

He is so damn good looking.

God, how did I get myself into this mess?

What mess?

The mess where I'm dating a man who doesn't want kids, who is in the public eye—not to mention, he's younger than I am.

THAT MESS!

I shift my gaze and give my muddled brain a shake, glancing to the counter where some cooking supplies are still out. Fresh tomatoes. Containers of sugar. A rolling pin. Flour scattered across the cold stone.

"Wait." My jaw drops open as I connect the dots. "Did you make the pasta from scratch?"

He shrugs humbly. "Cannot confirm or deny."

"You have got to be kidding me." He has to be lying—even *I* don't make my own pasta—*never, not once* have I attempted it. Never wanted to! And here is this grown man—a man-child, really—who has prepared it for our date. "How long did that take you?"

Another demure shrug. "I don't know, like twenty minutes."

"Twenty minutes!" I shriek, voice shooting up a million octaves. "Stop it, there is no way."

Dex blushes. "Maybe it was more like an hour. I wasn't keeping track."

I relax back into my seat. "Even so, making your own pasta is . . . impressive." Like, wow. My stomach grumbles. "I can't wait. I'm starving."

Dex chuckles softly, the sound vibrating through the kitchen air. He moves closer, scooting around the counter to my side, the scent of fresh basil clinging to his clothes.

Oh my God—yum.

My eyes trace the lines of his face, his jawline dusted with stubble, eyes crinkling at the corners. He looks good.

Good enough to eat.

Down, girl. You haven't had dinner yet; stop thinking about making him dessert!

I try to focus on anything else, but my mind drifts. I can't help but imagine him kneading the dough to make the noodles, the muscles in his forearms flexing with each motion. I find myself wondering if those same strong hands could be just as skilled in other areas . . . *if you catch my drift.*

"So." I swear my voice cracks as I try to steer my thoughts back to a normal conversation. "What's the secret to your pasta? Besides an absurd amount of patience?" I know how tedious sauces can be.

Dex grins, a playful glint in his eye. "If I told you my secret, I'd have to kill you."

I laugh, the sound a bit too loud in his cavernous kitchen. "Guess I'll have to live in suspense."

He leans in, his arm brushing mine as he reaches for the wine bottle. The contact sends a shiver up my spine.

Spellbound, I watch as he pours himself another, the liquid swirling and catching the light.

"Cheers. To homemade pasta," he says, raising his glass.

"To homemade pasta," I echo, clinking my glass against his.

"And us," he adds, winking.

Us.

"Seriously," I say. "Thanks for offering to cook—the best food is the food I don't have to make myself."

He chuckles. "It's not that hard. Just takes a bit of practice."

"I'll take your word for it." I set down my glass. "But you might have to show me sometime."

"A private cooking class?" he asks, one brow raised.

He steps closer, the space between us shrinking. My breath catches in my throat as his hand brushes a strand of hair behind my ear. The touch is gentle, almost hesitant, but it sends a thrill through me.

But.

Now we're interrupted, this time by the timer on the oven.

Chapter 27

Dex

My goal was to impress Margot, and it worked.

I breathe a sigh of relief when I open the oven and see the bubbling, cheesy pan of lasagna that had been delivered personally, by the restaurant, a mere thirty minutes before Margot arrived.

It was a close call that had me sweating.

Phew, baby.

I watch her savoring each delicious bite, and I know my erratic heartbeat was worth it. Her eyes light up with every forkful, and the satisfied hums and moans escaping her lips are a swift kick to my nut sac.

My dick tingles watching her lick her fork, damned if it doesn't.

"I actually can't believe you made all this," she groans, voice filled with genuine amazement. "You're full of surprises."

I grin, trying to mask the guilt gnawing at me because, technically, I cheated. "You know me, always aiming to please."

She laughs, a soft, melodic sound that makes my heart skip a beat. "Well, consider me thoroughly impressed."

We continue eating, conversation flowing easily.

She tells me about her day and her latest project at work, and I hang on every word. She even tells me about her ex calling while she was in the driveway, and the sarcastic tone of his voice when she told him she had a date. *The lasagna may be a fucking lie, but the connection between us is real.*

After dinner we move to the living room, wineglasses in hand.

The ambiance is cozy, the dim light casting a glow around us. I sit next to her on the couch, wanting to pull her onto my lap so she can wrap those smooth legs around my waist.

I want to make out with her like we're in high school.

I want . . .

"This was perfect." Margot leans into me slightly. "I love how quiet it is here."

"Um. Me too."

"Dex," she whispers, her breath warm against my lips.

"Yeah?" My voice is barely audible.

"Show me more of your surprises," she murmurs, a playful glint in her eye.

I smile, closing the distance between us.

Her lips move against mine, inviting, and I lose myself in the moment. My hand travels to the small of her back, pulling her closer. She responds by threading her fingers through my hair, a gentle tug that sends a shiver down my spine. When we finally break apart to stare at each other, Margot's eyes are sparkling with desire.

"That's making me tingle."

"I'll fucking make you tingle," I promise with a chuckle, stroking my thumb along her jawline until she tilts her chin, moving so my mouth touches her skin.

Margot's breath hitches as my lips find a particularly sensitive spot on her neck. "You're really good at this," she says, her voice breathy. Gasps.

"Just wait," I tease, pulling back to look into her eyes.

"Wait for what?" She pauses, and when I don't respond, she shakes her head, frustrated. "Wait for what?!"

Clearly unable to stand it, Margot pushes me back onto the couch cushions and straddles my lap with a confidence that makes my heart rate skyrocket. Her hands roam over my chest, the heat from her palms searing through the fabric of my T-shirt.

I groan when she leans in, her lips against my ear, her tits brushing my chest.

"Tell me, Dex," she coos, her breath sending shivers down my spine. "Besides dinner, do you have any more surprises for me?"

I swallow hard, my pulse quickening. "Why don't you find out?"

Her laugh is sultry. "You better not be referring to the surprise in your pants."

No doubt she can feel it straining against my jeans, hard and hot and ready. *Always ready, damn him* . . .

Margot kisses me again, deeper this time, tongue teasing mine. My hands go to her hips, guiding her movements as she grinds against me, the friction making it hard to think straight. She's dry fucking me, and I feel like a teenager.

I sit as still as I can, letting her be in charge.

She breaks the kiss and gazes down at me, lips swollen and red. "You're not going to make this easy, are you?"

"Where's the fun in that?" My voice is husky. "I thought you liked a challenge."

"I do," she admits. "But I also like winning."

"So do I." And with that, I pick her up, flipping her so she's on her back, pinning her beneath me on the couch. "Let's see who comes out on top, then."

Her laughter is cut off by my lips capturing hers again, our bodies pressing together in a deliciously intoxicating rhythm.

I grind my hips into hers.

She lifts her hips so they meet mine.

Fully clothed, we let our hands roam, exploring every inch of each other with a growing hunger. I can feel her responding, her nails digging into my shoulders as she arches into me, tugging at my shirt so she can touch my bare skin.

"Dex," she moans, her voice a desperate plea. "Don't stop."

Don't stop . . .
Don't stop . . .
"Don't worry. I won't."
Her wish is my command.

Her fingers tug at my shirt, and I help her pull it up and over my head. The cool air hitting my skin is a stark contrast to the heat in my kitchen.

Margot runs her hands over my chest, watching me with wonder, her touch igniting a fire that blazes through me.

"God, you're perfect." Her breath is another quiet murmur as her eyes roam my body appreciatively. "I've never touched anyone with an eight-pack."

I don't have an eight-pack but do not argue with her.

Tipping my head back, I give her a shaky laugh before leaning down to capture her lips, pouring all my pent-up desire for her into this kiss. All the frustration from lying to her, all the attraction I feel for someone I told myself I wasn't going to date.

Yet here she is beneath me. Because I am a liar.

"You're the one who's perfect," I murmur against her mouth, my hands finding the hem of her shirt.

I want to see her naked too.

With a quick tug, her shirt joins mine on the floor. I take a moment to admire her. The way her skin glows in the dim light. The curve of her breasts above the lace of her baby blue bra. Her smooth clavicle.

Margot's breath is coming in short, ragged gasps.

The sight of her lying there in nothing but a bra and shorts is intoxicating.

Her soft palms travel from the middle of my chest down to my waistband, her touch sending sparks through my body when her nails scratch my skin.

"Let's see what you're keeping in here," she teases, fingers pulling on the button of my fly.

I can barely nod my assent.

Brain dumb.

She undoes the button, deftly and somewhat confidently. No flinching, no hesitation.

The anticipation is electric, every nerve in my body on high alert.

As she tugs the zipper down, her teeth flirt with her bottom lip, biting. *She's excited too* . . .

My zipper whirs down further.

"Oh my God, I feel like a virgin," I joke, voice strained.

"Which we know isn't the case." She smirks as she slides south, her touch sending a jolt through me.

I try to chuckle, but it comes out more like a groan. "You're killing me, Margot."

I groan again when she removes her hands from my ass, fingers gripping my waistband. With a quick, decisive motion, my jeans are down around my thighs.

Together we shuck them off so I'm left in nothing but my boxer briefs (bright blue if you're wondering), Margot's gaze traveling the length of me, taking in every detail.

"I was impressed before, but now . . . I'm speechless."

Her words are all the encouragement I need. My hands move to the waist of her shorts, and with a gentle tug, I add to the growing pile of clothes on my living room floor.

Margot in nothing but a pair of lacy panties, lacy bra, tits practically spilling over the cups.

I want to suck on her nipples.

Her skin.

All of her . . .

Slowly, I run my hands over her, feeling the warmth of her flesh. Her breath hitches as I explore, body responding to my touch, chest heaving.

Then.

Margot reaches for my boxers and, without preamble, removes them. We're both bare now, the heat between us *so fucking unbearable.*

I move her closer.

Skin against skin.

I capture her lips again, this time more urgently, my hands sliding beneath her and up her back, hunting for the clasp of her bra. With a flick of my deft fingers, it comes undone.

The baby blue lace falls down her shoulders. Panties melt off.

"Fuck, you're sexy," I whisper, hands trailing down her sides, feeling the soft curve of her waist, her hips. Her belly.

Her tits.

She moves her arms to the side so I can look my fill: boobs, pussy—the whole pretty picture . . .

"Then do something about it," she taunts.

"You little troublemaker."

Even though she's buckass naked, Margot rolls her eyes. "Stop procrastinating."

I don't need to be told twice.

My hands cup her breasts, thumbs brushing over her nipples in slow, teasing circles. She gasps—good girl—back arching slightly, pushing herself into my hands. Oh, the invitation . . .

The sight of her responding to my touch, the sound of her pleasure, *is intoxicating*.

I am so unbelievably hard.

For a mom—can you believe that shit?!

Leaning in, I take one of her nipples into my mouth, sucking gently, then flicking it with my tongue. Blow on it, the cool air making it harden.

Her moan is soft but filled with desire, and it spurs me on—not that I need any more encouragement.

My other hand continues to caress and squeeze, reveling in the way her body moves against mine.

Her fingers tangle in my hair, pulling me closer. I switch to the other breast, giving it the same attention.

I want more.

I need more.

"Oh my God, Dex," she whispers, voice filled with pleading. "I want you."

I need you.

The words send a jolt of arousal through me, and I kiss my way back up to her lips, capturing them in a searing kiss.

"I want you too," I murmur against her mouth. "So fucking much."

Our bodies press together. I can feel the slickness of her arousal against my thigh, and it takes everything in me to not lose control.

I want to take my time, to savor every moment—not dump my load after three minutes. I haven't been inside her yet; how fucking embarrassing would that be?

I kiss my way down her torso, nipping and licking at her skin, drawing those glorious soft gasps and moans from her lips. When I reach her pussy I pause, staring up her body, my breath hot against her most sensitive spot.

"Yes, do it," she begs, hips lifting slightly, seeking more.

"You little beggar," I tease. "You want me to fuck you with my mouth?"

I love how she's completely undone.

I lower my head, tongue tasting her.

The taste of her—the way she cries out my name—makes me want to make lapping her up my next career. I lick at her slowly, teasingly, building the tension.

Frustrate her beyond belief.

Her hands grip my hair, her hips rocking against my mouth as I increase the pressure, sucking gently on her clit. Her moans are louder now. Desperate. Unfulfilled.

I know she's close.

"Oh my God, don't stop," she demands, bossy little thing.

I have no intention of stopping, but I have no intention of telling her that.

I want to drive her over the edge; I want to feel her come apart in my mouth.

My fingers slide inside, just right. Margot cries out, her body tensing, shuddering as she climaxes.

Fuck yesss . . .

I watch, mesmerized by the sight of her lost in pleasure, her body arching, fingers gripping the fabric of the couch—a couch I will never sell or get rid of.

And then, when she finally relaxes, I kiss my way back up to her, capturing her lips in a tender kiss.

"That was . . ." Her legs quake beneath me. "Amazing."

"Was it?" If there's one thing I love, it's a compliment.

"You know it was."

"You stop rolling your eyes at me," I reply, brushing a strand of hair from her face. "Because we're not done yet."

Her smile is lazy, and she stretches. "Are you finally going to fuck me?"

Finally going to . . . "You sassy brat."

I move over her, positioning myself at her entrance, and she moves too, wrapping her legs around my waist, pulling me closer.

So wet.

So hot.

I slide into her slowly, savoring the feeling of being inside her, the way her body welcomes me.

Tight as fuck.

"Holy shit." I can barely breathe.

Jesus Christ, she feels amazing.

So much so that I have to remind myself to pump my hips, to drive into her.

We move together until we're in sync, each thrust, each moan, each kiss, each time she clenches so she feels tighter.

I am going to lose my mind.

"Faster," she commands, nails digging into my shoulders.

It hurts so goddamn good . . .

Chapter 28

MARGOT

I wasn't digging in the garbage, honest I wasn't.

I was simply tossing a wrapper.

In my opinion, Dex should have been smarter with his subterfuge, but if there's one thing I won't accuse him of, it's being a rocket scientist.

"Dex." *Babe.* "What's this?"

Because to me, it looks like a bag for an Italian restaurant. And a receipt. And cooking instructions.

That son of a bitch lied to me!

I pull out a white half sheet of paper that had been stapled to a paper bag, then hold it up toward the light.

"Mama Lucia's Lasagna," I read. The name of the restaurant is printed at the top, followed by step-by-step reheating instructions.

I feel a mix of amusement and annoyance bubbling up inside me.

"Dex!" I call out, wanting his ass in the kitchen so I can get answers. "You've got some explaining to do!"

Dex saunters into the kitchen, a smug smile on his face—the afterglow a man might display after getting thoroughly laid—until he sees the object in my hands.

His eyes widen, and he stops dead in his tracks. "Uh, I can explain."

"Oh, can you?" I wave the paper instructions in the air, lips pursed. "I cannot believe you lied and told me this was homemade lasagna."

He scratches the back of his head—if he's trying to look bashful, the attempt fails. It comes off as immature.

"Okay, you caught me." His hands go up. "It wasn't homemade. But I swear, I made the pasta from scratch!"

I cross my arms. He so did not make that pasta from scratch—it's part of the entire dish!

"Stop lying, dude!"

He gives me what I assume he thinks is another sexy grin. "Don't call me dude."

"Don't change the subject." I feel myself scowling, deepening the already dense wrinkles between my eyes. Ugh!

"You're seriously pissed about this?" He sounds perplexed. "I just wanted to impress you."

I sigh, tossing the bag back into the trash, where it belongs. "You didn't have to lie to impress me, Dex. It's the effort that counts."

The lasagna could have seriously been a gross pile of slop, and I would have been thrilled he'd attempted it.

He takes a step closer, his expression earnest. "I know, I know. I just thought . . ." Dex shakes his head. "I don't know—I thought that you'd think I was more serious about dating you if I did something special and went through all the trouble."

I soften a little—*just a little, teensy bit*—at the sincerity shining in his eyes.

"I already think you're serious about us. People are allowed to change their minds, and I know we started off on the wrong foot, but . . ." I step closer to him, walking into his open arms. "You don't have to pretend to be someone you're not. I like you for you, even if you can't cook Italian food."

He visibly relaxes. "Really? You don't hate me?"

Hate would be a bit harsh, eh?

"No, I don't hate you for lying about fake cooking. But next time you have something to tell me, maybe tell me the truth."

He chuckles, looking down at the floor. "Deal. I promise, no more lies."

My eyes roam to the counter across the kitchen where flour is generously dusted. "And I'm *not* helping you clean this mess up."

"You're not?"

I shake my head. "No."

His hands go to my hips. "Are you sure?"

Dex picks me up, carrying me to the counter space where the rolling pin, flour, and measuring cups are strewn about. Lifts me so my ass is on the cold stone surface.

"I think you are going to help me clean this up."

"You literally set me in your mess." I try to glance backward. "There's flour all over my ass cheeks."

"I can help you with that." Dex steps between my legs, pulling me so everything is at the edge of the countertop—all my best parts. Bare legs because I hadn't gotten to the part of the program where I put all my clothes back on.

Just my top.

"You're good enough to eat."

Speaking of eating. "You haven't fed me dessert yet."

He leans into me, so tall his hard-on and pelvis are pressed into the apex of my thighs.

With hot breath against my ear he murmurs, "How about I give you a taste right now?"

A taste . . .

His hands slide down my sides, gripping my hips firmly before adjusting my position on the counter. The stone might be cold against my skin, but the heat between us more than makes up for it.

Damn, he's sexy.

Dex's lips find mine in a searing kiss, his tongue exploring my mouth, both of us suddenly hungry all over again. His big rough hands travel up my thighs, spreading them wider as he steps even closer still.

I can feel his hard length as it strains through the fabric of his pants.

"Stay right here," he whispers with a wicked smile, then turns and goes to the fridge. He stands in front of it for several seconds while he searches, finally holding up a canister of whipped cream.

Victory.

Shaking the can vigorously, he's back between my legs. He sprays a dollop onto my inner thigh. I gasp at the sudden chill. At the sudden delight. At the anticipation.

It makes my breath hitch watching him.

Before I can say a word, his mouth is back on me—on my skin—warm and ravenous, licking and sucking the sweet cream.

The sensation has me shivering, electricity shooting through my body, my hands instinctively clutching the edge of the counter for support. Transfixed, I watch as his tongue works its way up my stomach, pushing my shirt up, all the while leaving a trail of fire in its wake.

"You are way too good at this."

He pauses long enough to glance up at me, a mischievous glint in his eyes. "You taste like I want to taste more of you."

A sudden burst of boldness has me pulling my shirt up and over my head. I toss it to the kitchen floor, then unhook my bra. Arching my back as his mouth moves higher.

I sound as if I've just run a mile, my breathing ragged.

I feel needy and greedy.

Dex's fingers slide over my flesh, slipping between my legs to find me already wet and ready.

His touch is gentle and demanding and driving me wild with eagerness.

I can barely stand it.

Craving closeness, I lean forward, wanting him to touch me all over. I want to kiss him—but I'd rather have him kissing me . . . *if you catch my drift.*

Dex does not disappoint.

With a low growl, he drops to his knees; the whipped cream has melted into a sticky, sweet treat.

My pussy? That's sticky and sweet, too, and he buries his face in it, tongue licking over my most sensitive spots, shock waves of pleasure coursing through me.

I grapple, hands tangling in his hair.
Sucking.
Licking . . .
Sucking some more.

"Dex," I moan, unable to do anything but beg. And whisper. "Oh my God . . . don't stop . . . oh shit . . . yesss."

He doesn't stop.

Of course he doesn't.

Instead, he sucks harder, his tongue and fingers working to bring me closer and closer.

Ohmygodohmygodohmygod . . .

My body trembles, legs too. If I had to get up and walk right now, I'd fall. I'd be incapable.

I can feel the climax building, threatening to push me over the brink. I'm not ready, but at the same time I want it so bad.

So bad.

So so bad . . .

Just as I'm about to let go, he pulls back, leaving me teetering on the edge.

"Nope. Not yet," he murmurs, voice husky with desire. "I want to be inside you when you come."

Yes, please.

My mouth opens to say the words, but before I can get them out, he has me off the counter and on my feet. Pushes down his jeans. Watching him while my limbs shake, I'm then turned to face the cold stone surface as his hands resume roaming my body.

Dex grasps my hips.

Bends me forward.

I am at his mercy—or that's how it feels.

It feels naughty and I love it.

His breath is hot against my neck; it tickles.

"So fucking sexy."

He positions himself so that with one slow and deliberate motion he can enter me from behind. He fills me completely, and I gasp, the sensation overwhelming. *Literally no one has ever fucked me from behind before*, and I relish being bent over.

My fingers grip the counter for balance and support.

Dex's pace is relentless, each thrust driving me closer to the edge.

Yes...

Yes...

Yes!

So close.

He pumps his hips. Thrusts.

Grunts.

Groans.

With one arm around my waist and the other near my shoulders, it's a push, pull. Hard. Fast. Wet.

I can barely stand it.

I bite my bottom lip when he demands that I come for him, his voice thick with need.

"I'm so fucking close." He groans into my neck. "Come for me."

And because I am a good girl who listens to directions, I comply. With a shuddering cry, I let go, my climax crashing over me like a tidal wave. My body convulses. My legs can barely keep me standing.

As Dex holds me steady, his own release follows moments later.

He moans loudly before pulling out and coming on my ass, the wet, hot part of him branding me.

Our bodies tremble.

Then.

Dex presses a gentle kiss to my shoulder before pulling me away, reaching for a kitchen towel, and wetting it under the faucet.

"You are a total mess." He laughs as he cleans my skin—back side and front, the towel moving across my ass.

"You started it," I manage, eyes scanning for my clothes.

Dex chuckles, nuzzling my neck. "It was worth it."

Chapter 29
Dex

Dang.

Women's bathrooms are sure different than men's.

I pick up a tiny pink soap shaped like a seashell and give it a sniff. Then I pick up the blue one, decide I like the smell of that one better, and use it to wash my hands.

It's dinky.

When I'm done, I glance at the decorative towels hanging on the rack. They're embroidered with delicate patterns, clearly meant for show and not for actual use. I dry my hands with one anyway 'cause I have no idea how the hell else to dry them, then give the tiny lotions and perfumes a once-over.

On the wall next to me is a sign: **Empowered women empower women.**

I chuckle to myself. Of course Margot would have a sign like that in her bathroom, the goof.

In the back pocket of my jeans, my phone buzzes, and when I check the screen, I see that it's Trent. Perfect timing because I have a bit of privacy.

"What's up?"

"Where are you?" He gets straight to the point, no chitchat.

"Margot's house. I'm here to pick her up for a—"

He cuts me off. "Have you seen the headline online?"

I shake my head, staring at my handsome self in the mirror. "No."

"You're on the front page."

"Front page of what?" I scrunch up my face. "I thought the internet was digital."

He sighs—loudly. "*Please* follow along, Dex. *Please.*"

I thought that's what I was doing, but whatever. He doesn't have to sound so goddamn frustrated.

"You and your new girlfriend. It's a nice article about how you're dating a single mom. It's fucking brilliant! Makes you look like a Boy Scout."

"It does?" This is great news. Really great fucking news.

I lean against the counter, holding the phone to my ear. "What did they say about her?"

Trent's tone is brisk, as usual. "Just the basics. They mention she's a single mom, a teacher, and that she's got a good head on her shoulders, blah blah blah. They even included a picture of you two from the other night, but obviously they blurred out the kid."

I don't love how he refers to Wyatt as *the kid* but don't make an issue of it. The less he knows, the better, even though Trent goes digging on his own. In fact, he probably hired the guy outside my house to take pictures of Margot coming and going.

"You look happy. Nice work."

I smile at my reflection, feeling a surge of pride. "That's because I am happy. It's not an act."

"Sure." Trent chuckles. "Sure it's not." He pauses. "Just be ready for more attention—this kind of coverage is going to put you in the spotlight even more, which is exactly what we want. But keep it positive, and don't dump her until we have a plan in place."

Don't dump her until we have a plan in place . . .

My stomach drops to the floor.

"Yeah, yeah. I hear you." I run a hand through my hair, not sure what else to say because suddenly this conversation is making me ill. It's a reminder about how I was prompted to contact Margot again—not because I was dying to see her, but because I need to make myself look good. Better.

In the media.

Not because I want to *be* good or *be* better.

Then.

I'm saved by the bell—literally.

The doorbell rings, and I pause. "I should go. There's someone at her door."

"So? It's her door. Let her take care of it."

Sometimes Trent is such an asshole.

"I'll call you back," I say before ending the call and shoving my phone back into my pocket. "Dickhead."

But Trent's words echo through my mind as I pull open the bathroom door and head back toward the front of Margot's house, curiosity piqued by the unexpected visitor. As I reach the living room, I hear voices and pause.

Stand still in my spot around the corner, listening.

"What are you doing here?" Margot is saying.

"Mind if I come in?" asks a man's voice. It's deep and low and raises the hair on the back of my neck.

"I'm kind of in the middle of something," she says, and if I had to guess, I'd say her arms were crossed right now. "Where's Wyatt?"

"At Target with Gretchen."

"Ahh. Gotcha."

The tension in Margot's voice is palpable, and I feel my muscles tighten as I lean, trying to stay out of sight but within earshot.

"I won't be long," the man continues. "I just need to talk to you about something important."

"Is everything all right? Is this about you and Gretchen? Because if it is, I'm sure that—"

"No, this is about you being plastered all over the fucking news."

There is a pause long enough to fill a room.

"I have no idea what you're referring to. I'm not plastered all over the news."

Of course she wouldn't have a clue; she seriously has better things to do than sit online and read about herself or the latest celebrity gossip. Since I've known her, she hasn't brought up things like that. She'd rather read and talk about books, or be outside, or—

"Tell me this is a joke."

"I'd have to know what you were talking about first." It sounds like her hackles are raised.

"There is no way you're dating someone famous." A sarcastic laugh follows.

Margot sniffs. "Why would you say that?"

"Because. You're . . . *you*." He laughs again. "You're a teacher, and you hate going out in public."

"Okay, if you say so," she returns, not taking his bait. "Not that you would know what I like and don't like."

"So are you? Seeing someone?" He clearly cannot stand not knowing.

"Yes, I'm seeing someone."

Her ex hesitates. "Is he actually a football player?"

"Yes."

"You know." His voice goes up a few octaves. "Even though I'm seeing Gretchen, you know it's not really serious, don't you?" The guy pauses before continuing his butt-hurt bitch fest. "I really thought there was a chance we would get back together someday, but I guess not."

What's this now? This bag of shit did not go there with her. I don't know shit about emotional blackmail, but even I know emotional blackmail when I hear it, and this dude just went there.

"Are you being serious right now? What is wrong with you?" Margot gasps. "Why the hell would you say that?"

"I thought we were friends," her ex goes on to say, sounding like a complete gaslighting toolbox.

"You're making my head spin right now, Colton. You should stop talking."

Her blunt comment almost causes me to laugh from my hiding spot and give myself away.

I watch and wait, warring with myself between giving her privacy and giving this blowhard a piece of my mind.

The tension in the room is tangible—I can feel it from here, and I can certainly hear Margot shifting uncomfortably on the living room carpet. *It's crazy how well I've come to know her in a short amount of time, so much so that I can predict her movements even when I'm not in the room.*

That is some wild shit.

"So you're dating a celebrity now?" the man accuses, voice rising. "What kind of mother are you?"

"Excuse me? First of all—he's not a celebrity." Margot's tone sharpens at his judgment of her. "And secondly, I'm a damn good mother and you know it. What does my personal life have to do with you? Or Wyatt?"

"It has everything to do with her!" he snaps back. "Do you know what the press is going to do when they find out about her? About *us*?"

"You? Of course you're going to make this about *you*." Margot's response is calm but firm. "There is no us. There almost never was and hasn't been for a long time. And secondly, I won't let anyone exploit Wyatt."

I take a deep breath, deciding it's time to make my presence known. Stepping out from my hiding spot, I clear my throat.

"Oh hey." I pretend as if I'm hearing and seeing him for the first time, my eyes doing a quick scan of a man I've only heard about in passing.

Tall. Blond.

The cocky arrogance of a guy who knows he's good looking, who looks as if he plays golf four days a week and probably gets hit on by his girlfriend's married girlfriends—and is regularly tempted to cheat.

Polo shirt, jeans.

Yup. I was right: Colton is a total toolbox.

He looks as shocked to see me as I was to see my mother that time I was eating out Shelby Sullivan in our basement in high school.

"You must be Wyatt's dad." I try to smile, but even I know it doesn't reach my eyes. This guy is a complete grade A douchebag, and I have no desire to be friendly. Not after the shit I just overheard him say to Margot.

Not today, Colton.

He finds his voice box. "Who the hell are *you*?"

His tone is rude, which I don't deserve.

I raise a brow, a laugh escaping my mouth. "Dude, you totally know who I am. You said so yourself, it's all over the internet. Isn't that why you're here? To make sure what you read was bullshit?"

He doesn't respond, but the blush spreading across his cheeks is enough of an answer for me.

I put my hands up. "Surprise! Margot has company!"

Colton has zero idea what to do with himself or how to react now that he's face to face with me and Margot isn't alone to defend herself against his onslaught of negativity.

Sucks to be him.

"I'm Dex." I do not offer him my hand. "And she's not wrong—I'm not a celebrity. I'm more like an athlete." I hesitate, then add, "And not to brag, but you may have seen me in the Super Bowl a few times."

Salt, meet wound.

This dude is so obviously butt hurt.

He nods. "I'm Colton. Wyatt's dad."

"I gathered."

The room is silent as everyone racks their brain for something new to say.

Then,

"Clearly you've met my daughter." He sounds unhappy about it.

I nod. No denying it. I've met his kid, and "She's awesome."

"I know my daughter is awesome," he sarcastically replies, not remotely impressed with meeting me, a legend.

Whoa, calm down, dude. I was giving her a compliment, *which is basically a compliment to both you and Margot since you raised her.*

"It's not necessary for you to be so defensive," Margot points out, biting on her bottom lip. She looks nervous, like she wants to get the hell out of here and out of the situation.

It's awkward and uncomfortable, no doubt about that.

His eyes turn to me, sizing me up. Which is laughable because, well—I'm me, and he's him, and if this were a dick-swinging contest, I would win because like I said: I'm me.

Like how can you compete with me?

Men want to be me, women want to fuck me.

It is what it is.

"You know, Colton, you could have just called." I can't stop the words from slipping out of my mouth, knowing they're going to piss him off. But like I said—this is a dick-swinging contest, and he needs to know he can't just show up at Margot's place and start bullying her because of who she's dating.

It's not like I'm a loser. "We could have video chatted to save you the trip. No need to drive all the way over."

I'm coming off like a prick, and I know it.

Not the best way to get to know a dude, but hey, he started it.

Colton stuffs his hands in the pockets of his jeans for lack of a better place to put them, and I can see the tension in his shoulders.

"Guess I could have. But I wanted to see the guy who's been spending so much time with my family."

His family.

I take a step back, trying to defuse the situation. "Look, Colton, I get it. You're protective. You care about Margot, and you love Wyatt. I respect that."

"It's . . . complicated."

Complicated? How? If he's trying to tell me he still has feelings for Margot, he's way too late. He had his chance, and now I have mine.

You snooze, you lose.

"Most things are." I try to keep my tone neutral, my back ramrod straight. "But I'm not here to make things harder for Margot. I'm here to support her."

Margot steps between us, her expression a mix of frustration and concern. "Can we please not turn this into a confrontation? Colton, I appreciate you stopping in, but this isn't the time or place for this discussion."

Colton's gaze softens slightly as he looks at her. "I just want what's best for Wyatt, Margot. That's all I want."

And you.

I want what's best for you.

I create the dialogue in my own mind. He's not speaking the words, but they linger in the air like a cloud.

"Same. I want what's best for her—and so does Dex." She nods in my direction. "We can handle this together without making things more difficult for each other. You cannot show up unannounced like this again. Especially now that I'm dating someone."

I smirk at him over her head, damned if I don't.

There's a moment of silence as Colton considers her words, glancing between the two of us. Finally, he concedes.

"All right." His jaw clenches. "But we need to talk soon. *Privately.*"

It takes every ounce of self-control I have not to roll my eyes.

"All of us," I put in. There is no way in hell I'm letting him in a room with her alone. *Not* after the way I heard him speak to her earlier. No fucking way.

"Sure." He levels me with a long look before walking toward the door, his gaze then bouncing between Margot and me as if to make sense of it—of us.

Our relationship.

He looks so baffled I'm tempted to say, "Hey, man, I get it—I don't understand it, either, but somehow it makes perfect sense."

When he's gone, I try to be cool. Unfortunately, that lasts all of three seconds, and I'm blurting out the words "Is this normally how it goes with him?" 'Cause he was acting like a fucking douche canoe.

"No." She shakes her head. "He's never talked down to me like that."

"Jealousy has a way of rearing its ugly head."

"He is not jealous." She keeps shaking her head, quite certain her ex's ego isn't bruised. "Trust me, Colton does not have a jealous bone in his body."

I'm a guy and know how guys think, and that dude is jealous or my name isn't Dex Motherfucking Lansing.

"Wanna make a bet?"

I try keeping my thoughts to myself; pushing the issue will not help right now. But this is me we're talking about, and I have a tendency to blurt out whatever the fuck is inside my brain.

"Maybe he's stressed out," Margot tries. "Learning your ex is dating someone new is a lot to handle, especially when you hear about it on the news. I was single a long, long time, and he's not used to seeing me with someone."

I almost snort. Is she serious right now? "He can date someone, but *you* can't?"

Her expression remains troubled. "I just don't want whatever that was to affect Wyatt. She needs stability."

"I'm sure the reason he was being a dick was from shock." That's putting it mildly and as kindly as I can say it. "We'll make sure Wyatt has stability, I promise."

Obviously I have no idea how to make *that* happen, but stability sounds pretty damn good—I mean that, I truly do. How hard can stability be?

Margot looks at me and smiles. "Thanks, Dex. It means a lot."

"Maybe . . ." I swallow, hating the words about to come out of my mouth, but I say them anyway. "Maybe I should head home. Let you clear your head. Process."

Give her some space. Unless she doesn't want me to leave?

She frowns, nibbling her lip again, clearly torn.

"I don't want you to go," she admits, her voice barely above a whisper. "But maybe you're right? I should probably give myself the space to process everything and maybe talk to Colton again once he chills out."

I nod, even though the last thing I want is her to contact that jealous douche nozzle.

"You can text me if you need anything," I let her know, giving her hand a gentle squeeze and tugging her into an embrace. Kiss the top of her head. "And we can talk more later. Or tomorrow. Okay?"

"'Kay. Thanks for understanding."

I lean down to kiss her softly on the lips, lingering there, bummed that I just told her I was going to leave and give her space.

"Text me later," I whisper against her mouth before finally pulling back, suddenly feeling alone.

Chapter 30

Margot

I let him leave.

I let him leave, and I didn't want him to.

In fact, the one thing I don't want *is* to be alone.

The house is empty again.

Silent.

Wyatt is obviously at her dad's, and when Dex offered to give me space, I agreed that was for the best, but in all honesty it's the last thing I need.

He's right, though; I need a hot second to process what the hell just happened between Colton and me, and between Colton and Dex. Colton's words rear back at me in flashes.

I really thought there was a chance we would get back together someday, but I guess not.

What a liar.

There is no way he thought there was a chance we would get back together. No. Way. What a load of gaslighting bullshit. Ten years ago the conversation came up; we tried to be a couple when Wyatt was still a baby, but could never see eye to eye.

Some things aren't meant to be . . .

For him to weaponize those words? Appalling. I've never heard him speak to me that way, with that tone—condescending and patronizing—making me feel as though I could never date a man like Dex because I'm not good enough.

How dare he?

"What an asshole! Way to ruin my night." I stomp through the living room, then into the kitchen, where I yank open the fridge and search the shelves for a bottle of wine.

"Wine, wine, where are you?" I mutter to myself because wine is exactly what I need, and it appears that I'm out.

Drinking away my worries is not going to happen—at least not tonight.

I slam the fridge closed. Leaning against the kitchen counter, I pick up my cell and tap open the web browser. Can't hurt to poke around, right? Find out what Colton was so upset about?

Tap, tap.

Tap.

"And here they are . . ."

Pictures, links, and articles for the very same stories that brought Colton to my front door:

DEX LANSING DATES SINGLE MOTHER

DEX AND HIS DATE: THE MOTHER OF ALL SINGLES?!

DEX LANSING DOMESTICATED?! *Click for the full story!*

The headlines glare up angrily at me, taunting me to click them with their bold, sensationalistic fonts. Dex Lansing, NFL heartthrob, domesticated by little old me? Imagine! Me, a single mother, dating America's bad boy of football!

It might have been laughable had it been anyone else but me.

This was *my* life, my relationship, my privacy.

Headlines I can handle—I think. My ex-boyfriend and the father of my daughter getting pissed about it? Well, that makes the fantasy of dating Dex unravel faster than I can stitch it back together.

Tears sting as they threaten to spill over; I blink them back. *I refuse to cry.*

The audacity of Colton to show up at my doorstep and spew his self-righteous nonsense! Over the judgment of the media, who knows nothing about my life. My struggles! My heart!

Ugh.

I shove away from the counter and pace the length of my small kitchen, eyes on the sink Dex tried to help me fix—a tiny smile threatens to bend my lips.

I need to do something to distract myself from the chaos swirling in my mind.

Glancing around the kitchen, my gaze lands on the messy pile of dishes in the sink.

Perfect.

I roll up my sleeves and plunge my hands into the soapy water, scrubbing furiously. The monotonous task allows my mind to wander, the physical exertion a balm to my frayed nerves.

"Men," I grumble, scouring a plate. "I swear."

Bubbles cover my arms, water wrinkles my skin.

So satisfying.

The dishes done, I dry my hands on a towel and, because I am a glutton for punishment, reach for my phone again.

I stare at the screen and debate long and hard before tapping open a fluff piece on a pop-culture website using Dex as its clickbait.

IS ARIZONA QUARTERBACK SCORING OFF FIELD?

Rumors have been swirling for weeks about the nature of Dex Lansing's—Arizona Sentinels' quarterback—relationship with a mysterious woman spotted with him on numerous occasions. Today we can confirm that the woman is none other than single mom Margot Mahoney. Ms. Mahoney is an elementary school teacher.

Sources close to Dex reveal the pair have been on and off for several weeks and met on the social app Kissmet. Dex has been spotted in public with Margot's daughter, aged 10.

However, those same sources report this romance is far from picture perfect. Just yesterday, Dex was spotted storming out of Margot's home. Is there trouble brewing in their so-called paradise?

Only time will tell if this relationship—and his career—can withstand the pressures of the spotlight. One thing is clear: Dex Lansing is no longer the carefree bachelor. He is officially off the market. For now.

Seriously?!

"He did not storm out of my house after a fight!" I announce loudly to no one. "He wasn't even here yesterday!"

How do they know all this? My God, talk about an invasion of privacy!

Is this how it is? Lies printed about people for clickbait?

"Yes. The answer is yes."

Frustrated, I shut off the screen, heart practically pounding outside my chest.

I'm the first to admit the article was way less sensational than I expected it to be, but it still feels incredibly invasive. They mention my child *and* her age? And the fact that I'm a teacher? My relationship with Dex isn't meant to be fodder for gossip columns. It's private!

What if reporters show up and are standing outside school Monday morning when I arrive for work? Then what? Will I get fired for dating an athlete and putting my job in the spotlight?

Am I in jeopardy of getting fired for drawing attention to myself?

I bite my fingernail nervously.

Shit.

Shit, shit, shit!

Before I can dwell on it any longer, the doorbell rings, and my pulse quickens as I walk to the door, not knowing who's on the other side of it.

Thank God it's you.

Dex stands there with a concerned expression.

"Dex." I can't keep the shock off my face. "What are you doing here?" He's only been gone a short time. Twenty minutes maybe?

"I never actually left," he admits, stepping back over my threshold and pulling me into a hug. "I was outside googling shit and thinking. And I texted my buddy Landon, so I didn't get very far." He chuckles, and I love the sound of his voice. His explanation is perfect and exactly what I need right now.

The tension seeps out of me, and I relax. "Well, now that we're confessing things . . . I hadn't actually wanted you to leave. I'm glad you came back."

"Did you look at your phone?" He wants to know.

"If you're asking if I read any articles and went on the internet, the answer is yes."

"What'd you think?"

"Er. I guess I've seen far shittier, more sensational articles."

He nods his agreement. "You should see some of the articles that have been written about me—there have been some doozies. Do you know how many times I've been called a piece-of-shit womanizer?"

My eyes get wide. "*Are you* a piece-of-shit womanizer?"

He laughs. "No. Not at all."

My head hangs as I walk toward my bedroom. He trails along after me as I explain, "I was seriously hoping our relationship wasn't going to become tabloid fodder."

"It's not." He pauses. "We could have gotten ahead of the story and leaked some information, but that would be like jumping the gun, yeah? And we didn't exactly disguise ourselves when we were rock climbing. Or when we went to eat."

Dex sits on the edge of my bed, watching me, when I go into my bathroom so I can remove my makeup. "Know what I discovered tonight?"

"What?"

"Your last name is Mahoney." His chuckle makes me shiver. "Never would have guessed."

"We've been out how many times and you didn't know my last name?"

"You didn't tell me. It never came up." He shrugs. "It suits you though. It's cute."

"You think my last name is cute?" That's a new one. I turn back to the mirror, dabbing at the last traces of mascara. "Well, I guess I can live with cute."

"Good," he says, his voice suddenly serious. "Because I like it. And I like you, Mahoney."

"Do not start calling me by my last name. I'm not one of your bros."

"Bros before hoes." He grins when I scowl at his ridiculous mantra, and I gawk at his reflection in the mirror.

His phone rings, and he looks at the screen, then glances up at me. "It's my agent. He wants to video chat—is it okay if I take this call?"

"Of course! This is work, you can't ignore the call."

Dex stays in the room, sitting on the edge of the bed as he answers the call. I can hear his agent faintly through the phone.

"Hey, Dex. You have a second?" His agent's voice is deep and direct. "I want to go over this situation with your new girlfriend."

Situation? New girlfriend?

This perks me up—his agent didn't mention my name, but he's obviously speaking about me. That's a good thing, yeah? His agent knows I exist! Yay, me!

"What about it?"

"I ran a short focus group with some fans who were touring the stadium today, and the survey came back favorable. Seventy-five percent of the results show you in a more positive light than they did before it was released that you're dating a single mom."

What's this now?

I stop running a toner-soaked cotton ball across my face so I can listen, not wanting to be noticeably eavesdropping.

"Uh-huh." Dex's finger taps the side of his phone as if he's futzing with the volume button.

"Case in point," his agent is saying. "According to the numbers, everything we discussed is working. Good job."

"Thanks," Dex deadpans, no expression on his face.

His eyes dart and meet mine in the mirror.

"I say you give it another few weeks, then pull the plug on your fun. Tamryn Clarke's people followed up about the Daytime Goldie Awards and wanted to circle back around to see if you were still interested in being her date."

I recognize that name.

Tamryn Clarke is a singer slash actress slash influencer with millions of followers who is probably more famous than Dex is. I wonder what his agent is going on about. Is he trying to set them up on a date? How can he do that when Dex is dating me? Why would Trent even mention her?

What is Dex pulling the plug on? The fun?

By fun does he mean . . . me? I'm so confused but try to stay occupied, keeping one ear on the conversation.

"I'm not interested in the Goldie Awards with Tamryn." He pauses. "Look, Trent, let's drop this. Now is not a good time."

There's a brief silence, and I can almost feel the tension in the room. His agent seems to pick up on it too.

"Ahh, I get it now. You're in the room with her."

Dex says nothing—only stares into the phone, eyes hard.

"Noted." His agent laughs. "We'll talk later. Keep me posted, will ya, buddy?"

"Will do," Dex replies curtly before ending the call.

Then.

He sits for a moment staring down at his phone, a mix of frustration and exhaustion on his face. Like he's afraid to lift his gaze and meet mine; like he has no idea what to do besides clear his throat.

I step out of the bathroom, toner in my hand, not sure what to say to him. "Everything okay?"

He looks up. "Yeah, just . . . football stuff."

It did not sound like football stuff. "Tamryn Clarke is work related?"

He gives a jerky nod. "Yes." Shakes his head. "No, she's not. I meant that was my agent."

"I know that was your agent. I could hear him rather clearly." Unfortunately. I lean on the doorjamb, watching him curiously, waiting for him to say more. "Explain to me what he was talking about. Please."

"Sorry you had to hear that."

"Sorry I had to hear *what*? Which part?"

He inhales, then sighs, running a hand through his hair. It sticks up this way and that, looking utterly freaking adorable. He is so cute . . .

"I know we had a rough afternoon—and the last thing I want to do is make it worse."

"My ex was here posturing, remember? You won't ruin our day." *Not if you're honest with me.*

Dex's laugh is rueful. "Don't be so sure—you haven't heard what I have to say yet."

"Does this have to do with your agent?"

"Yes. It's about a conversation we had a few weeks ago."

"Oh?" I know nothing about agents, other than contract negotiations. I have a feeling I'm about to get a crash course in the intricacies of agents' involvement in their clients' personal lives.

"One of the things most people don't understand is PR relationships." When I look confused, he goes on. "A PR relationship is when a couple is set up by their public relations people because it's good for their career to be seen together—not because they're in an actual relationship."

"Ah." I nod. "Makes sense." Sort of.

"I've had a bunch of those, mostly 'cause I'm lazy," Dex explains. "And I figured if I met someone in the industry or someone in the spotlight, it would make it hella easier 'cause they already know how this shit works." He scratches his pants with the nail of his index finger. "Turns out, it doesn't—it mostly makes it worse."

I don't ask him to expand on what he means by that.

"And as you know, when we met on Kissmet, I hadn't wanted . . ." He hesitates, breezily waving a hand through the air. "To date someone with a kid."

"Uh-huh." I cross my arms, not sure where this discussion is headed.

He blows out a puff of air. "So a few weeks ago, I mentioned you on a call with Trent, and he had a bunch of questions about you—and when he found out you were a mom, instead of telling me to block you, he thought it might be a good idea if we started dating."

For a moment, I was sure I hadn't heard him right.

A good idea? His agent told him it might be a good idea if we started dating because I'm a mom?

"But . . . we're already dating."

Dex crosses his arms and gets comfortable. "What I should say is—he and I had a conversation before you and I started dating, and he thought it would be a good idea."

I tilt my head.

Brain tries to make sense of his words.

Thought it would be a good idea . . . thought it would be a good idea . . . thought it would be a good idea . . .

"Huh?" I'm lost.

"Part of Trent's job is to guide me through shit," Dex rushes to explain as if he's already regretting telling me this information.

"What kind of shit?"

"I already told you. Relationships. Investing. Appearances. He's basically my agent and the guy who puts out fires." Dex leans back on my bed casually, settling into the explanation as if it makes perfect sense. "I don't know if you know this, but I haven't always had the best reputation."

"No. I didn't know that."

Never mind the earlier implication he made about being labeled a womanizer. But that was only gossip created for attention, right? Unless I understood him wrong.

"It's not a big deal to never have a steady relationship, is it? You haven't had one in a long time, and it's been the same for me." He pauses. "If you don't count the occasional actress or whatever."

The occasional actress or whatever . . .

At least he didn't say "the occasional supermodel."

"I thought you were going to say you haven't had the best reputation because you get into fights or do drugs." I muster a laugh, but when I catch my reflection in my bathroom mirror, that laugh doesn't even come close to reaching my eyes.

He holds his hands up. "Ha ha—it's nothing like that."

"Say more, please," I encourage him from the doorway of my bathroom, stuck in my spot.

"My agent, Trent, suggested that if we were seen together"—he points between the two of us, his finger going back and forth—"it could generate some buzz. You know, the whole 'celebrity romance' thing."

Dex uses air quotes when he says the words *celebrity romance* and confuses me further.

"I'm not a celebrity."

"I know that, babe." He smiles sweetly. "But I am."

I stare at him, trying to school my expression so it's not one of complete horror and shock as I process the absurdity of what I'm hearing.

"Are you saying Trent wanted you to pretend date me for publicity?"

Dex shakes his head quickly. "Not *pretend*. Actually date. And I did."

"Dex," I say slowly, trying to keep my voice steady. "Are you telling me that you're only dating me because your agent thinks it will help your career?"

"I mean—he might have suggested it, but after giving it some thought, I really did want to work things out."

My mouth falls open. "Are you out of your fucking mind?"

This is the perfect occasion for cursing, don't you think?

Dex, for his part, barely flinches at my harsh tone or my harsh words.

"I'm just telling you what he said! Don't shoot the messenger."

Oh. I want to do so much more than shoot him right now—is he fucking kidding me? I narrow my eyes in his direction, steam practically pouring out my ears and nose.

"You know I *am* looking for a long-term relationship," I say. "Someone who wants to have a *family*, who wants to spend time not only with me but with my daughter. I have a kid, Dex—this isn't a joke to me."

I feel my nostrils flaring in the most unflattering way.

His hands smack his knees, and he blows out a puff of air. "I can't help it if this is my reality."

Yes. Yes he can.

"Are you listening to yourself?" I practically shout. "Relationships are supposed to be about feelings—not strategic career moves." I pause only for a second. "The one and only reason you met my daughter the first time is because it was an *accident*. I never in a million years would have allowed her to meet you this soon." Ever.

Dickhead.

Dex stares, looking perplexed. "Why? I'm a decent dude."

"Decent dude?!" My voice has risen a billion octaves. "Oh my God, you're fake dating to make yourself look good! They write romance novels about this, it's not real!"

And yet.

It is.

It's happening and it's happening to me.

It cannot be normal to be sitting around, thinking about your personal life as a potential career move, but this is why he's him and I'm me and it was never going to work.

My heart races, anger and disbelief forming a boiling rage in my chest. I cannot freaking believe I let myself get caught up in this charade! Dex's eyes soften, but I refuse to be swayed by this asshole who pulled the wool over my damn eyes. I'm too furious to be drawn in by his good looks and unrelenting charm.

"This was supposed to be different." My voice is cracking. "I thought *you* were different. I thought you gave a shit. Yes, you're a big kid, but I'm the idiot who thought our differences would be a good thing."

Dex moves from the bed so he's standing, hands immediately reaching for me. "I never meant for it to get this complicated—I didn't think this would be a big deal. I really do care about you, Margot. I care about Wyatt."

"Oh my God, stop talking," I snap, shaking my head. "You care? Ha! You've allowed your agent to manipulate you for your own gain, and the only thing he cares about is making money off you."

How can he be this naive?

I turn on my heel, storming out of the room, my mind racing with the implications of what just happened. How could I have been so blind? So stupid. The realization hits me like a ton of bricks: I need to protect my daughter from this mess.

"Why am I the one leaving?" He's the one who needs to get out of my house!

I stalk back to my bedroom. Dex is standing in the same spot I left him in.

"You can't just decide to date me because it might be good for your image," I spit out. "It's not fair to any of us, and I cannot for the life of me believe you thought this would end well. Or didn't you care about that?"

"Margot, I'm just telling you what Trent and I discussed, that's all. I'm not saying he meddles in my business, but he likes to meddle in my business." He attempts to make a joke, the cheeky grin never making it to his eyes.

"*Is* it his job?" Why am I allowing him to keep talking?

Dex nods. "Kind of, yes. The more money I make, the more money he makes. The more popular I am in the news, the more my stock goes up for the team I play for, the more money I make."

"Wow. That's . . . sad." I pat him on the arm sympathetically. Sarcastically. "Listen. I'm so sorry you're in this position, but there is not a chance in hell I'm going to pretend to date anyone. It's insulting."

I don't want to see him again. Not to go to the movies, not to go for ice cream, not for a free afternoon or a free dinner.

"I think we're done here," I breathe out. "You need to figure out your shit. What you really want. If it's not me, and you're only after some calculated move, then we have nothing left to say to each other."

"Margot, come on."

"Margot, come on," I repeat. "That's all you have to say?"

He nods. "I'm scared to keep talking because I don't want to get yelled at."

Oh my God.

I almost laugh—almost.

At least he's honest.

"Please just get out of my house." I stand aside so he's able to walk out of my room without touching me. The last thing I want are his lying, traitorous hands on me.

He stops in the foyer, turning to face me, and from the looks of him, he's going to plead his case one more time. "Margot . . ."

"I said *get out*."

Chapter 31

Dex

I am a fucking idiot.

For real.

Why was I stupid enough to take that phone call with Trent with Margot in the room?

Why didn't I lie to her to spare her the details?

Because, asshole, you're a fucking idiot!

It doesn't take a rocket scientist to know that you should NEVER tell a woman you're dating her because someone told you to because it would be good for business.

I am seriously a bona fide jackass.

Spiraling into self-loathing typically isn't my MO, but today I haven't been able to stop myself from wallowing in my bad decisions.

My cell phone rings, snapping me out of my thoughts. It's Trent, again. Of course it is, the timing of his call not lost on me. God must be punishing me for being a douchebag.

I hesitate before answering. Take a couple of cleansing breaths.

"Yeah?"

"You said you were going to call me back when you were alone," he barks, getting straight to it.

"I don't recall telling you I'd call back." And even if I had, it would have been a lie. "I don't even know why we need to have a conversation about this in the first place. Things are going great."

Are.

Were.

Past tense.

"The paps got a picture of you leaving her house last night, and you looked pissed, so we should get ahead of it. Damage control."

The paps catching me looking pissed isn't news, and it isn't new. I'm a big dude and often look angry—why the hell should I have to stomp around blowing sunshine and roses up everyone's ass all the time?

"Damage control?" I run a hand down my face. "That's all you can think about right now? My relationship has gone to shit."

"You know how this works." My agent ignores my whining. "They get pictures, we post a comment. Whatever you did to make your girlfriend mad, apologize—make a grand gesture, do whatever it takes because it's too soon for a breakup announcement. Not when we just leaked that you're dating her."

Unfuckingbelievable.

I feel a surge of anger. "Jesus Christ, if only it was that simple. You are my agent, not my publicist. This isn't just about my image or my career. This is about Margot, her daughter, and the mess I've made."

"Margot isn't my responsibility—you are. No offense, but I really couldn't give a shit about how some random woman you're dating feels right now."

I am not on her payroll. His unspoken words linger.

Trent sighs, clearly frustrated with my lack of cooperation the same way I'm frustrated by his lack of consideration for Margot.

"Dex, you have to separate your personal feelings from your professional obligations. This is what you signed up for."

"No. I signed up to play football—I didn't sign up to fuck with someone's emotions."

"Listen, man, you—"

But I don't give him a chance to finish his sentence; I hang up without another word.

He doesn't get it.

I hear Carrie fussing in the kitchen, so I walk to my office door, shutting myself in—and her out. I pause, hand on the doorknob.

Carrie has always been a sounding board; perhaps I should talk to her.

No way, she'll tell you to your face that you're a stupid bastard, and she would be right.

I need someone who won't kick me while I'm down . . .

Someone who knows what I'm dealing with because they've been where I've been.

I flop down in my massive leather chair and settle in, dialing the only person who can talk me off this ledge.

"Dude. Why do you look like you have to shit your pants?" he greets me, and from the looks of it, he's in the backyard of his house, tongs in hand.

For once in my life I don't have a smart-ass comment for my friend. "I fucked up."

"Sorry to hear that, man." Landon's tongs go down, and I can see him lean against his grill, sobering up when he realizes I'm being serious. "What's going on?"

"Margot thinks I'm only dating her because it boosts my reputation." He knows the backstory, so I spare him the dirty details. "She's furious, and I don't know how to fix it."

"Do not tell me you listened to Trent." Landon stares at me through the phone. "Harlow would claw my fucking face off if I pulled a stunt like this—no offense."

"None taken." Tons taken. I need help, not to be made to feel worse. "I fucking *like* her, man. She and I were texting a lot and making each other laugh before Trent made his suggestion. So I didn't think it would hurt to go out with her a few times to see how things went. And if it, you know, made me a media darling—great."

He rolls his eyes. "Don't ever call yourself a media darling. It makes you sound even douchier than you already do."

"Sorry."

Landon hums. "I think you need to provide me with a few more details. Catch me up to speed."

That I can do. "Honestly, bro, I didn't mean to tell her. Everything is great—totally falling for her. Wyatt is awesome, too—if I'm gonna date someone with a kid, this would be the one. But Trent called while I was in her bedroom, I had him on speaker, she overheard everything and now wants nothing to do with me."

Landon whistles low. "He called while you were fucking? No way."

"She was taking off her makeup, and I was sitting on the bed keeping her company, calm down," I mutter, frustrated. "It was already a rough day, and the convo with Trent made it so much fucking worse."

I give him the scoop about Colton stopping by—what I'd heard and the things I had said.

"Sounds like a game of 'who's the bigger moron' when it comes to Margot." He laughs.

I sigh. "I need advice, dude, not you sitting there stating the obvious."

He rubs the back of his neck. "Give me a damn second, I'm processing. This is such a major fuckup."

"Gee, thanks."

He nods. "You're welcome."

I scowl. "Not helpful."

After several long, painful seconds—after staring out into his yard aimlessly, as if the answer to my problems were written in the clouds—Landon addresses me again.

"Real talk: I think the best way back into her good graces is through her kid."

Is he out of his mind? I can't use Wyatt to win her back—she would kill me!

"Her kid? Now you're talking crazy. That's fucking creepy."

"You don't even know what I'm gonna say!"

I doubt he knows either. "Spit it out then!"

Landon clears his throat. "What I meant was—if you plan to apologize, enlist the kid's help. If you have the kid on your side, it's two against one. Hasn't her daughter gotten you out of trouble once before?"

He knows all about my date with Madisson and how Wyatt came to my rescue.

I rub my chin. "That's not a bad idea." Still, "It's a kid. I can't contact her."

So how would I get her help? I can't text her—even if she does have a cell phone, you cannot slide into a child's DMs. *I might occasionally be a dipshit, but I'm smart enough to know at least that much.*

"Don't show up to her house without gifts," Landon adds. "Like flowers or something expensive. Earrings always work."

"For her or for the kid?" I grab a pen and notepad from the side table and scribble away.

"Her."

Gifts for her. Earrings, I write. "Wait. So am I not going over there, or am I?"

This has got me so fucked up I have no idea what I'm doing anymore.

"In my opinion, you're going to have to convince her to see you again," Landon instructs with the authority of a man who bosses other men around for a living. "Invite the daughter, and when Margot leaves the room to pee or whatever, you begin plotting against her with her kid."

"Leaves to pee, plot with Wyatt." I scribble that down. "Right. Got it."

"Don't fuck this up."

"'Kay. I won't."

I mean.

I'll probably fuck it up . . .

Chapter 32

Margot

Dex:
Hey.

Me:
Hey.

Dex:
Oh thank God—I thought for sure there was a chance you'd blocked me.

Me:
That would have been the smart thing to do, wouldn't it? But it seems I've made some really bad decisions since meeting you.

Dex:
Ouch. Guess I deserved that.

Me:
Guess you did.

Dex:
K, you don't have to keep agreeing with me, I already feel like shit.

Me:
OH! I'm so sorry! I keep forgetting this is about YOU and your CAREER and what's going to make YOU look like a rockstar.

Dex:
If you heard me sing, you wouldn't compare me to a rockstar.

Me:
I'm not even remotely amused by you right now.

Dex:
Sorry, I'm just trying to lighten the mood.

Me:
Yes, well. Don't bother.

Dex:
Margot, I know I fucked up—it's not the first time, but you're the last person I want to hurt. Can we get together and talk, please?

Me:
What's there to talk about, Dex? You made it pretty clear where your priorities lie.

Dex:
I know I messed up. I really do. But I want to explain. Face to face.

Me:
As much as I LOVE it when you beg, I don't think there's anything you can say that will change how I feel right now. The entire situation is so fucked up, pardon my French.

Dex:
You are owed an explanation. I did a shitty job last night—I was caught off-guard and an idiot. Please. One chance to explain myself. If

> you still feel the same way after, I'll leave you alone.

Me:
> Why should I believe anything you say? How do I know Trent didn't put you up to this too?

Dex:
> My knee-jerk reaction is to say, "Trust me," but I know you don't. And that makes me feel like a bag of shit. I wish you'd believe me when I say Trent has nothing to do with me wanting to . . . make this right.

Me:
> Make this right. Ahh. Well. If all you're going to do is apologize, I can save you the trouble and the drive over. I can forget this happened and we can go on with our lives and PRETEND this never happened.

Dex:
> I see what you did there.

Me:
Thanks, I was laying it on pretty thick. And I love a pun.

Dex:
So you're teasing me now, does that mean your ice is thawing and you're willing to hear me out????

Me:
My ICE???

Dex:
You know I don't have a way with words! Cut me some slack, I'm a football player not a poet. Jeez. I say stupid shit—A LOT of stupid shit

Me:
Okay, you're right. You don't have a way with words. I can't fault you for that.

Dex:
Thanks.

Me:
I'm just not sure seeing you is a good idea.

Dex:
Because I'm your kryptonite and you might accidentally want to make out despite yourself???

Me:
Something like that.

Me:
AND STOP SAYING THINGS LIKE THAT. I'm mad at you.

Dex:
Margot...

Me:
And stop saying my name like that.

Dex:
Please talk to me.

Me:
I am talking to you.

Dex:
I need to see you.

Dex:
Pretty please.

"What guy says pretty please anymore?" Cora's lips are pursed as she sets my phone on the table in the teachers' lounge, head shaking. "I still cannot believe he's begging to see you. The audacity of this guy."

"I know." I pluck at my ham-and-cheese sandwich, not hungry anymore, picking the crust off. "What should I do?"

Her eyes are wide. "I wish I had better advice for you, but you're dealing with an entirely different kind of man than I'm used to. I mean, last night Mark and I put an IKEA dresser together while eating a frozen pizza."

So relatable—unlike Dex and his signing events and huge house and personal chef.

"Okay, pretend he's normal, though. What would you do if you were in my position?" I can't tell my mother about this; she would die. She would also tell me to do whatever I had to do to keep him because of all the money he has.

Money, in her eyes, equals stability.

"I don't know—I run right toward red flags." She laughs.

"What do you mean?"

Cora shrugs, digging a Cheez-It out of a lunch-size bag of them. "One, when Mark and I started dating, he almost never made plans in advance—and never on the weekends. Two, I didn't meet his parents until six months in. Three, he called me his 'friend' when I met his grandmother, after we'd already been living together for eight months."

Oh shit. I did not know that about their relationship.

I gulp. "Uh. Okay, wow."

"You should see your face." Cora pauses. "My point is, I'm the wrong person to ask." She eats a cracker and chews, thinking. "You know what you should do, though? Trust your gut. If something feels off, it probably is. And if it feels right—" She shrugs. "You're the one who has to live with the consequences, and I won't judge you, whatever you decide."

My stomach turns. "I just don't know what my gut is saying."

Cora continues to snack. "Maybe you need to give it some time? It's okay not to have all the answers—you don't have to respond to him right away. You could take a step back, focus on other things, and see how you feel in a week or two."

I don't actually want to wait a week or two to see Dex, if I'm being honest. I want to see him now.

He's fun.

Sexy.

I consider her words, though. "That's probably a good idea. But . . . what if he thinks I'm not interested anymore?"

"If he's worth it, he'll understand. Communication is key, right?" She crushes the now-empty cracker bag in her hand. "Just be honest with him. Tell him you need some space and want to think things through."

Do I want space?

"Or," she goes on, "you could text him back and tell him you want to see him?"

My friend wiggles her eyebrows up and down.

"Should I?"

"Yeah, fuck it. You only live once. But if he pulls something like this again, he can kiss your ass goodbye."

I pick my phone up and go back to our chat, worrying my bottom lip. Type out a reply.
Delete it.

Me:
Begging will only get you so far.

Me:
Just because you're hot, doesn't mean I'm going to fall for your bullshit.

I delete those too.

Me:
Fine. I'll let you give your side of the story—but if you're going to tell me more lies or gaslight me, I'll go to the press myself and tell them what a PLAYER you are. Agreed?

Dex:
Deal.

I show my response to Cora, whose mouth falls open. "Damn, you're way braver than I am. I would have invited him to have sex with me in my car in the parking lot."

I stand and grab my garbage, glancing around to make sure the sixth-grade science teacher hasn't overheard her.

"You're a terrible influence."

And that, my friends, is how I ended up in the park with Dex.

He's here waiting when I arrive with Wyatt in tow. It's a park—she loves parks and can play while he and I talk. She insisted on accompanying me, and normally I'd never allow it, but she's obviously not old enough to stay home alone and no freaking way was I taking her to Colton's so he could keep an eye on her.

No. Freaking. Way.

He'd use it against me. I realize he's capable of that now.

"Thanks for seeing me," Dex says. "I know I don't deserve it."

"You're right, you *don't* deserve it." I can't resist snarkily pointing out that he's lucky I agreed to meet him in the first place. My lips are pursed, and I'm doing my best not to look directly at him. He's too damn good looking; it's like staring at the sun—hot and bright and makes me want to melt.

Dex shifts uncomfortably on the bench, his usual confidence dampened by the heavy weight of this moment. "I know I messed up. But I'm here because you deserve an explanation."

Obviously I do.

I raise an eyebrow, daring to glance at him. "An explanation? Or another excuse?"

"Shots fired." He winces at my words, and for a brief second, I feel a pang of guilt. *So briefly* because I remember the sleepless night I had, the tossing and turning, how embarrassed I felt overhearing that phone call between him and his lame agent.

I steel myself, determined not to let him off the hook.

I am not here to make up with him; I'm here because he wants closure.

"I swear I'm not a piece of shit." He leans forward, his eyes pleading with mine. "I swear I never meant to hurt you."

I cross my arms, trying to keep my voice steady. Chin up. Strong and resilient. "Then why did you?"

He runs a hand through his tousled hair. "I've never dated anyone stable. When I heard you were a teacher, I didn't know what to do with that information."

Oh brother. "'Cause you're so used to dating actresses and models? Boo-hoo, poor you."

"Hey—I'm speaking my truth, could you dial down the sarcasm?"

Crap. He's right. There's no need for me to be a bitch. Not with my daughter on the swing set nearby, watching me like a hawk.

"Look, I know it sounds pathetic, but I've always been surrounded by people who thrive on chaos. Yes-men. People I pay, people who don't care to get to know me. I went on Kissmet looking for something real but realized I couldn't handle it."

I raise an eyebrow. "That's all fine and good, but how does that help me right now?"

He scrunches up his face, concentrating on his words. "It doesn't. But it helps *me* understand why I allowed Trent to fuck with my head. I wasn't prepared for something real, something stable. And I messed up because of it. I know it sounds ridiculous to say that the teacher thing and the single-mom thing scared me, but it's true. I was intimidated by how grounded you are, how you have your life together."

Teacher thing.

Single-mom thing.

Give me a break. Grow up.

I roll my eyes, but something in his tone makes me pause. "I get the fact that dating a single parent is not for everyone, but being intimidated because I seemed grounded? That's a new one. You didn't even know me. I could have been a monster."

He nods, chuckling. "Yeah, I guess you could have been a monster. But it's not an excuse. It's just the truth." He holds his arms out. "I mean, look at me. Do I look like I know how to process emotions? No."

No, but he looks mouthwateringly good and makes me want to laugh.

What a big lovable dope.

Still. I cannot cave—he really screwed up big time.

"That argument is *not* helping your case."

From the corner of my eye, I watch Wyatt swinging higher and higher, her eyes darting between Dex and me. She knows he made me mad—doesn't know why, only knows I got little sleep last night.

My daughter doesn't miss a thing, so I owe it to her to handle this with a bit of grace and not lose my shit on this dude. Not here, anyway.

"Look, Dex," I say, my voice softer now. "You're a nice guy—I really, *really* liked you. I get that you have your issues. We all do. You met my ex, you know what a roller coaster that can be. None of us are perfect. But that's not really a reason to use someone." I let out a heavy breath. "You *used* me. Do you have any idea how that feels?"

Good people do bad things.

"I did not see it that way." His voice is quiet, mingling with the breeze and the rustling of the trees and Wyatt's occasional laughter.

I sigh, leaning back against the wooden picnic table. "For a few weeks we had a good thing. I was living in Delulu Land."

"I don't love the fact that you're using past tense."

"Good intentions don't erase the damage that was done." I feel the need to remind him, anger and sadness bubbling up. "I understand that you're here trying to make things right, but it's going to take a lot more than *words*. It's about actions, about showing that you're committed to changing." Surely he knows that.

"I get it," Dex says earnestly. "I'm willing to do whatever it takes."

"Do you even know what that means?" I shrug, agitated. "Because I do. Relationships are about trust and companionship. They're not just about saying the right things—they're about consistently doing the work. Relationships are work, Dex. And small moments, not just the big gestures. They're not about the media and Super Bowl wins and fans blowing smoke up your butthole."

I exhale. That was a lot of talking *at* him, and I wince when the telltale sign of needing to use the bathroom tingles in my lower half.

Worst.

Timing.

Ever.

I spot a public restroom not too far from where Wyatt is swinging. She's slowing now, feet dragging in the wood chips beneath her to busy herself.

"Ugh, can you hold that thought? I have to pee."

Dex grins. "Amazing."

I tilt my head. What a weird thing to say. "Be right back."

"Take your time," he calls after me as I beeline for the park bathroom.

As I quicken my pace, I can't help but feel a bit self-conscious. My mind is racing through our conversation, replaying his words in my head, a weird mix of relief and anxiety that's not helping my bladder situation. I'm a nervous pee-er!

The restroom is empty, thank goodness—and I rush in, locking the door behind me.

After taking care of business, I lean my forehead against the cool tile wall in an attempt to steady my breathing. The whole situation is overwhelming. The last thing I need to do is have a breakdown in a public restroom.

I finish up, wash my hands quickly, and take a deep breath before stepping out.

"You can do this."

Chapter 33

Dex

I move quick when Margot gets up to use the bathroom, motioning for Wyatt to get her rear over here. I have planning and plotting to do, just like Landon told me.

Except, I'm not sure what that plan to win her back is.

I'm hoping Wyatt will tell me.

"Dude, I need your help," I hiss, not wanting her mom to hear me, knowing I'd be in deep shit if she knew I was dragging her daughter into my drama. I have no idea how much this kid knows about our breakup or fight.

"No kidding," she says once she's done stomping over. "You seriously pissed her off."

Dang, she looks like her mom when she's irritated.

Ha!

"Hey. Are you allowed to talk like that?" She's only ten years old. Should she be allowed to use words like *pissed*?

"We don't have time for semantics," she informs me, glancing over her shoulder at the bathrooms where her mom disappeared. "You're a mess."

I am?

I rub my temples, feeling the tension in my shoulders mounting. "I know, I know. But I didn't expect things to blow up like this. Can you at least tell me what she's thinking?"

She crosses her arms, giving me a scrutinizing look that makes me feel about two inches tall.

"How the heck would I know what she's thinking? She doesn't talk about you, but there are signs." Her little voice takes on an ominous tone as she dramatically tosses her ponytail.

Trying not to take offense at this tiny, formidable person, I see the wheels turning in her brain.

"You know how she's been really stressed about work?" She has? I did not know that. "Maybe you could help her with something she doesn't like doing. Like, if she has a bunch of papers to grade or something, offer to help out. I do it all the time."

"I am not going to help Margot grade papers, good God, that would be a disaster."

Wyatt scrunches her face in concentration; then her expression brightens again as she comes up with another idea.

"Oh! You could make a card. A real one with, like, drawings and stuff. You don't have to be fancy, just make it look like you put some effort into it. And use stickers. I always do, and she *loves* them."

I chuckle, appreciating the simplicity of her suggestions. "A card? That's actually not a bad idea."

I rub my chin and Wyatt rubs hers.

"Have you said you're sorry yet?"

"Yeah, a bunch of times, but this is more about trust, and I don't know how to get her to trust me when I fuc—when I screwed up so bad."

Margot's daughter tilts her head and looks up at me. "What'd you do exactly?"

Let's see, how do I put this in a way this kid can understand?

"Um. A guy told me that dating your mom would be a good idea, instead of me just trusting my own gut and making the decision by myself."

Wyatt squints up at me. "How old are you?"

"Uh—twenty-five."

"Dude, why are you letting other grown-ups tell you what to do? Adults are supposed to adult."

How is she so wise? And why is she calling me dude?

"Because I'm a dumbass."

Her nod is sage. "Yeah, I can see that." She pats me on the arm to comfort me.

Once again, she's insulted me, but I deserve it. No one wants a child agreeing with them when one calls oneself a dumbass, but here we are. This is my life now, I guess.

"You're cool, do you know that?" I tell her. I've never met a kid like this, not that I've met many kids—not including the children that have come to meet and greets with their parents.

Another nod. "I get that all the time."

I laugh, surprised at her candor. What a little shit.

A cool little shit, but a shit nonetheless.

"So to recap," I begin. "You think the only way to get back into your mom's good graces is to make her a card and do something nice for her, like grade papers?"

"It's a start."

"What's something I can do now? Right now?"

We both turn our heads to see Margot exiting the bathrooms. She's brushing her hair back and wiping her hands on the fabric of her jean shorts.

Wyatt nudges me in the leg. "Just so you know, if you screw this up again, I'm not covering for you."

"I won't."

"Eh."

Surprised, I look down at her.

"I'm just messing with you," she teases, grinning like the goofball she is.

"Could you not? I'm a mess here."

"I see that."

"What are the two of you up to?" Margot has her hands on her hips, standing at the edge of the picnic area.

"We're plotting against you."

"Oh brother, here we go," Wyatt groans. "You lasted an entire two seconds."

It's not like I can bust out the craft supplies and start whipping up a card for her mother, for Christ's sake, and I'm not sure how the hell a picture is going to win me any points.

Margot's expression is stern as she glances back and forth between the two of us.

"I should've known I couldn't even pee without the two of you scheming." Her sharp gaze homes in on me. "Of *course* you dragged Wyatt into it. I suppose you want me to be flattered that you're making the effort?"

"I didn't drag her into anything," I protest. "She just—"

Margot doesn't let me finish. "Let's cut to the chase. What exactly have you two been scheming?"

She glares at us both.

"Welp! Oh gee, look at the time," Wyatt announces. "I'm going to grab a soda from the vending machine if that's okay. I'll just"—she steps backward, away from us—"give you a second."

"You are unbelievable." Margot whirls toward me to huff, throwing her hands in the air. "Wyatt already loves plotting against me, and she loves you, so what chance do I have?"

Wyatt loves me? This is news.

It hadn't occurred to me that the kid might . . . grow feelings. I mean, she's a kid. They watch TV and play and get messy; I forgot that they love stuff too. And people. Obviously she loves her mom and dad, but me?

Whoa.

Margot's nose is scrunched up as if I stink like crap. "Great. This is just *great*. What the hell was I thinking bringing her along with me?" she complains. "Why on earth did I think I could date a football player? I should be dating a banker or an accountant or—"

I pull her to me, cutting her off with a kiss, mouth silencing her.

Her lips are warm and soft, and for a moment the world around us fades into the background—unless you count the sound of Wyatt cracking open a soda can in the background, loudly slurping her first few sips.

I chuckle as the tension in Margot's body melts, the surprise of my kiss giving way to a tentative warmth.

Mmm . . .

I hold her face in my hands, fingers brushing against her smooth cheeks, feeling the slight tremor of her breath.

The kiss is tender—a mixture of apology and affection—as if I'm trying to tell her everything I can't articulate in words.

I'm an idiot, my kiss says.

I'm foolish.

I'm not the guy who's going to let you down . . .

My mouth lingers on hers, savoring the connection. The way her breath mingles with mine. The quiet reassurance that speaks louder than our argument.

Margot's initial rigidity slowly dissolves, her hands tentatively moving their way up my chest. Up, up her palms go, settling on my collarbone, and her kiss softens, becoming more responsive. It's as if she's finally letting herself be swept away by me; it's as if she's letting her guard down.

I pull back just enough to look into her eyes, seeing her surprise and something else. The beginning of forgiveness? Please say that's what this is . . .

I would miss her if she told me to fuck off and never contact her again, I seriously would.

"Look," I murmur, my voice barely above a whisper, hands on her shoulders. "I know this thing with my agent was fucked up. I'm not perfect, but I don't pretend to be."

She cocks her head and purses her lips, so I rush to say more.

"I can apologize until I'm blue in the face, and like you said, words don't mean shit if I can't show you I mean them. So. I'm just gonna have to ask you to trust me—no more fuckups." I search my word bank for a phrase I've heard Landon throw around. "Total transparency from now on."

My shoulders sag with relief when she slowly nods. "Then I should tell you that my parents have been actively campaigning to meet you." Margot nibbles on her bottom lip. "My dad is a good judge of character—so maybe I should let him decide if we continue dating."

"Does your dad like football?"

She nods again, snorting. "You think you'd get brownie points because you play football for a living? Puh-lease. I'm his baby girl. If he catches one whiff of shit, you're toast. And if I told him everything that's happened, oh my God. I'd be the least of your worries."

I cock my head. "You want me to meet your folks, hey?" That's a big step, but we've already jumped in headfirst. The whole world knows we're dating.

"Yes, I think we need to have dinner with them. They've obviously seen the news, they've seen the pictures. They're the only people who have been there for me since Wyatt was born, and it doesn't seem fair to keep this from them."

"Okay, let's do it." I can do dinner with them. I ain't got nothing to hide anyway, so how hard can it be? I rub her shoulders, fingers pressing into the tension located there. She relaxes when I concede to meeting her parents, melting into me. "When does Colton have Wyatt next?"

"The plan is for me to drop her off on my way home tonight—his nephew is having a birthday party, and they live in Tucson, so he wants to head out early."

Ah. Nice.

I exhale, about to take a giant leap. "Do you want to do a sleepover at my place tonight? We can put on jammies and do each other's hair. Get to know each other better. I can rub your feet."

Feet.

Back, tits.

Whatever.

Margot's eyes widen slightly, but a warm, amused smile plays at her lips. She tilts her head, considering my offer. "A sleepover at your place? That's quite a shift from our earlier conversation."

I try to maintain my casual demeanor despite my nerves. She makes me so fucking nervous sometimes.

"Yeah, I know it's a bit of a curveball, but I think it could be good for us. Just a chance to unwind and be ourselves without any pressure. Maybe take a bath."

"A bath?" She raises an eyebrow, clearly still cautiously deciding if she wants to join me. "And this is your grand plan to prove you're serious about things?"

"I mean, it's not the best but it's a start. I can feed you, too—there are a few meals in the fridge." Not meals that I made, but meals just the same. Ha!

I kiss her on the forehead. "So what do you say? Drop Wyatt at her dad's and then head over so I can spoil you?"

Chapter 34

Margot

He wants to spoil me?

I mean—if he insists . . .

I run my fingers over the fabric of the pajamas he has laid out on his massive bed—my first time in his bedroom—staring down at a matching set. His and hers.

Dex's.

Mine.

"How did you get jammies so soon? Did you assume I would cave this fast?"

He sits on the edge of the bed, looking all big and cute and like I want to climb in his lap . . .

"An assistant. He was here earlier when I called on my way home from the park." Dex smiles. "I was driving at least fifteen over the speed limit to get here, though. Surprised I didn't get pulled over."

Dang. He works quick.

I pick up the pajamas and hold them up to my chest.

Dex's is a two-piece set, top and bottom, and mine is more of a nightgown but with matching material. Baby blue with little stars and moons.

"I figured if we're doing a sleepover thing, we might as well do it right." He comes up behind me, sliding his hands around my waist, and I have to crane my neck to peer into his eyes. "I had him pick them up because you deserve to be spoiled."

Damn right, I do.

"Are you one of those guys who likes matching Christmas pajamas and stuff with your family?"

He shrugs. "I think I mentioned that my family isn't close—but yeah, if I'm at a buddy's house for Christmas, we've done the matching-group thing."

That I would pay to see.

"Flattery and pajamas—very smooth. It will get you some places," I tease, holding up the nightgown. "So, what's the plan? A movie marathon, or are we going for the full sleepover experience with face masks and maybe a little gossip?"

"Well, no. First, I have something for you."

Another something? Say more.

I wait as he disappears into another room, returning with an envelope and holding it out for me.

"What's this?"

I mean, obviously it's a card. But what's inside it? And when did he have time to run to the card store if he didn't have time to buy the pajamas himself?

My thumb peels up the edge of the paper, tearing it so that I can pull the card out, and a little tingle of disbelief bubbles up inside my throat.

"Did you . . . *make* this?" I stare at the paper in my hands, at the construction paper heart and the glitter that falls from it like confetti. Foam hearts also adorn it, stuck all over, weighing it down.

"Yeah." He shuffles his feet, suddenly looking bashful.

Margot, his manly scrawl begins. *Let's go back to the beginning and pretend I wasn't an asshole. Will you go on a first date with me all over again?*

Please check one. YES or NO

I don't know what to say because this is a first for me. My daughter has made me cards before, but a man? Never.

"You are so freaking cute!" I throw my arms around him, kissing his jawline, landing my lips on his mouth. "Yes. Yes, I'll go back to the beginning with you, and we can pretend this is our first date."

"Yeah?"

"Yes." I kiss him again. "You do realize, though, that I don't put out on the first date."

"You don't? Oh." His face falls. "Well fuck that, then."

I shake my head, laughing. "Maybe I could make an exception?"

"Good, because I have stuff planned for us." His grin widens.

"Stuff?"

"You know. Movies, snacks. And if you're up for it, we can do some of that *other* stuff too." He wiggles his eyebrows like a creep, and I giggle.

And other stuff . . .

"Oh yeah. Like what?"

His massive shoulders shrug. "Thought maybe you could take a bath while I sit and talk to you? I have a huge tub."

Oh? My ears like the sound of that. "I haven't taken a bath in ages. My tub is small and not all that relaxing."

Eagerly I follow him to the master bathroom—the sight has my breath catching. Shiny tile. Gold hardware. An enormous glass-enclosed shower.

The room is spacious—larger than my entire bedroom at home—the soak tub like a small pool. He already lit candles (or his assistant did) and they cast a soft, flickering light that makes everything seem dreamlike. The flames reflect against the surrounding glossy tile.

"Oh my God," I whisper. "This is incredible." My fingers glide along the edge of the tub. "It's like being at an actual spa."

Not that I've been to a spa in ages. Last time was a friend's bachelorette party three years ago. It was magic.

"I'm glad you think so. I don't use it that often." Dex steps closer. "Let me grab you a robe while you get comfortable. I'll get the water running."

I watch as he turns the gold faucet handles, adjusting the temperature until steam begins to rise. Then, he adds a giant blob of bubble bath, filling the room with the calming aroma of eucalyptus and mint.

I inhale. *Ahhh, it smells fantastic.*

"I'm impressed." I already feel relaxed, and I haven't gotten into the water yet.

Dex's eyes roam my face. "Anything for you."

I shiver and slowly begin to undress, a mix of anticipation and exhilaration thrumming through my body. He's seen me naked—of course he has; we've had sex and fooled around—but when he doesn't look away, I shiver again. His gaze is appreciative and filled with desire, and he isn't shy about it.

My shirt hits the floor.

I ease off my bottoms, and those land around my ankles.

I bend, sliding off my underwear—wishing I'd worn something sexier—trying to be smooth and casual about it, as if I were a dancer in an exotic club.

He watches me, transfixed.

Once my bra joins the rest of my clothes, I walk to the tub and dip my toe over the edge, into the bubbles.

Perfect.

One leg in, then the other, I ease myself in and let the hot, rushing water envelop me. I let out a sigh of contentment as bubbles surround my breasts, stomach, and legs, just my shoulders above the waterline.

"This feels amazing," I murmur, sinking deeper. "Mmm."

There is a chair at the vanity, and Dex pulls it next to the tub, close enough to put his fingers in the water. "You deserve to be pampered," he says softly. "The last twenty-four hours have been stressful, and it's been my fault."

Eh, that's not entirely true. My ex and my daughter add a certain amount of stress, too, and let's not forget about my mother, whose nonstop meddling in my life does not help.

I close my eyes, the soothing sound of his deep voice above me. "You're right. This is exactly what I needed."

Dex moves forward, leaning over the side so his lips can brush mine in a tender kiss.

The warmth of the water and the softness of his touch combine to create a heady sensation that gives me goose bumps all over my body. God, I feel like I'm in a movie—or at least one of those reality shows where the contestants climb into a bath together and sip champagne.

I kiss him back, more passionately than I ever have before, the water against my skin and the fact that I'm naked making me feel sensual and seductive. Dex responds with a low, appreciative moan deep in his chest.

As the water laps around me, our kisses grow more intense, the tips of his fingers trailing up my arm and across my collarbone, leaving a path of tingling skin in their wake.

More goose bumps.

More shivers.

When I pull back to look up at him, my heart is racing in a way only he can make it race.

The heat between us is literally unbearable.

Maybe it was meant to be?

"Why don't you join me?" My voice is husky with desire.

He doesn't need to be asked twice. The man stands so quickly to shed his clothes I think he might topple over.

But my laugh is caught in my throat when he begins tearing off his shirt, revealing his sculpted body. Abs. Chest.

Yum.

As he pushes his pants and boxers down to the floor, I can't help noticing he's already hard, his dick bouncing when he steps gingerly into the water. It sloshes as he settles himself on the other side to face me.

My feet find his chest, and he immediately begins rubbing them, our best body parts pressed together beneath the hot water. I sigh, toes curling as his hands move up my calves, massaging and caressing muscles I didn't realize were sore.

"That feels so, so good." I lean my head back, closing my eyes.

"Not as good as you," he replies.

I raise my head to look at him and giggle at his cheesy comeback. "When is the last time you were in here?"

"It's been a while. Maybe a few times since I bought the house."

"Why did you buy a house so big?" *If you didn't have or want a family . . . ?*

"Don't know. Guess it's because I had the money." Dex sniffs. "At least I'll make money on the investment when I go to sell it."

"Are you moving already?" I laugh.

"I'm not planning on it, but there's always the chance I'll get traded."

Oh.

Ohhh, duh.

I hadn't thought of that—the work stuff. How the football industry works and how unstable their positions can be.

Dex's hands are still working magic on my feet, thumbs pressing into the pads as he says, "Every year during the draft, we risk being traded if the team picks a newer, shinier, and less expensive version of ourselves."

I nod, understanding. Sort of.

I'm still learning.

His large palms move higher below the water, running slowly up my legs. Down again.

Lord, I wish I'd shaved . . .

I cringe every time his hands splay over my thighs—kneading there the same way he kneaded my calves—dying inside because of the hair on my legs, but I remind myself that I'm naked *and men love naked women* . . .

Chapter 35

Dex

"You drive me crazy."

"In a good way?"

Margot's hair is beginning to curl at the tips from the steam in the tub, and her cheeks are flushed in the most adorable, sexy way.

I watch as she adjusts herself, staring at her tits when they rise above the water. *Goddamn, they're pretty.* Not the biggest boobs I've ever seen, but definitely the sweetest. My mouth is watering for a taste.

"In the *best* way." Her voice is filled with desire and sends jolts of need to my groin.

I lean toward her to kiss her neck. Trail my lips down to her collarbone. Give her wet flesh a lick, because why not?

Salty. Sweet.

The combination of the hot water and the heat between us is almost overwhelming, and I cannot stop myself from muttering "You're so beautiful" against her skin, my hands moving to grip her hips, guiding her so she fits to my body. "I can't get enough of you."

Her chest rises and falls. "Did you draw me this bath just so you could seduce me?"

My laugh is tortured because my dick wants to be part of the conversation too. "No. I'm not that smart." I chuckle. "But in the short time I've known you, I know you like to multitask."

"Plus, if we get dirty, we won't have to get cleaned up?"

"Exactly." My voice is husky, my body hard as the water sloshes every time we move, giving me glimpses of her wet, slippery tits.

I am so fucking turned on it's stupid.

Her hands move to my chest, fingers tracing the contours of my muscles, the tip of her index nail trailing the curve of my pec. Over my nipple. Down the center of my clavicle.

Margot tilts forward, so much so that the tip of my cock pokes her pussy—I can't see it, but I know a pussy when I feel one—and I can feel her breath against my skin. Hot. Warm.

She tilts her head back, eyes locking on to mine with an intensity that makes my pulse quicken.

She's turned on too.

Yes . . .

I press my mouth to hers in a slow, sensual kiss. Her taste is intoxicating—like peppermint gum or toothpaste—and it only makes me crave more. I deepen the kiss, my tongue teasing hers, drawing a soft moan from her lips.

Margot is eager, her hands sliding over my naked skin, up the column of my neck to tangle in my hair. She pulls me closer still . . .

Slides onto me.

The water laps around us, threatening to spill over the side of the tub and onto the tile floor.

My lips trail kisses along her jawline. I kiss the spot beneath her ear I've recently discovered makes her wet, savoring the feel of her beneath my lips.

More.

I want more 'cause obviously I want to fuck her.

"Bath time is so fun. I should do it more," I murmur into her ear.

"Not without me."

She has my full attention. "I'm listening."

Margot shrugs, plunging her hands beneath the water, swallowed up by the bubbles. "That's it. Just . . . no baths without me."

I like the direction this is headed. "Does that mean you forgive my douchebaggery?"

Her mouth twists, noncommittal. "Jury is still out, but they're thinking about it."

"Can't argue with that."

Margot's fingers tangle in my hair, her nails scraping lightly against my scalp as she rides me. Her movements are slow and deliberate, each one sending waves of pleasure through me.

She's taking the lead, and me likes it.

Me likes it a lot . . .

Her hands reappear at the surface with a bar of soap. She lathers it up against her palms, then sets it aside before running them over my shoulders and chest, her movements both tender and sensual.

My skin puckers.

Her fingers glide along my arms, down my back, and then lower. Exploring and teasing. Each touch sends shivers rippling through me, despite the hot temperature of the water.

I want to shout HALLE-FUCKING-LUYAH, satisfied when this time the water does slosh onto the floor, splashing a decent-size puddle I'll worry about later.

I can't resist pulling her closer, hands on her ass.

Fingers gripping.

She grinds slowly, pussy running the length of my cock.

Teasing.

Testing my willpower.

It's paper thin at this point.

Worse when her movements become more deliberate, each roll of her hips driving me wild. Each roll of her hips makes me want to slide inside her and thrust.

I'm only so patient . . .

Finally, we cross the line.

Slide into her.

The tension between us builds, our eyes now locked as she fucks me.

"You're driving me crazy," she whispers, her breath hot against my ear.

"I drive you crazy?" I groan, hands sliding up her back to pull her closer. "You're making me lose my goddamn mind."

"You like it though, don't you?"

I give a jerky little nod, brain coming undone. "Yes."

Please.

Please keep fucking me . . .

"Don't stop," I beg, my voice hoarse.

She slides over me, over and over again, and we both moan.

Loudly.

"Oh shit . . ." I groan. "Fuck."

Tits jiggling, she moves up and down.

Water splashes everywhere, but neither of us gives one single fuck.

Her hips move faster. Urgently. The friction and heat build to an almost unbearable level, and I can feel the tension coiling in my core, ready to snap.

No. No, no, no—it's too soon to come.

Still. It's not my choice. Her nipples and boobs and the bouncing, along with her glistening skin, are enough to put me over the edge.

"Margot, I'm close," I warn, my voice strained.

"Oh God, me too," she gasps, her nails digging into my shoulders. "Don't stop."

Don't stop . . .

I grip her tighter, our bodies moving in perfect sync as we chase the edge together.

Slosh.

Splash.

It's a mess.

But so motherfucking good . . .

Chapter 36

Margot

"You look so cute in those pajamas."

"Do I?" Dex looks down his body at the bottoms that match my sleep shirt.

"It would have been even cuter if you had the top on. Then we'd actually be twinning."

"Do you want me to put the top on?"

I shake my head, hand sliding over his bare chest. "No. Then I can't feel you up." I bite down on my bottom lip. "And now that we're on the subject, you should probably not ever be allowed to wear a shirt."

His body is too damn good.

Eye candy.

I could eat him up.

Cora would be pissing herself if she could see me now. Not that I want her to see my, uh, boyfriend's naked chest, but you get the point I'm trying to make.

My finger runs over the hair on his chest, tracing a lazy, hypnotic path. Dex's breath catches slightly, and he gives me one of those looks, a mix of amusement and affection.

He looks . . .

Smitten.

I find myself blushing.

"Glad you like the view." His voice is low and playful.

"I'd say that's an understatement." Like? No. I love the view.

I don't say the words out loud. You don't throw the *L* word into a casual conversation even if it's not a declaration. Feels too heavy and weighty, and it's still early for that, even if I'm just speaking about his amazing bod.

Dex guides my hand along his chest in a slow, deliberate motion. "You're making it hard to stay focused on anything."

My voice is soft. "I think that's the general idea."

"What are you planning to do with me, exactly?"

I lean over, my lips brushing his ear as I whisper, "I'm planning to enjoy every second of tonight."

And hey, if we bang a few times before I have to leave in the morning, great.

For once I'd like to be the woman walking sideways from having been fucked thoroughly. Is that too much to ask?

His grip tightens slightly on my hand, and he tilts his head, his lips brushing against my temple. "I think I'm okay with that plan."

I pull back just enough to look into his eyes, my fingers still tracing patterns on his chest. So comfy and content.

"Careful where you're putting your hands," he warns me with a chuckle. "You don't want to reactivate the launch sequence."

"I don't?"

He glances down his body at me, brows raised, and pushes the hair out of my eyes. "You know—you're full of surprises. I didn't think an elementary school teacher was as sassy and sexy as you. You couldn't have paid me to believe it."

"I don't know if that was a compliment or not." So I just nod. "Thanks."

Dex's grin widens, and he tucks a loose strand of my hair behind my ear. "Oh, it's definitely a compliment. I'm just amazed by how you manage to balance that sweet, caring teacher vibe with . . . well, this."

This.

"Are you trying to tell me you can't get enough of me?"

"Totally."

He's teasing, but he's also serious—so I'll take it.

I raise an eyebrow playfully. "It's okay to be pleasantly surprised by how someone is in real life. Like . . . I was with you. Clearly I thought you were a dick at first. There's no bigger stereotype than that of a professional athlete."

Facts.

He nods his agreement. "You've got this incredible way of being both charming and downright irresistible, which is so fucking . . . sexy."

"Ugh," I sigh dramatically. "I could listen to you compliment me all day." Keep them coming.

Dex's smile softens as he looks into my eyes, the playful glint in his gaze suddenly turning serious. Dang. I haven't seen this look on his face before. He's usually so playful and *un*serious, if that's a thing.

His fingers trace the edge of my jaw gently. He looks me in the eyes as his palm smooths along my skin.

"So. There's something I need to say, something that's been weighing on me, and that's obviously the reason you're here." He swallows, Adam's apple bobbing. "I know I've been kind of selfish since day one, and I've taken advantage of how amazing you are—and how sweet—without considering your feelings, which is why I fucked up."

"By fucked up do you mean that thing with your agent?"

That thing = using me to make himself into a family man and not a manwhore to the public.

"I mean. Yeah." He shakes his head, the weight of his apology clear in the tone of his voice. "I don't know when I turned into the type of dude who disregards the feelings of others—probably college, when everyone kissed my ass. I could do no wrong—I was, like, the golden kid for four years."

How nice for him.

He goes on. "It's not an excuse. I just want to illustrate that . . . I haven't had anyone tell me I'm being an asshole, and at the same time I have a guy working for me that encourages it to a degree."

"Lovely."

Dex shakes his head, frustrated. "My parents are users, so I actually know what it's like being in your position—not that I realized that's what I was doing, in a roundabout way."

"Your parents are users?"

He nods. "Yeah. As soon as I got famous, they were up my ass about money and paying off their house. I mean, plenty of guys can afford to do that, but usually they do it because their parents were the ones supporting their craft. Mine didn't. I rode my bike to practice and had a job to pay for camps. Why the fuck would I pay off your house—or buy you a new one?"

He sounds bitter, and I know he has a lot to unpack with this subject, perhaps on another evening.

Dex blows out a puff of air. "Anyway. You're so fucking amazing. I knew it from the beginning, and I was an idiot to let Trent think I was only dating you for clout. Because that is not why I'm dating you."

I raise my brows as he rubs the fabric of my sleep shirt. "You kind of were. Isn't that the reason you backtracked after putting me in the friend zone?"

I'm no lawyer, but I object to his argument.

His face is grim. "I think it was an excuse to take you out of the friend zone."

"An excuse." Okay, that makes a bit of sense. I can wrap my brain around it. "You didn't want to admit to yourself that you were falling head over heels in like with a woman who has a kid?"

I'm teasing, but I hope he agrees with me.

"I thought if I could keep things casual between us, it would be easier for me to handle if things didn't work out. But obviously Wyatt is cool as shit and you're sexy as hell, and why the fuck would I want to date anyone else?"

In all his nonpoetic words lies the biggest flattery, and I blush. Dex is no wordsmith—they are not his forte, but they aren't mine either. But if he's saying what I think he's saying, I'm . . .

Happy.

"Do I make you happy?" His question invades my thoughts, and I gaze at him sharply. Is he a mind reader now?! Holy crap.

"I think so."

"You're not sure?"

My head lolls. "Listen, we had a rough week. You dragged my kid into our argument—slick moves, by the way—and I overheard your agent telling you to stick with this a month or so before pulling the plug." I worry my bottom lip. "I guess the better question is do I think you can make me happy?"

He waits for my answer.

"Yeah. I do think you can make me happy." Pause. "Do you think I can make you happy?"

"Margot, you already do." He pulls me over to him and shifts me so I'm flat on my back, pillows beneath my head. Braces himself above me, bending to kiss my neck. Jaw. Corner of my mouth.

"I thought we were going to watch movies."

"We will." His fingers work the buttons on my sleep shirt, his nose trailing along my skin. "How is it possible that you smell like baby powder?"

I chuckle softly, my hands sliding over his broad shoulders as my body is bared to him, one button at a time. "Mom magic," I whisper.

Dex kisses the valley between my breasts, moving down.

My breath catches as his lips explore my skin, his touch electrifying.

I let out a soft moan, arching my back slightly, my hands gripping the sheets beneath me . . .

I like where this is heading . . .

I feel so spoiled by him tonight and wonder if it will always be like this.

A girl can dream.

I moan to encourage him.

He pauses, looking up my body with a mischievous grin, fingers plucking open the last of my buttons. "You like that?"

"Yes." I pause. "I do."

I didn't realize I loved having a man go down on me as much as I do. In the past I've always been so . . . prudish about it. Dex, though? He can go down on me all day long. In the offseason, he can make it his second job.

Ha!

He continues his journey south, lips trailing lower, kissing the soft skin of my belly. Beneath my belly button. My pelvic bones.

Every touch sends a wave of pleasure through me, my body quivering with anticipation.

Keep going, my brain says.

Don't stop . . .

I close my eyes, losing myself in the sensations. Our worries from the past week, the arguments, the doubts I might have had, all those fade—at least momentarily—replaced by the warmth of his big hands. I am putty in his damn hands.

Dammit! I'm one of those women now!

The kind who let sex addle their brain!

Who knew . . .

Dex's hands slide beneath me, lifting my hips as he kisses along the elastic of my thong. It's lacy and see-through and gone before I can say "Houdini."

He glances up at me, seeking permission before he puts his mouth there.

I nod, my breath hitching in my throat.

How can my temperature be this hot when he hasn't even put his tongue inside me yet?

Magic.

His mouth opens, pressing gently against my most sensitive spot, *and I gasp*, tensing. It already feels so amazing. Incredible. Climactic.

I grip the sheets tighter. My knuckles are surely some shade of white.

His touch is firm, his hands splayed on my inner thighs, keeping them open, thumbs brushing back and forth close to my folds. It only adds to the pleasure.

His tongue works, exploring. Teasing. *Driving me wild with need.* Driving me closer and closer to the brink I already know is coming because he's given it to me this way before.

Flick.

Flick . . .

Every suck sends waves of pleasure coursing through me, building like a crescendo, lifting me higher and higher.

My back arches again.

I can hardly think or catch my breath, and I remind myself to feel and stop thinking.

My hips move of their own accord, as if his dick were inside and not his tongue, seeking more . . . more of the exquisite pleasure. The pain of waiting.

I let out another soft moan to urge him on, my body beginning to tremble with the intensity. Things quake. I try to make them stop, but they're not cooperating.

Oh my God . . .

"Dex," I whisper, my voice shaking too. "Please . . ."

"Please what?" He looks up at me, eyes dark with desire.

I can't say anything.

The sight of him with his face buried between my legs is enough in itself to send me over the edge. He holds my gaze as his tongue licks me, as his mouth sucks.

He's just so fucking good at this . . .

Too good.

I clench my inner muscles, knowing that the tension will make the orgasm stronger.

I am a tight coil ready to snap.

"J-Jeezus . . . ," I mutter, grasping for his shoulders, fingers brushing his flesh.

Reach for his hair—it's the only thing I can cling to other than the sheets.

My breath comes in short gasps as I strain toward my release.

Just when I think I can't take it anymore, that coil inside me snaps like a rubber band.

I cry out, convulsing with the force of my orgasm.

Tremors.

Shivers.

Racks of delicious, pleasurable pain.

But Dex doesn't stop. He keeps at it. Sucking. Licking. All the things to prolong my pleasure until I'm a limp, breathless mess. When he finally pulls away, I can barely move, lifeless and sated.

I find my voice. "Oh."

Oh = oh my God.

Oh = orgasm.

He crawls up the bed and gathers me in his arms. When I'm finally able to move my arms, I wrap them around him and rest my head on his chest, listening to the beat of his heart. It's steady but fast, thumping as wildly as mine.

His hand strokes my hair, his touch soothing and comforting.

He kisses me.

"You're amazing," I whisper, my voice still shaky.

"No, you are."

I won't argue with that.

I can feel him smiling as his warm breath caresses the crown of my head.

"Wanna know something?"

"Hmmm? You want to watch a sports movie because you're not in the mood for a rom-com?" I joke, brain barely functioning at the moment.

Dex laughs. It rumbles in his chest.

His big, broad, beautiful chest.

"Literally not at all what I was gonna say."

What was he going to say, then? "Hmm?"

"I, uh..."

I wait, shifting so I can glance up at him. But I don't press—he seems to be struggling for the words, not that that's unusual for him.

"I love you, Margot."

What?

I move so I can sit up, so I can look him in the face. In the eyes. Shock. Disbelief.

"What did you say?" I ask, voice barely a whisper.

Dex's eyes meet mine, unwavering and sincere. "I love you, Margot," he repeats, steady and resolute. Mostly. "I know we've only known each other a hot minute, but when I picture what a relationship and love should be like, I picture you. Is that weird?"

My head gives a shake. "No, it's not weird. It's..."

Beautiful.

Nice.

Sweet.

And. True.

"I might not have pictured myself in a relationship with a professional football player. And we haven't seen much of each other, but I think I can imagine myself as part of your life." Whatever that looks like.

I mean, how hard can it be to attend football games and cheer him on? How hard can it be to splash around in his pool during the summer and hold his hand and go for ice cream, something he loves very much.

We've already had a few conflicts, and we worked them out.

"If you can tolerate Colton, I can tolerate Trent," I tease, running a hand down his bare chest.

"I can tolerate that prick too."

I laugh despite myself. "He's not bad—he's just butt hurt."

"You mean jealous?"

I hate assigning feels to someone else but, "Yeah. I guess."

"Don't blame the poor bastard. He lost out on you, and now I'm going to be the best fucking boyfriend ever." He kisses me on the forehead. "Wyatt is my new best friend."

I shiver. "Do you hear that?"

"Hear what?"

"My ovaries bursting."

Dex chuckles, his chest vibrating under my touch. "I have no idea what that even means."

"It's something a woman says when a cute guy gets her all hot and bothered, and she wants to, you know, make more babies."

He holds his hands up in surrender. "Whoa whoa whoa. Let's not get ahead of ourselves."

"I'm kidding." I kiss him below the chin. "I love you too."

He snorts. "I was wondering when the hell you were going to say it back. I was getting worried—my testicles are about to shrivel up inside my body."

We laugh as he adjusts us both so he can murmur against my lips. "I think we're going to be just fine."

I grin happily, resting my forehead against his. "I know. I'm excited," I whisper.

As we settle back into each other's arms, I feel the warmth of contentment spreading through me.

I begin rebuttoning my sleep shirt while he reaches for the remote on the bedside table.

"This dating stuff is so easy," he boasts, clicking the television on. It's massive, anchored to the wall opposite the bed, and comes to life almost instantaneously.

"You think so?" I roll my eyes.

Of course he thinks it's easy. He has it made.

I'm amazing.

My kid is awesome.

I'm fun. Smart. Cute.

I don't exactly think it's going to be a cakewalk 100 percent of the time, but I think I'll be able to hold my own with him, and he with me—as long as we treat each other with respect.

"I do." Dex hesitates. "I mean, how could it not be? I get to date the most incredible woman ever."

"True." I laugh playfully, swatting at his chest and leaning into him. "You're just saying that because my daughter thinks you're Thor."

He catches my hand, pressing a kiss to my knuckles. "Well, yeah, the hero worship is a definite bonus," he admits. "But I'm serious, Margot. I've never felt this way about anyone before. God, listen to me. Gross. I make me want to vomit in my helmet."

Oh Lord. He's so dramatic.

Still. His praise melts my little heart, and I lean in to kiss him softly. "You make everything feel right too," I whisper against his lips. "I love you."

He kisses me deeply. Open-mouth kisses that are wet. Hot.

I can *feel* the intensity of his emotions in the way he kisses me, in the way his body responds to mine.

When we finally break apart, we're both breathless. His hand caresses my spine, up and down . . . up and down, lazily.

"I love you too."

Chapter 37

Dex

It's like I said—my parents weren't involved in most of my shit, so I have no idea what to expect when I meet hers.

We're at the scene of the crime, a.k.a. the first place we met in person, a.k.a. the restaurant where I paid Wyatt to ruin my date with Madisson.

We thought it would be an ironic and fitting spot to meet her folks.

Margot is fussing with her hair, glancing nervously at her reflection in the window of the restaurant, tightening the sleek ponytail that she already tightened at least four times on the ride here.

"Mom, you look perfect." Wyatt takes her hand. "Stop fussing."

Honest to God, in the few short weeks we've been dating, I have grown to seriously respect that little shit. I have no idea how most kids are, but this one is intelligent as fuck and hilarious besides.

"Listen to Baby Yoda, Margot. She's very wise."

Wyatt giggles, pleased with the nickname.

She lets go of her mom's hand, and I take it instead, squeezing it reassuringly. "Hey, it's going to be fine." I try to sound more confident than I'm starting to feel. "Your parents are going to *love* me."

She gives me a skeptical look as I pull open the door for them. "You don't know my parents."

Uh—what's that supposed to mean? I don't ask; instead I guide them into the lobby.

"No, but I know you," I counter. "And if you love me, they'll love me too." Here I go boasting about things I know nothing about. Like meeting parents and blended families.

She takes a deep breath and nods. "You're right, you're right. They're going to love you. After all, they never stop hounding me to date."

Yeah. She's told me all about how her mom is always trying to set her up with her friends' divorced sons, or men she meets in the grocery store.

We walk into the restaurant, the familiar scent of Italian food wafting through the air. My stomach grumbles on cue as the hostess leads us to a table toward the back where Margot's parents are already seated.

They stand as we approach, her father's expression stern, her mother's more curious.

They both give me a once-over.

"Mom, Dad, this is Dex," Margot says, her voice slightly trembling. "Dex, these are my parents, Robert and Lydia."

Robert is a tall dude with distinguished gray hair at the temples and an imposing presence. He extends his hand to me. "Nice to meet you, Dex."

His grip is firm.

Super firm.

Wyatt hugs her grandpa while he's shaking my hand, giggling the entire time.

"Nice to meet you, sir," I reply, our fists moving up and down, and I do my best not to wince at the strength of his handshake. What's he trying to do, crush my palm?

Damn, Robert, relax.

Her mother, a petite woman with sparkling eyes, steps forward next to hug me.

"Please sit," she says after giving me a squishy, warm hug. "We've heard a lot about you."

Wyatt, Margot, and I take our seats at a big round table—not too far from the one I was at with Madisson and within earshot of the bathrooms. Ha!

"I hope she didn't tell you the story about my agent." I throw out a zinger, verbal diarrhea rearing its ugly head. Since when am I nervous around parents? Fuck. I told her they were going to love me, and here I am, talking out of my asshole.

Lydia tilts her head toward Margot. "I don't recall a story about your agent."

A foot nudges mine beneath the table to keep my mouth shut, and I do my best to look unfazed.

Once we're settled, the waiter comes to take our drink orders. Margot's parents order wine, but I stick with water, wanting to keep a clear head. The last thing I need is to spew more garbage about agents and fuckups since it looks as if that's the path I'm veering down.

Margot squeezes my hand under the table.

"So, Dex," Robert begins, taking on a businesslike tone. It's a fatherly expression to show me he's ready to get staunch and serious. "How did the two of you meet?"

This is it—*my time to shine*. The perfect opening to razzle and dazzle.

Margot and I exchange a quick glance. "Well, it's a bit of a funny story," she starts. "We actually met here for the first time. At this restaurant."

"Oh?" Her mother's eyes practically glitter with interest. "I would have guessed a dating app." She winks, attempting to be hip and in the know of the younger crowd.

I rub the back of my neck nervously, and her father notices. *He's like a hawk, this guy.*

"I was here, uh, on a date with another woman, and things weren't going well because—" I want to bang my head on the table. *Why did I just tell Margot's parents I was here with another woman?*

"Oooh, oooh!" Wyatt interrupts, waving an arm in the air as if she were raising her hand at school. "Can I tell it? Can I?"

Margot's eyes go wide. We're now entering dangerous territory. How will her parents feel about me paying a child to do my dirty work for me? Or the fact I tried climbing out a restroom window?

She nibbles her lip, concerned. "I don't know, Dex—*can* she tell the story?"

I nod slowly. "It's her story as much as it is ours."

Wyatt practically bounces out of her seat, thrilled to be the star storyteller, a captive audience ready to hang on her every dramatic word.

Beside me, Margot braces herself, slamming most of her wine in a single gulp.

"So." Wyatt pauses on that single word, glancing around the table. "Mom was here with us. Remember when we were here having that fancy dinner, Grandpa?" Grandpa tilts his head. "And Dex was here too. Except he was here on a *really* bad date. I mean, this lady was so horrible, right, Dex?" I nod sagely, waiting for what comes next in our story. "Anyway, Dex paid me a hundred and forty bucks to ruin his date."

Wyatt punctuates the sentence by sipping from her kiddie mocktail, then setting it back on the table with a thud.

Lydia's eyes are wide as saucers, but she looks more amused than appalled? *Thank fucking God.*

Robert's expression, on the other hand . . . not so much.

Thus far he is not impressed with my antics. Nor my charm. And no mention of football.

"You paid a child over a hundred dollars?" Robert repeats, his tone questioning, eyes bugging out. He turns his attention to his daughter. "And you were okay with this?"

"It was for LEGOs, Grandpa!" Wyatt interrupts again. "I told the lady I was his daughter and he had *ten* other kids." She giggles. "It was so funny. This was after he tried to escape through the bathroom window."

It's safe to say we're all horrified.

Margot's face is now a mix of embarrassment and laughter, while I try to gauge Robert's reaction.

Yup. Still pissed.

And by *pissed* I mean a vein is bulging in his goddamn forehead.

"Is that true?" Robert asks, turning his narrowed gaze on me.

The vein in his head threatens to burst.

I clear my throat. "Yes, sir. Er. Uh. It was one of those situations that wasn't going to solve itself. It was a first date, and the woman was making plans for our wedding and our children." I exaggerate for the sake of saving my ass. "I was desperate."

"Does that sort of thing happen to you often?" Robert is tapping the table with his index finger.

"No. That was a first."

"And *then*," Wyatt continues, not wanting to be ignored. "As soon as I told her he had so many kids, she bolted. Worked like a charm!" She puts her hand up so I can high-five her, and I don't want to leave her hanging, so I give her palm a halfhearted, light tap.

God, I hate myself right now.

Hearing this told from a child's perspective makes it sound so . . . not great. It makes me sound like a colossal dipshit, bonehead, asshole, thoughtless prick. Take your pick; any of the adjectives work.

"It's not every day you hear about someone paying a kid to sabotage a date. So much action." Lydia tries to ease the tension between her husband and me, winking at her granddaughter conspiratorially.

"I know, Grandma. It was really fun, and I got that LEGO kit I wanted." She takes a chug from her mocktail. "Ahhh." Wipes her mouth.

"Goodness, *then* what happened."

"Then Mom came around the corner and busted us."

Busted us.

"Well." My girlfriend finds her voice. "I was looking for you, young lady. You were gone a long time."

Her mother is studying me, but judging from her amused expression, she's less offended by my actions than her husband is. I wonder if I'll be able to win him over—or if I'm doomed for life.

I clear my throat. "Long story short, here we are, having dinner with you."

"Quite honestly, after seeing the news stories, I texted Margot about meeting you. Every time one of my friends called to ask about it, I had no details." Now Lydia sounds slightly put out.

The server comes and saves us all from more awkward conversation, and we order appetizers but not our entrées. I readjust myself in the chair—it has armrests and feels too small for my giant frame, the tops of my knees knocking the table with each movement.

Silverware clanks.

"What are your intentions toward my daughter?" Robert is staring at me from above his menu, doing his best to play the role of the intimidating father who only wants what's best for his daughter.

"Dad!" Margot groans, rolling her eyes. "His intentions? What about my intentions, huh? Maybe I'm the one he has to watch out for, gold diggers and all that."

That is a very good point!

"Well, someone has to ask the tough questions," Robert replies, not breaking eye contact with me. "It's a fair question."

I clear my throat, trying to suppress a grin.

I'm onto him now—his bark is worse than his bite, and I don't blame him for being a hard-ass. I mean, come on, look at me. I don't come off as the boy next door. I'm well aware of the fact that:

I have a reputation in the media that's probably well deserved.

Biggest Player

I look like an asshole. It's the haircut and the five-o'clock shadow, and the fact that I was born looking cocky certainly doesn't help. It's this million-dollar face—there is no helping it.

"Someone has to make sure this guy's worthy of my little girl," Robert goes on, protective dad and all that.

"Little girl? Dad, stop." Margot is grinning at him, so I know her feathers aren't actually ruffled. She's playing along. "You do realize I'm a grown woman with a career *and* a mortgage, right?"

"I appreciate your sentiment, Robert. Sir." I'm trying to keep a straight face. "But you know Margot can handle herself—she did manage to wrangle me, after all."

"Oh, I'm sure she did," Lydia says, laughing. "She gets her sass from me."

"I am not sassy," Margot protests. "I'm spirited, and my bullshit meter comes from Dad."

Robert sits up a bit straighter at the shout-out. "So, Dex." He leans toward me, elbows on the table. "You've managed to survive our little interrogation so far. What makes you think you're good enough for my Margot?"

Beside me, Margot almost chokes on her wine. "Dad!"

I thought we were through with this, but nonetheless, I take a deep breath, ready to lay it all out there.

No time like the present, eh?

"No, Margot, it's cool." A lump forms in my throat, and I feel like I'm on the spot, but it's fine, *everything is fine*. I can do this—I can lay my soul bare, in front of her family, because I'm brave. I'm brave, dammit!

"I love Margot. Not only is she amazing, but she's smart, funny, and incredibly strong. I've never met anyone like her—no one has ever told me to my face that I suck. She swept me off my feet."

She smacks me, grinning from ear to ear. "Oh my God, I did not tell you you suck to your face."

I shrug. "Not in those words, but you did call me an asshole at least a dozen times after we just met."

"That's true." She flips her hair, laughing.

"Is this your way of flirting?" Wyatt asks, quizzically gazing between her mother and me. "Because it is so weird."

We all laugh.

"It's no secret that we've had a few rough patches, but . . . you know. She's my best friend." I take a drink of my cocktail. "Don't tell my best friend Landon that, he'll kill me. But yeah—I love her."

The table falls silent for a moment, the weight of my words hanging in the air.

"What about more kids?" her mom asks, a hopeful look on her face.

Some things are private, and it's still too early for more kids, but yup, "I'm sure that day will come."

Margot's eyes glisten with unshed tears, and Lydia's face softens into a warm smile. Robert studies me for a long moment before nodding slowly.

"Well, Dex," he says, his voice gruff but kind as he moves to spread his napkin across his lap. "That's all I needed to hear. Let's eat, shall we?"

Epilogue

Margot

Two months later . . . give or take

I couldn't be more nervous if I tried.

Well.

That's not true—I could be.

I could have lain in bed last night, staring up at the ceiling, wide awake, conjuring up scenarios in my brain that aren't going to happen but could. Such as: I could say something stupid. I could ramble. I could tell his best friend I think their agent is an asshole who needs to mind his own business.

I could have and I did.

Stomach in knots—the kind of knots you feel when you're finally meeting your new boyfriend's best friend AND HIS GIRLFRIEND for the first time. *Say it with me*: They are normal people! They go grocery shopping just like us! They go on coffee runs JUST LIKE US!

I mean, let's be real—since when did I give a fig about football before meeting this man? Answer: I didn't.

And if I wasn't nervous enough, the date Dex has planned is giving me anxiety too!

Game night.

At his house.

Competitive much?

As I get out of the car, I spy Dex standing at the door, his large form taking up most of the doorframe as he waits for me to collect my stuff. His smile has my heart racing. He looks so relaxed. So confident. He looks like this is the most natural thing to be doing on a Sunday night.

Maybe for him, it is. But for me? I'm about to walk into a battlefield of board games—and first impressions. Could there be a worse combination?

Ugh.

I drag my sorry ass to his massive front porch and lean up when he goes to kiss me on the lips.

"Hey." Dex kisses me full on the mouth at the same time he's pulling me into his arms. "Ready for game night?"

"As ready as I'll ever be." I force a smile.

He chuckles, kissing my forehead. "Don't worry, it's just for fun. Landon and Harlow are pumped to meet you."

The knot in my stomach turns, and I put a hand there to quell it as he ushers me into the foyer.

As I walk inside, the sound of laughter and chatter greets my ears, the kind of good-natured laughter that calms me a bit.

I peek through the arched doorway to the living room to see a big dude—not as big as Dex but certainly massive—arranging games on the coffee table. He and Harlow look so comfortable and so at ease, like this is just another Sunday night to them.

Maybe that's because they live in the Midwest? Aren't things wholesome there? They do things like game nights and county fairs and fundraisers at the local fire department. Or so I've heard.

"Hey, you made it!" Dex's best friend stands and sets down a black game box, already moving in my direction with his arms out, ready for a hug. "I'm Landon, but my friends call me Andy."

Dex's brows raise. "Hey—*I* call you Landon."

His buddy laughs and folds me up. Gives me a squeeze. "Exactly."

"You're such an asshole," Dex grumbles unhappily, not at all pleased by his friend's jokes.

"And this is my better half, Harlow," Andy announces. "She keeps me honest."

His girlfriend is not at all what I was picturing, although I couldn't tell you what that was. Maybe someone blond? Someone glamorous? Who can't move her face? Sexy?

If I'd done a deep dive of them online, I wouldn't be as shocked to see that they're both relatively . . . normal. As I was praying they would be.

"Oh my God—finally!" Harlow hops up from the couch, immediately wrapping me in a hug. She squeezes me too. "It's so good to finally meet you! I've heard so much about you . . . and some doozy stories, too, but only because sometimes men are idiots."

I'm assuming she means that bullshit with Trent, but I don't have the mental bandwidth to question it.

"When did you get into town?" I ask.

"This morning. After we landed, we stopped and got smoothies, then went to the hotel to chill."

"I said you could stay here," Dex points out.

Andy laughs. "Nah. It feels more like a vacation when I stay at a hotel. We're at the Four Seasons—are you going to pamper me like they will?"

"I will if you pay me," Dex volleys back.

We all share a laugh, Harlow dragging me toward the couch, a bottle of wine and glasses on the coffee table already, waiting for the fun to begin.

"We were just debating what to start with—Cards Against Humanity or Scattergories," she explains. "Or Pictionary? Dex doesn't have a huge selection."

Oh God. My worst nightmares, all on the table.

Shit. I can feel my palms begin to sweat.

It's one thing to have dinner and try to make a good impression over a meal, but game night? There's a chance I'll be exposing my deepest, darkest flaws—like how I can become overly competitive when Monopoly is on the table because I hate losing money to other players or the bank. Or how I'm hopeless at Pictionary because I can't draw to save my life, not even a stick figure.

What if I embarrass myself?

What if we play Cards Against Humanity and I'm forced to look like a pervert because of an embarrassing sentence? If you know anything about that game, it's literally the worst. I want them to like me, not think I'm a jerk.

Margot, chill.

Channeling Wyatt's infinite wisdom, I blink back at three very excited, enthusiastic faces. They're watching me expectantly, and I sit up straighter, putting on my brave face. I teach kids, for crying out loud—they are the toughest crowd I've ever met! Harlow and Andy already like me from what they've heard about me from Dex; they've said as much.

This is supposed to be fun, yeah? Just a casual night in, getting to know Dex's best friend and his girlfriend, who have been harassing him for an introduction for weeks and flew here *specifically* to meet me. At least, that's what we've been told.

Hey. No pressure, right?

No big deal.

Except it *is* a big deal. This is my chance to show them I'm not just some random woman Dex is seeing. I'm someone he's serious about. And I want them to like me for both our sakes. I know how influential other men are in Dex's life because his parents aren't a part of it, so for Andy to give him his stamp of approval means the world to me.

It is what it is.

Harlow hands me a glass of wine. It's still cold, the glass chilly in my hands, and I quickly take a sip, hoping it will ease my nerves.

She is so nice!

I can tell we'll get along, hope fluttering in my soul, filling me up. I'm going to need allies once the season is in full swing, won't I? Being the girlfriend of a famous football player cannot be for the faint of heart, from what I've seen through extensive online research.

"So what game should we play?" With the tip of his toe, Andy gives the black Cards Against Humanity box a tiny nudge. Shoves it to the center of the table, a beggar's expression on his face.

"Oh no. No you don't." Harlow laughs. Picks up her glass of wine but then immediately sets it back on the table without taking a drink. Hmm. "Forget it, buddy. The last time we played this game, you caused such a stink they kicked us out of the sports bar we were hanging out at for getting rowdy." She and I share a look. "Landon has *zero* chill."

"I can relate to not having any chill," I say, sipping from my glass, doing my best not to chug it. "My daughter tells me to chill nonstop."

We're all seated around the couches, Andy and Harlow on one sofa, Dex and I on the other, facing each other.

"That's right, Dex keeps mentioning your daughter. He said she's hysterical. I wish I would have been able to meet her tonight, but maybe next time?" Harlow beams at me. So friendly. "I love kids."

Is it my imagination, or did Andy nudge her with his knee when she made that proclamation?

Huh.

I peel my eyes away and force them back onto the table, where the boxes sit, waiting for us to decide which one we're going to open.

"Can we please, please play Cards Against Humanity? Dude, I'm begging," Andy quite literally begs. "Please, dude? It's so fun, and I'm so good at it."

In the end, he wins—probably because of his extensive use of the word *dude*—and we commence the word game, my face getting redder and hotter with every turn. With every card that gets placed. With every politically incorrect or pervy phrase.

Then.

Andy lays a black card in the center of the table that says: **IT'S HERE. IT'S FINALLY HAPPENING, I'M FINALLY DOING IT. IT'S TIME FOR _____.**

"Harlow—your turn," he tells his girlfriend.

She seems to stew over her options, nibbling on her bottom lip, holding the ten cards in her hands close.

"Hmm." She hems and haws. Removes one card from her hand and goes to place it on the table. Hesitates. Adds it back to her collection and hems and haws again. "Ah."

"I'm finally doing it. It's time for—" Harlow reads Andy's card out loud at the same time she lays down a white response card.

MAKING BABIES.

For a split second, Dex goes about the game on autopilot, flipping through his cards to choose his next move, eyes roaming from Andy's card to his own. The humming sound emanating from his chest tells me one thing: he isn't getting the hint.

"Making babies," I repeat quietly.

I don't know Andy or Harlow all that well, but now they're holding hands, and all I can do is give Dex a tap, hoping he'll notice so I don't have to spell it out for him.

"Wait," my boyfriend finally says. "They have a card that says making babies? Since when?"

Honestly, I'm trying not to roll my eyes. I love him dearly, but occasionally he is too clueless, even for me.

"Since you can order custom cards."

"You can?" Dex scratches his head. Pauses.

Stares down at the table, the meaning of those two cards clicking into place at long last.

"Wait," he says again, gaze jerking to Andy's. "Are you guys *preg*nant?"

Harlow and Andy both nod.

"Holy shit! No way!" He stands, grabbing his friend and enveloping him in a hug at the same time I stand so I can hug them too. "This is fucking amazing. Holy shit, I'm going to be a funcle." They clap each other on the back, doing that bro thing. "A fun fucking uncle, get it?"

"Yeah, I get it." His best friend laughs.

"We should seriously celebrate, not sit home playing board games," Dex goes on, practically vibrating with excitement.

"No, man, this is exactly how we wanted to celebrate. It doesn't need to be a spectacle. We're trying to keep it as private as we can for as long as we can," Andy explains, his arm around his girlfriend's shoulders. "Especially since we're not engaged or anything."

She has her hand on her stomach now. "The only people who know are my dad and his parents. We're just now starting to tell our close friends."

"How far along are you?" I ask, over the moon for this couple that's going to be part of my life, honored to be counted as among their close friends.

"Four months—sixteen or so weeks. I feel like we found out yesterday, but it's actually been a bit."

"Is this the real reason you came into town?" Dex wants to know, a big goofy grin on his face.

It's contagious—we're all grinning from ear to ear—and I swear, my insides are melting, all my nerves completely gone as we get swept up in Harlow and Landon's joy.

A baby.

Could there be anything more exciting?

As Dex slides his arm around my waist, I feel him squeezing it, his body leaning into me. "You know what I think?"

"No, what do you think?"

"I think it would be sexy as hell to have a baby with you."

I look up at him, startled. He's recently come around to the idea of kids and not waiting, but it still surprises me that he'd bring it up now—and in front of his friends.

I swallow, gulping down my hormones. "Is that so?"

"Yeah. I say we start practicing tonight."

I roll my eyes, mindful that his friends are watching. "You're always practicing."

"But maybe this time we practice for real."

I lean back so I can look him in the eyes. "Okay, Mister Raging Hormones, you calm down."

But my hormones are raging too.

I am so desperately in love with this guy. This giant man-child who loves everything about me, most of all being part of my little family. My daughter, who counts him as one of her best friends.

He kisses me then, full on the lips, for Andy and Harlow to see, dipping me the same way you see two lovers dipping in the movies.

Dex Lansing has turned from one of the biggest players to one of the biggest softies—*and I cannot wait to see what happens next.*

Acknowledgments

Surround yourself with people who believe in your dreams and ideas . . .

I stared at this blank sheet of paper for the longest time, not sure where to begin these acknowledgments because I have so many people to be thankful for, and because I'm not actually writing this on paper.

If you follow me on social media—namely Instagram—you get a glimpse into my relationship. I have an amazing fiancé named Jeff . . . and if you look up his name in the dictionary, beside it you'll find the words: BEST SUPPORT SYSTEM EVER.

My family is incredible. My parents and brothers and sister are as proud and boastful as I am of them, and God bless their patience because lately, I've been writing nonstop. Which means sometimes I miss the important things. But it's my daughter M and stepkids who I work tirelessly for. My fam loves each other to pieces.

I have incredible friends. Amazingly talented author friends.

I start my days by texting several of them—and my assistant, Shauna Casey. And while occasionally she terrifies me, she's also one of my biggest fans. In all honesty, if she lived nearby and could follow me around all day wearing a cheerleading uniform and tossing confetti at me, she would. Get you a Shauna, but don't get mine, 'cause I need her.

Some people search their whole lives for the right agent . . .

There was a time when I had stories inside me that I craved for a wider audience to read. I'd been indie my entire career and knew I wanted to do trad too. Then I slid into Michelle Wolfson's @

WolfsonLiterary DMs as if I was single and ready to mingle, and that's what you call "going for it."

(Sidebar: what I actually did was send her a very professional query letter like everyone else does, and she didn't ignore me.)

You know that scene in *The Bachelorette* where the woman says, "Will you accept this rose?"

That was Michelle and I becoming a team. She knows I have dreams, and she wants to help make them come true. Do I frustrate her from time to time? Sure. Do I make her laugh most of the time? Not sure. LOL.

Michelle + Me = Maria Gomez at Montlake.

Maria gets me. It's been an incredible experience working with her from the beginning, and to say that I was excited to work with her for *Not Your Biggest Fan* (my first book with them) is an understatement. Her team is extraordinary, and Sasha Knight, editor, has such attention to detail, she has made me a better writer. More conscientious. I think about things as I structure them because WWSD? (What would Sasha do?!)

Another Montlake editor to thank? Karah Nichols, copyeditor. Another amazing and talented professional who is a delight to email and go back and forth with.

Hang Le creates such gorgeous covers—I have envied them from afar for years, never able to get on her schedule until these books. When I found out she would be creating them, I did a little shimmy.

Y'all, I am blessed. Truly.

Thank you.

I wake up every day excited to write. Go to my spot at Starbucks, order my drink, sip it while I check my emails. Live my dream.

Surrounded by all of you.

xx Sara

About the Author

Photo © 2018 Lauren Perry, Perrywinkle Photography

Sara Ney is an Amazon and *USA Today* bestselling author of new adult college and adult romance, notably the How to Date a Douchebag and Campus Legends series. She has two adult romance books releasing with Montlake beginning in spring 2025. Her books have been translated in many foreign markets, including Germany, Italy, Brazil, and Israel—to name a few.

Sara lives in a blended household overrun by four independent teenagers, alongside her partner, Jeff. She enjoys a weekly Cute Date Night, where they discuss TV shows they're bingeing and plot novels together, something Jeff is freakishly good at. Sara also loves *traveling*, because that's the only time she has the bathroom to herself.

For more information about Sara Ney and her books, visit https://authorsaraney.com.

Her socials:
Instagram: https://www.instagram.com/saraneyauthor

Facebook: https://www.facebook.com/saraneyauthor
TikTok: https://www.tiktok.com/@authorsaraney
Goodreads: https://bit.ly/35JrItR
BookBub: https://www.bookbub.com/authors/sara-ney
Amazon author page: https://amzn.to/3qb6e3a